A GAME FOR THE LIVING

He turned on the lamp at the foot of her couch. On Lelia's long table lay a bunch of white carnations that should have been put into a vase. On the table stood a bottle of Bacardi also, his favourite spirit, and he thought perhaps Lelia had bought it especially for him. He walked down the short hall, past the kitchen, to the bedroom. She was here, asleep.

'Lelia?'

She was face-down in bed, and there was blood on the pillow, lots of it, in a red circle around her black hair.

A GAME
FOR THE
LIVING

Patricia Highsmith

Hamlyn Paperbacks

A GAME FOR THE LIVING

ISBN 0 600 34103 8

First published in Great Britain 1959
by William Heinemann Ltd
First paperback publication 1962 by Pan Books
Hamlyn Paperbacks edition 1978
2nd printing 1981
3rd printing 1983
Copyright © 1958 by Patricia Highsmith

Hamlyn Paperbacks are published by
The Hamlyn Publishing Group Ltd,
Astronaut House, Feltham,
Middlesex, England
(Paperback Division: Hamlyn Paperbacks,
Banda House, Cambridge Grove,
Hammersmith, London W6 0LE)

Reproduced, printed and bound in Great Britain by
Cox & Wyman Ltd, Reading

To my friend and teacher, Ethel Sturtevant, Assistant Professor of English at Barnard College from 1911 to 1948, I affectionately dedicate this book, with a hope that it may add diversion to a very long and happy retirement.

And my gratitude to Dorothy Hargreaves and to Mary McCurdy for their empathy and for their house.

CHAPTER ONE

Faith has taken all chances into account . . .
if you are willing to understand that you must
love, then is your love eternally secure.
                                                S. KIERKEGAARD

JUST as Theodore had thought, something was going on at the Hidalgos'. He looked up at the four lighted windows on the second floor, from which came an inviting murmur of voices and laughter, shifted his heavy portfolio so that it balanced a little better under his right arm, and debated for the second time whether to ring the Hidalgos' bell or to look for another taxi and go straight home.

It would be chilly at home, the furniture covered with sheets. Inocenza, his maid, was still visiting her family in Durango, because he had not written her that he was coming back. And after all, it was barely midnight, the eve of the Fifth of February, a national holiday. Nobody worked tomorrow. On the other hand, he was burdened with a suitcase, a portfolio of drawings, and a roll of canvas. He hadn't been invited, either, though with the Hidalgos that didn't really matter.

Or would he rather call on Lelia? He had thought of it earlier, on the plane from Oaxaca, and he did not know what impulse had brought him to the Hidalgos'. He had written Lelia that he would be back in Mexico, D.F., tonight, and perhaps she was even waiting for him. She had no telephone. But she did not mind his dropping in at any hour, unless she was painting. Lelia was so good-natured! He decided to call on the Hidalgos, and to see Lelia later, if it did not become too late.

1

He walked to the door, put his suitcase down, and pressed the Hidalgos' bell firmly. He did not ring again, though it was at least two minutes before someone came to the door. It was Isabel Hidalgo.

"Theodore, you're back!" she greeted him in English. Then in Spanish: "Come in. How nice to see you. Come up. The house is full of people."

"Thank you, Isabel. I've just flown in from Oaxaca."

"How exciting!" Isabel went directly into the living-room, waved an arm, and announced: "Theodore's here! Carlos, Theodore's here!"

Theodore set his suitcase down as unobtrusively as he could in the little foyer, leaned his portfolio against it, and stood the roll of canvases up beside the suitcase.

Carlos came into the foyer, carrying a drink. He was wearing one of his boldly patterned tweed jackets. "Don Teodoro!" he cried, embracing Theodore with one arm. "Welcome! Come in and have a drink!"

Most of the guests were men, gathered in little knots in the corners and on the two square studio couches as if they had been talking in the same places for a long while. Theodore knew less than half of them, and didn't want to be presented to every single person, but Carlos, with his ebullient energy that always increased when he drank, took him around to every man, woman, and child—though the two children, both blond American children, happened to be asleep at the back of a studio couch against the wall.

"Don't wake them, don't wake them," Theodore protested quickly.

"Where've you been keeping yourself?" Carlos asked.

"I've been in Oaxaca, you know," Theodore said, smiling. "I've painted half a dozen pictures in the last month."

"Let's see them!" Carlos's face lighted with his big smile.

"Oh, not now. There's not enough room. But I had a

2

splendid time. I even——" He stopped, because Carlos had rushed off somewhere, perhaps to get him a drink.

Theodore turned slowly round, looking for a place to sit down. He glanced at a woman coming in from the hall, with a faint hope she might be Lelia, but she was not. Somebody jostled him. The room was full of the bland smoke of American cigarettes. There were five or six American men in the room, probably professors and instructors from Mexico City College or Ciudad Universidad, where Carlos Hidalgo taught stage direction. On a small table by one of the studio couches stood several bottles of gin and whisky and some glasses.

Carlos, with a fresh drink that was perhaps for him and his own dark, half-finished glass, was making his way across the room from the kitchen, tossing a few words at everybody. He was twenty-nine, but he looked younger with his smooth, compact face that made one think of a handsome little boy aged about ten. Theodore supposed that it was this boyish quality that had attracted Isabel, who was a bit older, but what a shame that it was a spoiled-boyishness, he thought. Carlos rated himself high in regard to women, and before he had married Isabel—who was as quiet a girl as a rake might have been expected to choose for a wife—he had had at least a dozen affairs a year. He had used to tell Theodore about them. Theodore preferred to hear him talk about his work, always hoping to see progress from the rather indiscriminate enthusiasm typical of Mexican directors, actors and playwrights to something approaching refinement. Carlos said, however, that one could not put on restrained drama in Mexico. The people just didn't appreciate it or understand it. Carlos finally reached him, thrust the glass of whisky and soda into his hand, and dashed off again, calling to his wife.

Seeing two men whom he knew slightly standing by a window, Theodore went over and said: "Good evening, Don Ignacio. How are you this evening?"

3

Sr. Ignacio Ortiz y Guzman B. was a director of one of the government-supported art galleries in the city. Once here at Carlos's house, months ago, he and Theodore had had a long talk about painting. The other man was Vicente something or other, and Theodore had forgotten what he did, though he had once known.

"Are you painting these days?" asked Ortiz y Guzman B.

"Yes. I've just returned from a month of painting in Oaxaca," Theodore replied.

Ortiz y Guzman B. looked at him but might not have heard him. The man named Vicente was graciously lighting the cigarette of a woman near him.

There was an awkward silence, in which Theodore could think of nothing to say. The two men began to talk to each other again. Theodore was reminded of other moments at parties and dinners when something he said—granted, not of much importance—had been completely ignored as if it had been either inaudible or an unspeakable obscenity. He wondered if it happened to other people as often as it happened to him. More insignificant-looking men than he were listened to, no matter how stupid their remarks were, he thought. Now the two men were talking about somebody Theodore did not know, and it occurred to Theodore too late that Ortiz y Guzman B. might have been interested to know that he had been asked to show four paintings in a group show in May at one of the I.N.B.A. galleries. After a moment, Theodore drifted away and stood by a wall. Perhaps being ignored did not happen more often to him than anybody else.

Theodore Wolfgang Schiebelhut was thirty-three, slender and tall, especially tall compared to the average Mexican. His blond hair, streaked with light brown, lay close to the sides of his head and was rather bushy on top, and unparted. He carried himself well, smiled easily, and there was a lightness in his walk and his manner which gave him an air of youth and cheerfulness, even if he happened to be in a de-

4

pressed mood. Most people thought of him as cheerful, though all his conscious ideas were those of a pessimist. Polite by nature and training, he concealed his depressions from everyone. His moods usually had no causes that he or anybody else could discover, and so he felt he was not entitled to show them in the social system of things. He believed the world had no meaning, no end but nothingness, and that man's achievements were all finally perishable—cosmic jokes, like man himself. Believing this, he believed as a matter of course that one ought to make the most of what one had, a little time, a little life, try to be as happy as possible and to make others happy if one could. Theodore thought he was as happy as anyone logically could be in an age when atomic bombs and annihilation hung over everybody's head, though the word 'logically' troubled him in this context. Could one be logically happy? Was there ever anything logical about it?

"Teo, we're so glad you dropped in," Isabel Hidalgo said to him. "Carlos said this morning he thought you were due back, and we wanted you to come tonight. We rang up your house earlier."

"Must have been a case of telepathy," Theodore said, smiling. "Carlos looks tired. Is he working too hard?"

"Yes. As usual. Everybody says he should take a rest." Her blue-grey eyes looked up at him rather sadly, in spite of her smile. "Now they're rehearsing *Othello* at the Universidad in addition to his classes. He takes on more and more. He worked late even tonight, and no dinner, and then he comes home and the drinks go right to his head."

Theodore smiled tolerantly and shrugged, though Carlos's drinking was a problem at social gatherings. The presence of people seemed to excite him, and he drank liquor as if it were water. He was not very drunk yet, but Isabel knew it was coming, and was already putting forth explanations. As for his taking on more and more, Theodore knew that was more a manifestation of egotism than of energy. Carlos liked

5

to see his name on as many programmes and posters as he could manage. "I don't suppose Lelia's coming tonight," Theodore said.

"She certainly was invited," Isabel said quickly. "Carlos! —Weren't you supposed to pick up Lelia?"

"Yes!" Carlos cried across the room in his loud voice. "But she phoned me at the Universidad at noon and said she couldn't come. No doubt because she was expecting *you* tonight, Teo." Carlos smiled and winked, swaying in time to a Cuban dance record he had put on the gramophone.

"I see. Has she——" But Carlos had already turned his back and was bending over the gramophone. Theodore had been going to ask if Lelia had done any painting for him. She occasionally painted backdrops for his plays at the Universidad. He did not want to ask Isabel anything about Lelia, because Isabel knew—or *must* know—that Carlos was very attracted to Lelia. Carlos had made a fool of himself with Lelia on several occasions, once in the presence of Isabel, who had pretended not to notice.

"Excuse me, Teo," Isabel said, touching Theodore's sleeve with a nervous hand. "People at the door." She went away.

Theodore watched Carlos thrusting a drink into the hands of a woman who was firmly but unsuccessfully refusing. It occurred to him that Lelia had phoned Carlos in advance, to avoid an argument over not coming to the party once he had arrived at her apartment. It was nearly impossible to make Carlos take no for an answer. Theodore looked up at a suspended mobile whose pieces seemed about to strike each other but never did, and thought how strange it was that in a room full of artists and writers and professors he could feel so isolated. Even the Americans with halting Spanish were faring better, he saw. He had been happier on the plane an hour or so ago, anticipating the welcome he would get if he telephoned Ramón or dropped in on the Hidalgos or Lelia. Theodore was quite fond of Carlos, but how often really had

6

they had a satisfying, illuminating discussion about any-thing? *Anything*, Theodore thought a little bitterly, remem-bering a conversation concerning the meaning of faith which had stopped exactly where Theodore had stopped, perforce, when he had been trying to think further for himself. There were answers that only time could bring, he supposed, and Carlos was young, but Theodore expected something also to come out of two individuals who put their heads together. Carlos seemed always to be in a state of over-excitement, as if he had just swallowed a half dozen benzedrines. One couldn't keep him on a subject for more than a minute. He jumped from a discussion of a Tennessee Williams play to the scenic designing of some Frenchman, to a Sarah Bernhardt recording he had heard at the Universidad, to a play a student had written for which he was contemplating asking government funds to produce. It might be stimulating, but it was unsatisfactory. And could art come from all that excitement? Wasn't art—most of it—emotion recollected in tranquillity? Even for a Latin? Theodore smiled at his own intensity. The smile brought an answering smile and a nod from a reddish-haired man Theodore did not know. Some-how this decided him. He'd go to see Lelia before it got any later. She did not usually go to bed before one, and even in bed she read for a while.

Theodore glanced around—and he would have said good-bye to Carlos and Isabel if they had seen him, though he was relieved not to have to argue with Carlos about his leaving—then walked to the foyer, picked up his portfolio, suitcase and canvases and let himself out.

He struggled two blocks to the Avenida de los Insurgentes and got a *libre* after a short wait. A last-minute hesitation as to whether to take the taxi home, which was nearer, or to Lelia's, then, "*Granaditas! Numero cien' vient'y siete. Cuatro pesos. Está bien?*"

The driver grumbled over the suitcase and the lateness

of the hour and the fact that it was a holiday eve, demanded five pesos, and Theodore agreed and got in.

It was a cool, crisp night. Ordinarily, the drive would have been no more than ten minutes from the Hidalgos', but tonight the downtown section was full of pedestrians and automobiles from Juarez to the Zócalo. The driver seemed to aim for the most congested streets just to slow them up.

A rowdy face poked itself through the window at a traffic stop and said: "Any person here named Maria?"

There was a burst of laughter from half a dozen young men's throats, and the drunken face was dragged back.

Theodore, who had started up on the edge of his seat, providently raised his window a little. Many people would be drunk tonight, especially in the section where he was going, behind the Zócalo. He had a present for Lelia, he remembered suddenly, and he began to imagine showing her his drawings and paintings tonight, and he sat up again and told the driver to hurry. Lelia was such a good listener, such a good critic, such a good mistress! She was what every man needed, Theodore thought, and so seldom found, a woman who was good to look at, a good companion, a woman who listened and encouraged, who even knew how to cook, and above all was good-natured about such things as moodiness, spells of solitude, and impulses that sent him flying to her at four in the morning, sometimes because he felt suicidal, sometimes because he felt unbearably happy and had to share it with her. Useless to try to think of such a woman as exemplifying an abstract ideal. There was only Lelia. Perhaps there was no one like her in the whole world.

Ramón might be there, too, might even be spending the night, Theodore thought. But that wasn't very likely tonight, and anyway he would knock first.

The taxi had arrived. Theodore paid the driver and got out with his things. It was a rather gloomy block at night with its shops all closed and its old houses presenting tall locked doors to the street. Lelia's front door latched from the inside, but could be opened by those who knew how with a stick lifted in the crack between them. For this purpose a stick which was a bar of a wooden bird cage usually leaned in the corner of the door and the house wall. It was there now, and Theodore took it and raised the latch. He went into a small, cluttered patio lighted only by the glow from several windows above. Lelia's window was one of the windows that were lighted, Theodore saw. He went through a doorless stone arch and began to climb the stairs. Lelia lived on the third floor. He walked down the corridor to her door and knocked.

There was no answer.

"Lelia?" he called. "It's Theodore. Let me in!"

She did not open the door for a caller she did not want to see, but Theodore was not in this category. Sometimes she was deep in a book, and if it were he, or he and Ramón together, she might take two or three minutes to come to the door, knowing they would be patient.

Theodore knocked more loudly. "Ramón?—It's Theodore!"

He tried the door, which was locked, and wished he had her key. He always carried it, but for some reason, perhaps to feel quite free of her for a while, he had taken it off his key chain before he left for Oaxaca. The transom was slightly open. Theodore reached up on tiptoe and pushed it still wider.

"Lelia?" he called once more to the transom.

Maybe she was visiting a neighbour or had gone out to make a telephone call. He set his suitcase flat against the door, put a foot on it, and gently pulled himself up. He stuck his head through the transom and looked to see what he might land on if he climbed through. The light from the bedroom was just enough to show that the red hassock was about two feet from the door. He listened for a moment to find out if any of the other tenants happened to be on the stairs, because he would have felt very silly to be seen crawling through Lelia's transom, but he heard nothing except a radio somewhere. He put his hands on the dusty bottom rim of the transom, stuck his head through, and pushed up from the suitcase. Once the rim of the transom began to cut him across the waist, he debated whether to push himself back out again. The pain forced him to move, and he wriggled forward until his hands lay flat against the inside of the door, his heels touched the top of the transom, and the blood rushed alarmingly to his face. Desperately, he struggled to get his right knee through the transom. It was of no use. He aimed for the red hassock and came down in a slow dive, clung to the hassock, and crumpled to the floor.

He stood up, dusting his hands, and glanced around happily at the familiar, spacious room with its ever-changing patterns of paintings and drawings on the wall, then unlocked the door and dragged his things in. He turned on the lamp at the foot of her couch. On Lelia's long table lay a bunch of white carnations that should have been put into a vase. On the table stood a bottle of Bacardi also, his favourite spirit, and he thought perhaps Lelia had bought it especially for him. He walked down the short hall, past the kitchen, to the bedroom. She was here, asleep.

"Lelia?"

She was face-down in bed, and there was blood on the pillow, lots of it, in a red circle around her black hair.

"Lelia!" He sprang forward and pulled back the thin pink coverlet.

Blood stained her white blouse, covered her right arm, where he saw a ghastly, deep furrow in the flesh. The wound was still wet. Gasping and trembling, Theodore took her gently by the shoulders and turned her, and then released her in horror. Her face had been mutilated.

Theodore looked around the room. The carpet was kicked

up at one corner. That was really the only sign of disorder. And the window was wide open, which was unlike Lelia. Theodore went to the window and looked out. The window gave on the patio, and from the patio there was not a thing anyone could have climbed up on, but from the roof, only one floor above, a drainpipe came down inches from the window jamb and stopped just above the top of the window of the floor below. Theodore had told Lelia a dozen times to have bars put on the window. All the other windows of the apartments on Lelia's floor and the floor above had bars. It was too late now to think of bars. A moment later his mind sank into a shocked despair. He sat down on a straight chair and put his hands over his face.

It came to him suddenly: Ramón had done it. Obviously! Ramón had a violent temper. He had stepped between Ramón and Lelia several times when Ramón had been about to strike her in some burst of petulant anger. They had got into another of their Latin quarrels about nothing, he thought, or Lelia had not been appreciative enough of some present he had brought her—No, it would have to be something worse than that, something so bad he could not imagine it now, but he felt sure Ramón had done it. Ramón also had a key. He could simply have used the door.

"*Ai-i-yai-i-i-i!*" cried a falsetto voice from the hall, and at the same time there was a pounding on the door.

Theodore ran to the door and yanked it open. Footsteps were running down the stairs, and Theodore plunged after them, reaching the ground floor as he heard the wooden door of the courtyard grate on the cement walk. He ran out to the sidewalk and looked in both directions. He saw only two men walking slowly in conversation across the street. Theodore looked around the dark patio. But he had heard the wooden door move. With a sense of futility and a feeling that he might be doing the wrong thing, he went back into the building and climbed the stairs. If it had been the murderer, even if it had been, it would have been useless to go running down the street after him, not even knowing in fact in which direction to run. And maybe it hadn't been the murderer, just a hoodlum from the street, or from the party that he now realised was going on in an apartment on the next floor up from Lelia's. But if it *had* been the murderer, and he had let him get away——

Just inside Lelia's door, he paused. He had to behave logically. First, tell the police. Second, stand guard in the apartment so that no one could destroy any fingerprints. Third, find Ramón and see that he paid with his life for what he had done.

Theodore went out and closed the door, intending to go to a *cantina* he knew of a block away where there was a telephone, but going down the second flight of stairs he ran into the woman who lived in the apartment next to Lelia's.

"Well, Don Teodoro! Good evening!" the woman said. "Happy Fifth of——"

"Do you know that Lelia's dead?" Theodore blurted. "She's been murdered! In her apartment!"

"*Aaaaaah!*" the woman screamed, and clapped a hand over her mouth.

Instantly two doors opened. Voices cried: "What is it?" "What happened?" "*Who* was murdered?"

And Theodore found himself simply struggling to get back up the stairs he had come down, back into Lelia's apartment, because her door was unlocked, and even now two men were running in.

"*Please!*" Theodore yelled. "You must get out! You must not touch anything! There may be fingerprints!" But nothing was of any use until twelve or fifteen of them had peeked into the bedroom and screamed and run out again, covering their eyes in horror.

"You're like a bunch of children!" Theodore snorted in English.

12

Sra. de Silva volunteered to telephone the police from her apartment, but before she went off she said to Theodore: "I heard something at about eleven o'clock, maybe a little earlier. This clatter on the roof. But I didn't hear anything else. I didn't hear any glass breaking."

"There wasn't any glass broken," Theodore said quickly. "What else did you hear?"

"Nothing!" She stared at him with wide-open eyes. "I heard this clatter. Like somebody was trying to climb over the roof. Something on the roof, anyway. But I didn't look out. I *should* have looked out, holy Mother of God!"

"Did you hear any sound of struggle in the apartment?"

"No. Maybe I did. I'm not sure. Yes, *maybe* I did!"

"Go and call the police, if you please," Theodore said to her. "I have to stay here to keep people out."

A murmuring crowd had gathered in the hall just outside the door, mostly boys from the street, Theodore thought. Some of them had been drinking. He closed the door as soon as he could persuade one of the young men to take his hands from the door's edge.

Then he sat down on the red hassock facing the door to wait for the police. He thought about Ramón, his Catholic soul trapped in his passion for Lelia. It preyed on Ramón's conscience that he could not marry her and could not give her up either. Theodore had heard Ramón say at least twice in fits of remorse, or perhaps in anger at some careless word of Lelia's: "I swear if I don't give her up from *this minute*, Teo, I'll kill myself!" Or something like that. And between killing oneself and killing the object of one's passion was not much difference, Theodore thought. Psychologically, they equated sometimes. Well, the beast had killed her instead of himself!

CHAPTER TWO

THE police arrived with a moaning siren. They sounded like an army coming up the stairs, but there were only three of them, a short, paunchy officer of about fifty with a Sam Browne belt and a large gun on either hip, and two tall young policemen in light khaki uniforms. The fat officer pulled a gun and casually pointed it at Theodore.

"Step over by the wall," he said. Then he gestured to one of the policemen to cover Theodore while he went into the bedroom to see the body.

The crowd from the hall was oozing into the room, staring and murmuring.

One after the other, so that Theodore was constantly covered and stared at by two of them, the young policemen also went into the bedroom to look at Lelia. One of them whistled with astonishment. They came back staring at Theodore with shocked, stony faces.

"Your name?" asked the officer, pulling paper and pencil out of his pocket. "Age? . . . Are you a citizen of Mexico?"

"Yes. Naturalised," Theodore replied.

"Keep them out of there! Don't let anyone touch anything in there!" the officer shouted to the policemen.

The crowd were seeping into the bedroom.

"Do you admit this crime?" asked the officer.

"No! I'm the one who summoned you! I'm the one who found her!"

"Occupation?"

Theodore hesitated. "Painter."

The officer looked him up and down. Then he turned to a short, dark man whom Theodore had not noticed, though

14

he stood in the forefront of the crowd. "Capitán Sauzas, would you like to continue?"

The man stepped forward. He wore a dark hat and a dark, unbuttoned overcoat. A cigarette hung from his lips. He looked at Theodore with intelligent, impersonal brown eyes. "How do you happen to be here tonight?"

"I came to see her," Theodore said. "She is a friend of mine."

"At what time did you come?"

"About half an hour ago. About one o'clock."

"And did she let you in?"

"No!—There was a light. I knocked and there was no answer." Theodore glanced at one of the revolvers, which moved a little and focused on him again. "I thought perhaps she'd fallen asleep—or that she had gone out to make a telephone call. So I crawled in through the transom. When I found her, I immediately went out to phone the police. I ran into Señora—Señora—"

"Señora de Silva," Sauzas supplied for him.

"Yes," Theodore said. "I told her and she said she would call the police for me."

The crowd in the room, which had ranged itself so as to be able to see Theodore and Sauzas at the same time, was listening with folded arms and blandly surprised faces, but Theodore had been in Mexico long enough to read apparently impassive expressions. The crowd was more than half convinced that he had done it. Theodore could see that also in the faces of the two young policemen who held their guns on him.

"What was your relationship to the murdered woman?" Sauzas asked. He was not making notes.

"A friend," Theodore said, and heard a murmur of amusement from the people around him.

"How long had you known her?"

"Three years," Theodore replied. "A little more."

15

"You are in the habit of visiting her at one in the morning?"

Again the crowd tittered.

Theodore stood a little taller. "I have often visited her late at night. She keeps late hours," Theodore said, trying to ignore the smile and the mumblings, some of which he could hear. They were calling Lelia *"una puta"*, a whore.

Then there was the matter of his suitcase. Was he moving in? No? What then? Why had he gone to Oaxaca? So he went to a friend's house after he left the airport and before he came here. Could he prove that? Yes. Who was Carlos Hidalgo? And where did he live? Sauzas dispatched one of the policemen to find Carlos Hidalgo and bring him back.

There was suddenly great confusion as two men in civilian clothes came in and loudly ordered the crowd to leave. The two men shoved some of the adolescent boys out the door. Señora de Silva protested against being put out and at Sauzas' intercession was allowed to stay. Briefly and carelessly, Sauzas repeated Theodore's story of how he had got in and ordered the two men to look for fingerprints in the bedroom.

"I believe I know who killed her," Theodore said to Sauzas.

"Who?"

"Ramón Otero. I do not know, but I have reasons to think it is possible." Theodore's voice shook in spite of the effort he was making to keep calm.

"Do you know where we can find him?"

"He lives in the Calle San Gregorio, thirty-seven. It is not far from here. Toward the Cathedral and the Zócalo."

"M-m. And his relationship to the murdered woman?" Sauzas asked, lighting another cigarette.

"A friend also," Theodore said.

"I see. He is jealous of you?"

16

"No, not at all. We are good friends. Except that I—I know Ramón is very emotional. He is even violent if he is angry. But I must tell you also that I heard somebody knock on the door and run down the stairs at about—two or three minutes after I got here. I ran to the door and tried to catch him, but he got away."

"What did he look like?" Sauzas asked.

"I never saw him," Theodore said, at the same time getting a mental picture of a boy in a soiled white shirt and trousers fleeing down the stairs, which was only because so many roughnecks who might have hammered in that manner on the door wore white shirts and trousers. "No, I did not see him, I am sorry. There was just an '*ai-i*' cry, like that, and the knocking, and then he ran."

"M-m," said Sauzas with faint interest. "However, you seem to think it was Ramón."

"Not the boy who yelled, no. But I think—yes, I think it is at least possible that Ramón did this."

"Do you know that Ramón was here tonight?"

"No, I don't know." Theodore looked at Sra. de Silva. "Do you know if Ramón was here tonight?"

Sra. de Silva raised her eyebrows and her hands. "*Quién sabe?*"

"The fingerprints will tell," Theodore said. He felt suddenly sure that Ramón's fingerprints would be in the bedroom.

"All right, let us try to find Ramón. Ramón Otero in the Calle San Gregorio thirty-seven," Sauzas said to the remaining policeman.

The policeman saluted and clattered down the stairs.

"You were her friend," said Sauzas, returning to Theodore. "You were not her lover, too?"

"Well—yes. Sometimes."

"And Ramón? He was not her lover, too?—Come, come. Señora de Silva has said that you both were."

Theodore glanced at the woman. She must have done some very fast talking to Sauzas before they entered the room. Theodore was quite used to sharing Lelia with Ramón, had long ago grown used to it, but he was not used to speaking of it before people. "That is quite true."

"And there is no jealousy between you? You're all good friends?"

"That is correct," Theodore replied, and returned the detective's unbelieving stare with composure. Theodore understood. Almost every day the front pages of the city's tabloids were covered with bloody photographs of mistresses and wives and sweethearts murdered by their husbands or lovers. Well, perhaps this was no different, except that the motivation had certainly not been jealousy.

"What weapon did you use, Señor Schiebelhut?" Sauzas asked. "Where is the knife?"

Theodore shook his head wearily, but in the next instant became alert as Sauzas slapped his pockets and felt down the inside and outside of his thighs. He even pulled up Theodore's trouser cuffs and looked in the top of his socks. Sauzas had a silver ring with a large skull and crossbones on it. Still without removing his cigarette, Sauzas said:

"Señora de Silva saw you coming down the stairs in a great hurry. You were trying to get away from the scene, weren't you?"

"But—I'd just found her! I was on my way to a telephone!" Theodore looked at Señora de Silva, whose face seemed frozen now in a frightened suspension of belief or even of opinion. "You should be able to determine when she died. Why don't you get a doctor to look at her?"

"A doctor is coming. And I have seen her," Sauzas said calmly. "I would say she has been dead between one hour and two. I have seen enough corpses." Sauzas was walking about, looking at Lelia's paint-stained table, at the white carnations, and at the bottle of rum, which had been un-

18

corked and apparently unsampled, because the rum was high in the neck. "Did you bring these flowers?"

"No," Theodore said. "They were here." It was not like Ramón to bring flowers, he thought. Lelia must have bought them, and then for some reason had not put them into a vase. "You might take the fingerprints on the rum bottle. Lelia always buys it for me. Her fingerprints will be on it and maybe somebody else's."

Sauzas nodded. "Enrique!" he called to one of the detectives in the bedroom. "Come and take the señor's fingerprints!"

The detective came in at once and got busy with Theodore's hands, using Lelia's work table to rest on.

"Señora de Silva," Sauzas said, "how often do you see Señor Schiebelhut here?"

She shrugged quickly, like an embarrassed schoolgirl. "I see him—maybe once a week. But Lelia has told me that he comes more often."

"You live in the next apartment. Have you ever heard them quarrelling?"

"Yes. Sometimes," she said with a look at Theodore. "Oh, not seriously, I think. I don't know."

"And how often does Ramón come here?"

She shrugged again. "The same. The same as Don Teodoro."

"What is he like? Do you like him?"

Sra. de Silva was looking for the answers in the corners of the room. "Ah, sí. He is nice. He is very handsome. He is all right."

"Which one of the men did she like better?"

A long hesitation.

The door opened. A short, plump man with a satchel came in, greeted Sauzas with a wave of his hand, and Sauzas gestured towards the bedroom.

"Well, which did she like better?" Sauzas repeated.

"I think—I do not really know, señor. I think she liked them both. Otherwise she would not have let them come here so often. Lelia had many friends. Many times her friends rang up my house to speak to her. I have heard her on the telephone. She was not afraid to say no to people she did not want to see," Sra. de Silva finished with an air of pride.

"This man's fingerprints are on the window-sill," one of the detectives said to Sauzas.

Theodore cursed himself for his clumsiness. "I think I leaned on the window-sill, looking into the patio."

"Are they facing out?" Sauzas asked the detective, who, not knowing what to answer, went back to the bedroom with the fingerprint papers.

Carlos Hidalgo arrived, escorted by one of the young policemen. He was drunker than when Theodore had seen him last—Theodore knew the signs—though he looked merely stunned and bewildered until he saw Theodore. Then he rushed to him and put his hands on Theodore's shoulders.

"Teodoro, old man! What has happened? Lelia's been *murdered*?"

Theodore started to speak and couldn't. Carlos wouldn't have been able to hear him, anyway, because the young policeman was bawling out Carlos's name and address as if he were announcing him at a ball; then Carlos started for the bedroom, where the detectives were prowling about, and the fat police officer caught him by the arm. Carlos staggered around, looking with wide, frightened eyes at the policemen, at the room itself.

"Was this man at your house tonight?" Sauzas asked Carlos.

"Yes." Carlos nodded vigorously. "He had just come from the airport. He had his suitcase with him."

"From what time to what time?"

Carlos looked cagily at Theodore, even in his drunkenness wary and mistrustful of the motives of the police.

But Theodore gave him no sign.

"I think from about twelve—to maybe about one," Carlos said, which Theodore found surprisingly accurate.

"You can't say exactly what time he left?"

"I didn't see him leave. There're so many people at the party. Maybe he said good-bye to my wife—" And it might have been a lie, from the furtive way Carlos glanced on either side of him as he spoke.

"I didn't say good-bye," Theodore said. "I didn't see either of you when I was ready to leave, so I just left. I then took a *libre* to Lelia's."

"A *libre* to Lelia's," Carlos repeated, as if he were trying to fix an unlikely fact in his mind.

"So," Sauzas said, turning to Theodore. "A *libre* to Lelia's after telling everybody at the party you were on your way way home, probably. You meant to come here, kill her as quickly as possible, and take another *libre* home, no? That way you would have an alibi."

"*Oh-h, no-o!*" Carlos said in his loud, stage director's voice. "This man here—"

"Or maybe you came here from the airport, killed her, then went to the party? But what did you come back for? Did you forget something?"

"My plane only arrived at eleven-five," Theodore said. "It is the plane from Oaxaca. That you can verify. It was at least forty minutes before I reached the city in all the traffic. I went immediately to the Hidalgos'."

"But why did you sneak out of the Hidalgos' house without saying good-bye to anybody?"

"I didn't sneak out. Everybody was busy!"

Carlos laughed suddenly. "That's right! Busy! We were very busy tonight!" Then he sobered, seeing that Theodore and Sauzas were staring at him. "Teodoro," Carlos said

21

sympathetically. "Hasn't anybody got a drink here?" He walked toward Lelia's kitchen, and Theodore saw him stop as he saw her body in the room beyond, then continue with drunken determination into the kitchen.

"Don't touch anything in there!" shouted the fat officer, who had started after him.

Theodore heard arguing voices and then the sound of liquor being poured into a glass, and he knew it would be Lelia's yellow tequila.

"My friend needs a drink," Carlos said with dignity, and walked towards Theodore with glass and bottle.

Theodore took the glass gratefully. It chattered against his teeth.

More questions. How long had Carlos known Theodore Schiebelhut? Had he known Lelia Ballesteros? How long? Did she have many men friends? She had many men and women friends. How had Theodore looked when he came to the party this evening?

"Fine," Carlos said, "absolutely fine." He took Theodore's glass from him and poured some more.

"That's enough of that!" said the fat officer.

"This is for me," Carlos said, and drank some from the glass, then passed it back to Theodore before the fat officer could take it from him.

Theodore felt suddenly exhausted. He walked to the couch, sat down, and leaned to one side on his elbow.

The plump doctor waddled slowly into the room, and Sauzas turned to him. "She has been dead—oh, two to three hours. And she has been raped," the doctor said wearily, fastening the last latch of his satchel.

Raped. Theodore felt the ultimate twist of disgust in his throat. He sat forward on the couch, holding his trembling knees down with his forearms. He pushed his cuff back nervously and saw that his watch said one-fifty.

The detective was questioning Carlos about Ramón.

"I don't know Ramón so well. He is in a different line of work," Carlos said somewhat prissily. "I have seen him perhaps three times in my life."

He had seen him many more times, Theodore thought, but it didn't matter. Nothing mattered until they saw Ramón. He was startled by Carlos shouting, *"Mutilated?"* in an astonished tone.

Carlos looked at Theodore blankly. "She was *mutilated?*" he asked, as if this somehow changed everything.

And then Ramón entered the room.

Theodore stood up.

Ramón looked around in a startled way, then fixed his eyes on Theodore. Ramón was of medium height, with black hair and dark eyes, and his body was strong and compact with that mysterious thing, a certain vitality, or perhaps only proportion, which was immensely attractive to women. His face could change expression in an instant, yet it was always handsome, even unshaven, even when his hair was tousled or uncut, the kind of face women always looked at; and now as he stood in the room in his inexpensive suit and with his hair mussed, Theodore felt that everyone must be thinking that Ramón had been her favourite.

"Where is she?" Ramón asked.

The policeman who held his arm pulled him towards the bedroom, and the detectives trailed after them to watch Ramón's reaction. Theodore also followed. Lelia lay on her back, and her head rested on her pillow, mangled arms at her sides. It was a horrible attitude of repose, as if she had just lain down for a moment, fully clothed, and something unbelievable had happened to her. To Theodore's battered senses it seemed that the blood might be dark red paint that they could simply wash off her. Except that if one looked closely, Lelia had no nose.

Ramón put his hand over his mouth. His shoulders crumpled. He made a strange muffled sound. The detective pulled

23

at his shoulder, pulled hard, but Ramón whirled out of his hold and flung himself down by the bed, gripping Lelia's knees, which the pink blanket just covered. He pressed his face against her thighs and sobbed. Theodore looked away, reminded of Ramón's Catholicism—of this aspect of it —that made him want to touch something, embrace something that was no longer alive. Theodore was at the time aware that he had *not* touched Lelia, not with any affection, that he had simply turned her over as a stranger might have done, and he regretted that, in the privacy before anybody had come, he had not touched her, not kissed her blood-smeared forehead.

"Where were you this evening, Ramón Otero?" Now it was the fat little police officer, beginning like a machine.

A detective crossed the room in two strides and pulled Ramón away from the bed. The question had to be repeated and repeated. Ramón might have lost his voice or his senses. He stared at Theodore again.

"Where *were* you this evening?" Theodore asked in his deep voice.

"Home. I was home."

"All evening?" asked Sauzas.

Ramón looked at him with dull eyes. One side of his face was wet with tears. He held his right hand against his stomach.

"You weren't here this evening?" Theodore asked him.

"Yes. I was here," Ramón said.

"At what time?" asked Sauzas.

Ramón looked as if he were trying to reach far back in time. He suddenly bent over, clutching his head.

"What's the matter with him?" Sauzas asked Theodore impatiently.

"Perhaps it's a headache. He's prone to them," Theodore said. "Sit down, Ramón."

One of the detectives pulled Ramón towards the long table

where there was a chair. Ramón collapsed in it, and a detective took his right hand and began inking the fingertips.

"At what time were you here, Ramón?" Sauzas asked more gently. "Did you have dinner here?"

"Yes."

"And then what? How long did you stay?"

Ramón did not answer.

"Did you kill her, Ramón?" Sauzas asked.

"No."

"No?" Carlos Hidalgo asked challengingly.

Sauzas waved Carlos back. "What time did you arrive for dinner?" Sauzas waited a moment, then approached Ramón suddenly as if he were going to slap him into sensibility, but he stopped as Ramón, without a change in his dazed expression, began to talk.

"I came here about eight, and we had dinner. We thought Teo might come. We were going to have a party. I brought some rum. Then I didn't feel well. I went home."

"At what time?"

"I think—about ten-thirty, maybe later."

"Did you have a quarrel with Lelia tonight, Ramón?"

"No."

"You didn't quarrel about Teodoro? You hoped he would come?"

"Yes," Ramón said, nodding.

"I sent Lelia a postcard saying I would be in tonight," Theodore said, but Sauzas did not seem to be listening.

"And did you bring her these flowers, Ramón?"

"No," said Ramón, looking at them.

"Were the flowers here when you were here?" Sauzas asked, feeling the flowers' stems.

"I don't remember," Ramón replied.

"Did you eat at this table?"

"Yes."

25

"Then the flowers must have arrived after you left. Did she say she was going out to buy flowers?"

Once more, Ramón tried to think. "I don't remember," he said miserably, shaking his head.

"Look in the kitchen for a paper that might have come around the flowers," Sauzas said to one of the detectives. "Look carefully!"

Theodore stared at the flowers, not knowing what to make of them. He had not thought that Ramón brought them. Lelia might have gone out to get flowers after Ramón left, but why hadn't she put them in a vase? Had the murderer accompanied her back to the apartment? But that was inconceivable to Theodore.

The detective came back and reported no paper that the flowers might have come in.

Sauzas turned to Ramón, frowning. "She washed the dishes after dinner, Ramón?"

"Yes. And I dried them."

One of the detectives, at Sauzas's order, was wiping Ramón's face with a wet towel.

"Does he take drugs for these headaches?" Sauzas asked Theodore.

"No. He's had no drugs. He's just stunned." As soon as he had said it, Theodore realised that if Ramón were stunned it would indicate that he had not done the crime.

"There was a noise on the roof tonight," Sauzas said to Ramón. "Señora de Silva said she heard something like running footsteps on the roof. Were you here when that happened?"

"Footsteps on the roof?" Ramón repeated.

"Ramón, wake up! We haven't all night to get a little information out of you!" Theodore burst out.

"Oh, yes, we have all night," Sauzas said with a chuckle and lit a fresh cigarette. He smoked Gitanes, and the strong bittersweet smell of their 'caporal' tobacco was beginning to fill the room. "Well, did you hear the footsteps on the roof?" Sauzas asked.

"I don't remember. I don't think so."

A detective stood up abruptly from the table. "His finger-prints are on the bottle," he said, pointing to the Bacardi on the table. "There is also one of his on the bedstead and on the table by her bed."

"What about the window-sill and the knives in the kitchen?" Sauzas asked.

"There is only one knife with fingerprints, and the finger-prints are those of the woman," the detective replied.

"Um-m," Sauzas said non-committally. "Were you in love with Lelia, Ramón?"

"Yes," Ramón said.

"Did you want to marry her?"

Ramón's lips pressed together, then he jumped up from his chair and strode to the door. A detective and the two police-men ran after him and yanked him back. As they turned Ramón round, Theodore saw for a moment a frantic, tired, bewildered expression on his face, then they bounced him into a chair again. He sprang up. "I didn't do it!" Ramón shouted. "I didn't! I didn't!"

"No one has said you did."

Ramón was standing and would not be put back into the chair. A policeman on either side of him held his arms akimbo. "Did you do it, Teo?"

"No, Ramón, but I found her. I came here and found her," Theodore said.

"I don't believe you! Are those your flowers? Do you deny bringing them?" Ramón's voice rose hysterically.

"That remains to be found out, Ramón," Sauzas said. "Señor Schiebelhut says he came here and crawled through the transom because he had no key——"

"But he has a key!" Ramón interrupted, jerking at the policeman's hold.

27

"I left it at home. I have no key with me. I saw a light, Ramón, and I called to her."

"Search him for a key," Sauzas said to one of the detectives.

Theodore patiently emptied his pockets on to the table—wallet, key chain with two keys to his car and two to his house plus a mail-box key, cigarettes, lighter, change, a button that had fallen from his raincoat—but the detective felt in every pocket for himself. The keys on the chain were tested to see if they fitted the door.

Sauzas turned to Ramón. "You have her key with you?"

Ramón nodded, reached into his trouser pocket and pulled out a key-ring with three or four keys on it.

"Which is hers?" Sauzas asked, and when Ramón singled it out and handed the key-ring to him, he opened the door and tried it. The key worked. "Did you lock the door when you left here, Ramón?"

"Of course I did not. She was here."

"Did you hear her lock the door after you?"

"No. I don't remember."

"Was she in the habit of keeping the door locked?"

Ramón hesitated, and Theodore knew there wasn't any answer to that. Lelia did not have habits like that. She just might or might not lock the door after someone left her.

"The señorita's keys," Sauzas said suddenly. "See if you can find them, Enrique," he said to the detective who was standing in the hall doorway.

The detective went back to the bedroom, and Sauzas walked after him.

Theodore looked into the painted clay bowl on the book-shelf where Lelia often dropped her keys. The bowl was quite empty.

The keys were not to be found. The detectives looked even in the kitchen for them. The keys were not in any handbag, not in the pocket of any coat, not in any drawer. Theodore and Ramón were asked where she was in the habit of putting them, and both said in the clay bowl on the bookshelf.

"She was not very orderly," Theodore said, "but we should be able to find them if they are here." He was wondering why Ramón would have taken them. Or if somebody else could have taken them, someone who now had access to the apartment.

"Why did you take her keys, Ramón?" Sauzas asked abruptly.

"I did *not* take them."

"What did you do with them?"

Ramón stared back at him and lighted one of his little Carmencitas.

Sauzas walked up and down the room thoughtfully. "They may still be here—or they may not." He shrugged. "This would seem to eliminate the drainpipe as a means of exit. The murderer could have locked the door from the outside when he left. We shall have to look over your apartment, Ramón, but that can wait for a little while. Now——" He paused to light a fresh cigarette and looked at Ramón as he inhaled the smoke. "Would you say Señor Schiebelhut is a good friend of yours, Ramón?"

This, Ramón refused to answer.

"How long have you known Señor Schiebelhut?"

"Three years," Theodore supplied.

"And how long had you known Lelia?"

"Nearly four years," Theodore said when Ramón did not answer.

"Aha!" said Sauzas. "So Ramón found her first."

"Yes," Theodore said. "But we soon all became friends."

"How nice. No disagreements even though you were both her lovers?" Sauzas asked.

"No," Theodore said.

"Is that true, Ramón?"

"You know it is true, Ramón," Theodore said.

"Let him do the answering, Señor Schiebelhut."

Ramón seemed suddenly to relax. The policemen released him guardedly.

"Where did you meet her, Ramón?"

"I met her at the Cathedral," Ramón said.

The policemen and the detectives suddenly laughed.

"At the Cathedral. You spoke to her? Why?"

Ramón sat down in the chair and covered his face. "I spoke to her," he mumbled into his hands.

"And you became her lover at once?"

"Yes," Ramón said, though Theodore knew this was not so. They had known each other for months before Ramón became her lover.

"Did you give her money, Ramón? Money when you slept with her?"

"No," Ramón said sullenly through his hands.

"Did you give her money, Señor Schiebelhut?" Sauzas asked.

"I gave her many presents. I did not give her money."

"And how did you meet her?"

"I met her—by accident. One Sunday in Chapultepec Park." The scene flashed before his eyes, Lelia sitting on the stone bench sketching under the huge ahuehuete trees and glancing up at him as he strolled by, glancing up with the same preoccupied smile she might have given a *charro* on horseback, a peasant in sandals, a stray dog. Theodore had said: "It's a beautiful day for sketching." Such a commonplace beginning, but sentimentally he remembered it.

"And then?" Sauzas prompted.

"Then I got to know her," Theodore replied.

More smiles and smirks.

Someone was knocking on the door.

"Did you ask her to marry you, Señor Schiebelhut?"

"No."

"He doesn't believe in marriage," Ramón put in.

"Did you ever ask her to marry you, Ramón?" Sauzas asked him.

"No," Ramón said.

It was an absolute lie, Theodore knew. Ramón had asked her many times. But perhaps through lies they would get at the truth.

"And why not?" Sauzas asked.

"Because I have not the money to support her." Ramón lifted his head proudly and smiled.

The knock came again, and a female voice said: "Would you open the door, please?" But no one so much as looked at the door. Theodore recalled that Ramón had asked Lelia to marry him shortly after he, Theodore, had met her. And perhaps that hadn't been the first time. He wondered if Ramón had asked her again tonight, just before he was due to arrive, and Lelia had refused him. Not that Ramón would have planned it far enough that he was to walk in and be found with her body. No, Ramón did things impulsively. But he might have been angry tonight because she refused him.

"Did Ramón want to marry her, Señor Schiebelhut?" Sauzas asked.

"It was Lelia who did not want to marry."

Sauzas went to the door and opened it very slightly. A shrill duet of female voices began, and he shut the door quickly and leaned against it. "How many other men friends did she have, Señor Schiebelhut?"

Sauzas simply wanted to label her a whore, Theodore thought, something he was familiar with. "She had many. Many of them are artists—painters like herself."

"That she slept with?"

"Oh no. None."

"Anybody who came here frequently? Who might have been in love with her?"

Theodore thought of one young and struggling painter

from Puebla. But he gave that up. It couldn't have been Eduardo.

"There weren't any other men," Ramón said slowly. "*We* were her friends, Theodore and I. The rest were just——"

"Boy friends," supplied one of the detectives, and all the men except Sauzas and Theodore guffawed at Ramón.

"Any former lovers, then? You two weren't her first, were you?" Sauzas looked at Ramón.

Seconds passed, and Theodore said:

"I, at least, have never met any of her former lovers."

"Do you know the names of any?"

"Only one—Cristóbol Wagner. She told me he now lives in California."

Ramón had plunged his face in his hands. Cristóbol had perhaps been Lelia's first lover, at any rate the one who counted most. She had told Theodore, and probably Ramón too, that he was the only man she had ever considered marrying. His name, infrequently as Lelia mentioned it, always piqued a little jealousy in Theodore, and no doubt it did in Ramón. Cristóbol had known Lelia from the time she was twenty to twenty-three. Theodore answered Sauzas's questions about him as correctly as he could. He would be forty now, and he was an architect, and had gone to North America seven years ago and lived in California. As far as Theodore knew, he had never returned to Mexico, and Lelia never wrote to him. For one thing, he was now married and had children. Theodore did not know of any other former lovers in Mexico, but Sauzas kept asking him to rack his memory.

"She was a painter!" Ramón yelled. "This is her work! Look at it!" He indicated the four walls with a sweep of his arm.

The men looked about with prejudiced eyes, smiling a little.

"She was as good as this man here or better!" Ramón said aggressively with a nod at Theodore.

Now there was a sharper knock at the door. Sauzas went slowly to the door and opened it.

"I am Señorita Ballesteros's aunt," a woman's voice said.

Theodore went immediately to her. "Tía Josefina," he said, embracing her and kissing her cheek.

Lelia's Aunt Josefina, a woman of about fifty with a shining bun of black hair pierced with a silver comb at the back of her neck and a touch of purple shadow on her eyelids, permitted herself to rest her cheek for one instant on Theodore's shoulder. Then she lifted her head and addressed Sauzas: "Where is she, please?"

"In the bedroom," Sauzas said.

Theodore went with her, holding her arm, and he would have held the arm of Ignacia, her twenty-three-year-old daughter, too, but the hall was too narrow for the three of them to walk together. Ignacia followed them, and so did three or four men who had come in from the hall with Josefina. Theodore recognised only one of them, a local shopkeeper whom Lelia sometimes greeted when she passed him in the street.

Josefina gasped, and then from her large bosom came pigeon-like sounds of repressed sobs.

"There is no need to look, Tía Josefina," Theodore said, patting her arm. He tried to dissuade Ignacia from looking, but she stood where her mother was, on the threshold, clutching her mother's arm. Theodore went back into the livingroom. "Why can't we put the sheet over her face?" he said both to Sauzas and the fat police officer. "Is that not allowed?"

Somebody was kicking at the door now. "This is the press! Will you open up or shall we kick the door in?"

"We are still taking fingerprints!" Sauzas yelled back in a stentorian monotone. "You are not allowed in! So stay out and shut up! And who are all of you?" he asked the men who had come in with Josefina.

"José Garvez, at your service," said a tall, stout man with his hat in his hands. "I am the señorita's liquor caterer."

"Hm-m," Sauzas said, rubbing his black moustache. "And you?"

The next man shrugged, with embarrassment. His eyes were full of tears, and he could not speak. This was the man Theodore recognised as the baker.

"Sit down, all of you," Sauzas said. "We have questions to ask."

CHAPTER THREE

THEY were still at it at seven in the morning. Only Carlos Hidalgo and three of the men had been allowed to go home. José Garvez, the liquor caterer, had been asked to stay. The press had been let in, and six or eight men had clumped through the apartment with flash-bulbs and cameras and photographed Lelia from every angle they could, in spite of Theodore's protests and his pleas to Sauzas to call a halt. Theodore had begun to dislike Sauzas.

Nothing of significance had been found on the roof, nor had any fingerprints been found on the drainpipe.

One of the policemen had gone out for coffee and rolls, and they made a disorderly breakfast on Lelia's table that was already covered with fingerprint samples, newspapers, jackets, ash-trays, even a gun among all the mess only inches from Ramón's limp right hand. Ramón had laid his head down on the table, and whether he slept or not, nobody knew or cared.

They asked Josefina if she knew of any enemies that Lelia might have had. No; well then, any debts that she had? Josefina knew of only one possible debt, a small one to a doctor for a slight rash she had got at Lake Pátzcuaro last September, but even that was not really a debt, because the doctor had liked her so much he had told her she did not need to pay him anything.

This caused a burst of laughter among the police and detectives, and Josefina looked around at them with dark eyes afire with pride and resentment. "I know what you are thinking! If a woman wants to paint, what is so strange about that? If a woman has imagination? Do you think she wasn't serious? Look at her work around you, and if that doesn't impress you, maybe it will that she has paintings in the permanent collection at the Bellas Artes! And also that her work has been shown in New York! And if she does not want to marry, isn't that her own concern? And if she has two fine men friends," she went on, patting Theodore's hand which he rested on the table, "isn't that her business, too? If they call on her in the middle of the night, must you all smile like schoolboys? Just because all of you would perhaps have only one reason for calling on a woman in the middle of the night?"

"Mama," Ignacia said gently.

The portrait of the small boy named José, which Lelia had painted in luminous, melancholic blues and greens, looked down on it all with childlike dignity.

"When Lelia was nineteen, she went with my husband and me on a great tour through North America. She has studied in New York. She is no little girl from the provinces. I myself was a concert pianist," Josefina said, tossing her head and sitting up still straighter. "But I gave up my career to marry. Lelia did not give up her career. And for another thing," she said, looking at the fat officer and then at Sauzas, "my husband has for years been giving her a stipend of four hundred pesos a month. She did not have to beg for her bread, I assure you. Or whore!"

Sauzas acknowledged all this with a deep nod and made no comment. Coolly he turned to Ramón. "Ramón Otero, have you ever been in trouble before with the police?"

Ramón raised his head slowly.

Sauzas repeated the question.

"Yes," Ramón said. "I was falsely charged and beaten nearly to death by the fine police of Chihuahua. I was sleeping by the roadside in a truck, and they came up and hauled me in for murder and robbery." He glared with loathing at the fat police officer, and pulled his packet of Carmencitas— the cheap miniature cigarettes—out of his pocket.

36

"When was this?" asked Sauzas.

"Five years ago. Six."

"How old are you?"

"Thirty."

"And you were found not guilty?"

"The guilty man was found a few days later. Otherwise they might have killed me. As it was——" He made an effort at a smile, but it was a grimace.

"They hit him with a metal bar," Theodore said to Sauzas, "and he suffered a concussion. It has——" Theodore shrugged. "It has changed him."

"Aha," said Sauzas. "Has he ever been in a mental institution?"

"No," said Theodore, "but he gets severe headaches sometimes."

"You are now defending him, Señor Schiebelhut?"

"No, I am not defending him!" Theodore said, frowning.

"And he has spells also of bad temper?"

"Yes," Theodore said firmly.

"And you think he got into a bad temper tonight and killed the woman?"

"I did not kill her!" Ramón shouted. "All right, beat me to death! Help yourself! But I didn't kill her!" He was half out of his chair.

"All right, Ramón! We are only here to find out the facts. Do you have a knife? A knife at home?"

"I have several knives. All for my kitchen," Ramón said.

"You never carry a knife?"

"Do you think I'm a guttersnipe?"

Suddenly everyone was talking at once.

"You were the last one here!" Sauzas was yelling. "Why shouldn't we suspect you? Do you think we're numbskulls?"

"Try it! Go ahead!" Ramón yelled wildly.

Sauzas threw up his hands and turned to Theodore. "Señor Schiebelhut, why did you come to Mexico?"

37

"Because I like Mexico very much."

"How long were you in the United States? Did you become a citizen?"

Theodore had already told Sauzas that he was born near Hamburg, that he had been taken by his parents to Switzerland when he was eleven, had received his schooling there and in Paris, and that he had come to the United States at the age of twenty-two. "I left before my citizenship papers came through in America," Theodore said tiredly.

"Then what did you do?"

"I travelled—mostly around South America—for three or four years. I lived here and there. Does all this matter?"

"Yes. Why did you decide to come to Mexico?"

"Because I like it best. Since I have an income, it doesn't matter where I live."

Theodore's source of income was discussed for perhaps fifteen minutes, though it was quite simple: he derived it from property that his family owned in Germany and from stocks which had become active and valuable when Germany had begun to recover after the war. All in all, he received about twenty-five thousand pesos per month. On which, of course, he paid the required Mexican income tax. He could prove that, if anyone cared to examine his papers. The subject bored him and made him feel sleepier than ever. It seemed to him that the police were deliberately keeping him and Ramón awake in a kind of slow version of American police grilling. There were no swinging lights or rubber cudgels; but in the long run the method was the same: extract a confession through exhaustion, through a collapse of sanity. His tiredness made him fretful, and he was particularly irritated by the stupid curiosity with which the police and detectives looked at him when they heard that he had an income of twenty-five thousand pesos per month. How did a man spend all that? What did he do with it? The more he cut short and evaded, the more closely they pressed him. When he said he owned a house in Cuernavaca as well as one in Mexico, D.F., they stared at him with the pleased, dazed expressions of people watching a Hollywood movie.

"I can only say that it is quite possible to spend twenty-five thousand pesos in Mexico, if one has a house, a maid, a car, repairs on the house—if one buys books and music——" Theodore had the feelnng he was talking in his sleep, arguing with irrational characters in a dream.

"And a mistress?" the gum-chewing detective sitting next to Theodore asked him with a nudge in his ribs.

Theodore edged away from him, but the nauseating mint-staleness of his breath had made Theodore's stomach constrict. He took a swallow of his execrable coffee, which was mouse-grey and mostly boiled milk. The rim of the paper cup was disintegrating. "Excuse me," Theodore said, getting up. He went to Lelia's bathroom off the hall. He could not throw up after all. There was nothing in his stomach. But he stood nauseated for several minutes over the toilet, holding his tie out of the way with his big, gentle hand against his chest. He washed his hands and face. His skin felt numb. Then he took some of Lelia's Colgate toothpaste and rinsed his mouth. He stood for a moment, staring at the array of perfumes and toilet waters on the little shelf on the wall. He looked down at the unlevel white tile floor and the oval blue bath-mat. He could see his own naked feet on it. How many happy day and nights—— Perhaps it was all not true what had happened, Lelia dead, raped, and with her nose cut off. His ears began to ring and the tiles grew unclear. Theodore bent over as low as he could, until his head was below his knees. A ridiculous position. He cursed his body.

"Señor Schiebelhut!"

He waited with eyes shut, feeling his heavy blood gravitating to his head.

"Señor Schiebelhut!" Steps approached.

"Coming!" Theodore called, straightening. He brushed his hand across his hair and opened the door.

They were questioning Ramón about his work and his income. Ramón replied in sullen, monosyllabic answers, Ramón worked in a furniture repair shop behind the Cathedral, only five or six streets away. He was a partner in the shop with Arturo Baldin, and they had two assistants. Ramón's income varied. He said from three hundred to six hundred pesos weekly, but Theodore knew that many weeks Ramón made only a hundred pesos or even less, sixty pesos, as little as the commonest labourer in Mexico. Theodore, hearing of Ramón's low wages from Lelia, often tucked a hundred-peso bill into Ramón's jacket pocket and sometimes insisted outright that Ramón take a few hundred from him. Ramón had a sense of economic justice and didn't mind accepting money from Theodore, because Theodore had so much more and did nothing to earn it. He could take Theodore's money with neither shame nor arrogance. He did not even show that he was glad to get it. This Theodore appreciated very much in Ramón. But Theodore noticed now that Ramón did not mention that he often gave him money. It was just as well, Theodore thought, because it would have confused things still more. They kept asking Ramón how he managed to live on so little money, or did he not try to supplement his income in other ways. Ramón certainly did not try to supplement his income in other ways, not even with the *Loteria Nacional*. He lived frugally, and he did not complain. When the police officer—there was no systematic interrogation, and anybody asked a question who wanted to—suggested that Ramón might have served as a pimp for Lelia, Ramón replied in the same dull tone: "No." How often did he come to see Lelia? Maybe two or three times a week, maybe every evening sometimes.

And sometimes, Theodore knew, he did not come to see her for two and three weeks. But always he came back, swallowing his pride, or rather concealing with debonair good humour the defeat of his pride once more.

A canary's trill came through the open window. A newsboy's *"Excelsior! Novedades!"* And the thunderous roar of a truck. It was another beautiful, sunny day.

"Señor Schiebelhut, do you think he killed her?" Sauzas asked suddenly.

"I don't know," Theodore said.

"You thought so a few hours ago," said the fat officer.

It was true, he had. Theodore could not think what had happened to make him doubt. Perhaps nothing.

"Who do you think killed Lelia, Ramón?" Sauzas asked him.

"Maybe he did," Ramón said indifferently. His dark eyes rested on Theodore. "After all, he was found here with her. He can't explain how he got in. She let him in."

"Ramón!" Josefina said in an admonishing tone.

Theodore felt only a slight start of fear, and yet his heart had begun pounding. He remembered a time when Ramón had thrown a platter of cooked duck out the kitchen window into the patio because he, Theodore, was a little late for dinner, and Ramón hadn't liked to wait. But with such a temper—if Ramón thought he had killed Lelia, he would certainly kill him, probably throttle him with those strong hands before anybody could stop him.

"Señor Schiebelhut did explain how he got in, Ramón. Ramón!" Sauzas said over his shoulder, "Get another wet towel, Enrique. Ramón, you have the key to this apartment. You have it with you. The lock is not automatic, so the door had to be locked from the outside—perhaps by you. The drainpipe would not bear your weight. We have tried it. The transom shows from its dust that *something* came through it. Now do you want us to suspect you?"

Ramón shrugged, and the very slightness of the shrug was an insult to Sauzas.

41

Everybody waited uncomfortably as the detective approached with the wet towel, put it over Ramón's face, and wiped it with a twist as if he were wiping a baby's nose. Ramón sprang up and threw a wild blow at the detective with his fist. Instantly the policemen were on their feet around the table. Ramón kept swinging violently, even when he slipped to his knees. A tall policeman was thrown completely down when he caught one of Ramón's arms. Then there was a cracking sound; Ramón sprawled on the floor, and a policeman hovered over him with bared teeth, holding by the barrel the gun he had struck him with.

"That's fine!" said Theodore, who reproached himself now for not having joined in the fight. "That's going to do him a lot of good! Six men, and you have to hit him with a gun-butt!"

Josefina was kneeling by Ramón, using the wet towel on his face. Ramón made feeble movements, as if he were fighting in a dream, but he did not open his eyes. His strong mouth looked calm and childlike.

When Ramón came to a little, Sauzas asked more questions, which Ramón scorned to answer by so much as a glance at him.

Then the door opened smartly, and Theodore jumped a little. A policeman he had not seen before came forward and saluted Sauzas. "The flowers were bought at a stand four streets from here," the policeman said, a little out of breath. "They were bought between ten-thirty and eleven-thirty. The man is not sure."

"Bought by whom?" Sauzas asked.

"A small boy. About—this high, the man thinks. These are the only white carnations sold in the neighbourhood last night to the number of two dozen, Señor Capitán." The policeman's face was tense and blank.

"A small boy," one of the men at the table echoed, and gave a low laugh.

CHAPTER FOUR

A LITTLE before eleven, Theodore got out of a taxi and carried his suitcase and portfolio and roll of canvases to his front gate. He was accompanied by the fat police officer and one of the detectives. Ramón had been taken off to prison for further questioning by Sauzas.

Theodore was irritated by the presence of the two men. They had stuck their noses in when he was talking with Josefina about the funeral arrangements for Lelia and had not offered the least assistance when he was searching on the street for a telephone to call an *agencia funereal*. All this had been most complicated, because the police were not through with the body. They wanted to measure the depth and width of the knife wounds and perform an autopsy besides.

Theodore opened his mail-box, took out some letters, and pocketed them without looking at them. Señora Velasquez, who lived next door, had been forwarding his important mail to Oaxaca.

He noticed that the ivy that overhung his iron gates needed water badly in the half nearest his house. Constancia, the Velasquezes' maid, would have watered it from his first-floor window, but he had not given her a key. Theodore and the two men entered a patio paved with pinkish flag-stones, at the back of which, under part of the second storey, was a garage. Theodore went on to a door at the side of the house for which he used his other key. The living-room was semi-dark, but Theodore's eyes were everywhere, looking first at his plants—the big begonia looked as if it had died, and it was a shame—and at the furniture Inocenza had covered with

43

sheets as he had asked her to do. He pulled a cord, and bright yellow sunlight filled the room. Then, ignoring the two men, he carried the begonia to the kitchen at the back of the house.

He had soaked the plant before he left and stood it in a bowl of water, but it was a big *semperflorens* and drank half a litre of water a day. And now, as he soaked the dry pot, Theodore reproached himself for fretting like an old maid over a plant, when Lelia had been dead only twelve hours.

He turned round and found the two men staring at him from the doorway of the kitchen. "Well, this is my house. You see that I have one."

"Why did you go to Oaxaca, señor?" asked the fat officer slyly.

"I went to paint, señor."

"You must have left very suddenly, not to be able to take care of your plants."

"I do things when I want to."

"You are a very careful man," the officer continued, shaking his head. "You wouldn't have left your house without preparation unless you had been in a hurry."

"You have Ramón Otero in prison. Why don't you go and question him?" With his begonia pot, he advanced towards the door, and the two men stepped back to make way for him. Then they followed him through the dining area and into the living-room, where they gaped for the second time at the stairway that curved up out of sight with no visible means of support.

"Would you like to see the first floor?" Theodore asked ungraciously.

The detective, bending towards a small nude of Lelia that Theodore had painted, did not answer. The fat officer yawned, exposing several gold teeth. They tramped up the carpeted stairs to Theodore's bedroom, his bathroom, the guest-room and its bathroom, the little front corner room

44

where he painted, and finally even Inocenza's room and bathroom, which were the only rooms on the second floor.

"Lots of bathrooms," commented the police officer.

The tiny red bulb was still burning beneath the effigy of the Virgin made of sea-shells and pink and white coral that a friend of Inocenza had sent her from Acapulco. A reproduction of a bad painting of the Last Supper advertised as well Bayer's Cafiaspirina, bore a calendar of the year with all the saints' name days on it, and wished to all *Prosperidad y Bienestar para el Año 1957*. They went downstairs.

"You are not to leave the house," said the fat officer, "without notifying us."

"I have no intention of leaving the house," Theodore replied.

They copied his telephone number from the telephone in the living-room, then drifted out of the door, taking time to bend and inspect one of the blossoming cacti that bordered the patio. Theodore made sure the iron gates had latched after them, then closed his house door.

He carried his suitcase up to his bedroom, interrupted his unpacking to take a bath, but the water was cool because the heater was not turned up. He went down to the kitchen, turned it up, collected his other plants and stood them in the kitchen sink and its wash-basin, then went up and resumed his unpacking. There was a little horse of glazed black Oaxaca clay that he had bought for Lelia, and a mermaid of grey unglazed clay, strumming a guitar, for Ramón. Besides this, he had bought Lelia an antique bracelet of silver set with garnets, and for Ramón half a dozen hand-woven ties. He tossed the presents on his bed and felt that the better part of his existence had been torn from him and destroyed. He bathed before the water was quite hot enough, but he was so eager to be clean he did not mind. Then he shaved and put on clean linen, a blue and red striped tie, and a freshly pressed grey suit.

He walked out of the room, down the stairs, snatched up his keys from the cocktail table and went out. He pressed the bell of the house next door.

Constancia, fat and brown and in a pink uniform, opened the door. "Ah, Señor Schie-bale-hoo!" she cried shrilly. *"Pase Usted! Benvenido! Com' está Usted?"*

He could see from her tentative smile that she had heard the news. "All right, Constancia. And you?"

"Well, thank you!" she said mechanically.

"And Señora Velasquez?"

"She is well, too, and so is the cat. Wait till you see him! Leo! Leo!" She preceded him through the grape-arboured patio, calling to the cat on either side, assuming in spite of the murder of his friend that he would be extremely interested in seeing his cat. "We do not let him out on the street. His girl friends have missed him," Constancia said, smiling.

The door of the house was open, and Olga Velasquez rushed across the foyer to greet him. She was about forty, small and small-boned and very chic with her short blonde-tinted hair and her tiny high-heeled sandals. "Theodore!" She reached up for his shoulders and made a gesture of kissing both cheeks, though she came only to the middle of his tie. "I have just seen the paper! How dreadful! Is it true?"

"Yes, it is true."

"You've been with the police?"

"All night. I've been home only an hour." The sight of Leo stepping forth from behind a hollowed log full of blossoming orchids sent a shock through Theodore, like the shock of seeing a close friend after a long time. For an instant, Theodore took pleasure in the colours of the picture: the orange of the orchids, Leo's blending brown and tan and his clear, bright blue eyes. Theodore stooped and caressed the cat's brown cheek and ear. "Leo—and how have you been?" The cat, miffed at Theodore's desertion of him for

46

a month, pretended interest in something in another direction. Then as Olga Velasquez began to speak, Leo looked at Theodore and opened his mouth in a monotone wail, holding the note like an operatic soprano at the climax of an aria, augmenting it even to drown out Olga, who, however, paid no attention.

"Doesn't he look fine? He has caught at least six lizards and *one snake*! Imagine! A snake *this* long in our patio!"

"He is angry because I went away and left him," Theodore said, feeling suddenly weak enough to drop on the floor.

Olga Velasquez's face took on an expression of distress. "You must be exhausted, Don Teodoro! Sit down. Would you like some coffee? I was just about to have some. Imagine, I had to get up at eight o'clock this morning to go to a traffic court about a ticket I got for speeding on the *autopista* to Cuernavaca. Imagine that one *could* speed on a speedway! That's why I didn't see the papers until just now when I got back. I couldn't believe it was true! You do take sugar, don't you?"

"Yes, Olga." He accepted the cup of coffee. It was in a little cup of transparent blue glass with a spiral design. The cool, beautiful blue made him think of diving head-first into some refreshing sea. He half listened to Señora Velasquez's voice, that went on and on about Lelia. Was it true, was it true? Was it true that he had just walked in and found her?

"And do you think it could have been Ramón?" she asked in a breathless whisper.

Constancia, who had not left the living-room after bringing the extra cup and saucer, stood a few feet away, listening agape.

"I don't know. I suppose it is better not to say anything until we know. He is being questioned by the police."

"Do you have any idea who else could have done it?"

"No."

47

"I never thought Ramón was quite right in the head."

"He is moody, he has a temper—but I don't consider him insane," Theodore said, looking at her.

Olga tossed her head a little as if to say, well, *he* might not consider him insane. "Such a beautiful girl! Such a sweet girl, Lelia! I liked her very much, you know, Teo."

But she had seen Lelia very few times, Theodore thought. She knew that Lelia was his mistress, but she probably did not think that he was really in love with her. Olga would have behaved with the same concern if Lelia Ballesteros had been merely a friend. Theodore and Olga were good neighbours, but they kept a certain distance. Señor Velasquez, though ostensibly a lawyer, dabbled unethically in several businesses, Theodore knew, but he never asked questions of Olga or of anyone else about him, and had no curiosity to find out anything about his business practices.

"How is your husband?" Theodore asked, as he always did.

"Oh, as fine as ever. But tell me, you mean they have no suspects except Ramón?" She leaned towards him on the sofa, pressing her soft, well-groomed hands together.

"Dear Olga, *I* am a suspect."

"*You?*"

"Because I was there, too. I'm not supposed to leave my house."

"Oh, they don't really suspect you, or you'd be in jail!" she said carelessly. "And Inocenza is not back?"

"No. I must phone her."

"I shall make Constancia go home with you and take care of everything you need today—marketing, cleaning, everything! You must take a rest after this terrible experience!"

"Thank you, Olga. And I can't thank you enough for taking care of my mail."

"Ah! I'm glad you reminded me. There's lots of mail here still. I sent you only the most important, you know." She

48

jumped up. "But we can get that later," she said, sitting down again. "Ramón was very fond of her, too, wasn't he?" she asked.

"Oh yes." Theodore stroked Leo's back. The cat was in his lap, turning round and round on the unsure footing of Theodore's thighs, unable to make up his mind whether to show enough affection to lie down or to express his annoyance with Theodore by leaving.

"And you're very fond of Ramón, aren't you?"

"Yes, I am. I considered him my best friend—at least until this happened."

"Then you do think he did it!" she cried.

"I don't know. But I have to suspect him. The facts——"

"That's what I mean, Don Teodoro."

She prepared more instant coffee for him, taking three generous *demi-tasse* spoonfuls from the glass jar imprisoned in its hand-wrought silver filigree case which stood always on her coffee-table. The coffee was quite good, being much stronger than American instant coffee, but it still seemed odd to Theodore that a country which exported quantities of coffee beans drank instant coffee almost to a man, preferred it even, and, moreover, thought so much of it that silversmiths made beautiful cases around ordinary instant coffee-jars of varying sizes to take their place among the family valuables.

Theodore stayed about a quarter of an hour, during which time he phoned Durango at Sra. Velasquez's insistence, and left a message with Inocenza's sister—Inocenza was at a neighbour's house, the sister said—that he was home and he would like her to come back at once by plane. He was grateful that the sister did not say anything about Lelia. They had probably not yet seen the papers. Theodore went with Constancia back to his house, he carrying the cat, and Constancia a pair of baked squabs, a litre of milk, and a casserole of egg-plant and cheese, freshly made, which Olga Velasquez insisted he

49

take. There was no need for Constancia to come back until four o'clock, when she had to prepare for a small cocktail party. Theodore was invited to the party, but he had declined.

After showing Constancia what had to be done in the house, Theodore changed into pyjamas and dressing-gown, made himself a pot of tea, and carried it to his room. He felt weak and half sick, hungry yet averse to anything he could think of to eat. He gave Constancia ten pesos and told her to go out and buy some rolls and fruit and the news-papers, but not to bother him with them when she came back as he might be asleep. She had not yet gone out, and down-stairs, as she worked, she was singing a popular song.

> . . . my heart . . . which is so heavy . . . cries for your heart . . . how can you leave me alone . . . my heart . . . when I bring you my heart . . . my heart . . . in my hands . . .

Mi corazón. The word *corazón* occurred over and over in Mexican popular songs. Theodore tried not to listen, but at the last line, each time Constancia came to it—and she was singing the same verse over and over—Theodore saw himself stumbling towards somebody with his own bleeding heart in his hands and a bleeding hole in his chest. He looked through the mail that Olga had saved for him. Bank statements. A telephone bill. Unsealed announcements of exhibitions and of a performance of *Lysistrata* at Ciudad Universidad under the direction of Carlos Hidalgo with sets by Lelia Ballesteros. It had come and gone. He got the mail he had received this morning out of his jacket pocket, saw a square blue envelope among it, and opened it frantically, letting the rest of the mail drop on the floor.

It was dated simply 'Friday'.

Amor mio,

I have a feeling you will be back in a day or so and did not want you to come home without a note from me. Welcome home! Did you paint well? We have missed you.

Let me know as soon as you are back and visit me and bring your work or if you have *so many* excellent canvases, I'll come to see you.

I think I am about to sell a painting to the man of San Francisco—that is to a man he knows. Remember the dealer from S.F. who took photographs of my Veracruz paintings? Much to talk about.

Ramón is fine. We both miss you.

Todo mi amor,

L.

It had been mailed on 1st February. Today was the 5th. He searched it foolishly for a clue, and could see nothing but Lelia's good spirits, energy in the crossed t's that carried over and began the next word and suggested the easy legato of her speech. He carried the letter to his opened desk and laid it gently down. Over the desk hung a pen-and-ink and water-colour sketch of a girl lolling in a hammock at Pie de la Cuesta, a bare foot and leg dangling, a string of green coconuts tumbled in her lap. "Just an Indian girl who was selling coconuts. Thank you, Señor, but it has no price. It is promised to a friend." And Lelia had laughed. Theodore remembered the sound of her laugh, expressing pleasure at the man's appreciation of her sketch, friendliness and apology all at once. Theodore frowned at the drawing until his tears obliterated the blue of the water, the sky, and finally all of it, and he sank into his chair and wept at his desk. He cried thoughtlessly, like a child over an unwarranted and undeserved disappointment.

Theodore wondered how little José would take it. He was

51

about nine years old now. Lelia had done four or five paintings of him, though behind her back he was apt to steal her jewellery or a handful of change that she left lying about. "Oh, he can't help it, Teo. I was not so fond of that pin, anyway!" Lelia would say when Theodore offered to give the child a good scare and get the jewellery back. Lelia loved innocence, which was why she loved most children and only some adults. She always said the ideal thing would be to grow more innocent instead of more wise, and when Theodore had done some absent-minded thing or had got rooked by a shopkeeper, Lelia would tease him and tell him he was certainly growing more innocent every day. He could see Lelia swinging her door open for him with a smile, could see her in tears late at night and inconsolable because a day's work had gone badly, could see her stooping to talk to a child on her block, buying candy for another, kissing another on the cheek as if it were her own, because the child had posed for her. It seemed to Theodore now that her equal love for Ramón and him, which he had often puzzled over, finding ever new and complex reasons for it, was simply in accord with her nature. To belong to one man would be to shut out all others.

He walked to his bed and lay down slowly, as unrelaxed as a figure of stone on a tomb. No more conversations with Lelia, no more happiness shared with her when she sold a picture, or when a reviewer wrote a word of praise. As a painter, Lelia was going to be judged by what she had done up until yesterday at the age of thirty years and one month. Theodore's blood began to stir with thoughts of revenge. Whoever had done it would pay with his life. He would see to that, even if there were no capital punishment in Mexico. This was no ordinary murder—with a bullet or even one or two knife stabs. He heard the scratch and tear of Leo's claws in the ivy, and the cat arrived at the window-sill and seated himself with his tail curled around his forefeet, staring into the room while his eyes adjusted to the dimmer light. Theodore lowered his hand at the side of the bed, and the cat came noiselessly to him and rubbed his face against his fingers, then jumped on to Theodore's chest. Leo purred loudly and gazed at Theodore as objectively as if he had been a picture on the wall.

As he drowsed, Theodore's thoughts about Ramón became ambiguous, as they had been for moments during the questioning. Ramón had a streak of cruelty, Theodore thought. He was not able to forget that, and not able to control his contempt and fear of Ramón because he had it. That parakeet he kept in his apartment! It drove Theodore insane when he was there. A dozen times Theodore had wanted to rush to the cage and free it and then open the window so it could fly out—but he never had. As far as Theodore knew, Ramón had never let the bird so much as fly around the room, and the little creature worked constantly to get the door of its cage open. Ramón had never even honoured it with a name. There was much more Spanish than Indian in Ramón. Ramón accused him of looking down on the Spanish, but Theodore did not look down or up, he simply tried to understand them, and they fascinated him because he couldn't. Ramón fascinated him with his mixture of Catholicism and cruelty and that extra enigma that was in him because of those four or five days of humiliation and beating in the Chihuahua prison. That beating had gone beyond mere mistakenness, the mere shame of being called a murderer: to Ramón the beating involved a concept of punishment for all his past 'sins' foisted upon him by the Catholic Church and created in his own mind. So that, in a curious way, Ramón had enjoyed the beating and the humiliation, though it had made him bitterly hostile to the police because they had inflicted it. Theodore did not want to think that Ramón had killed Lelia, but the facts and Ramón's character made it possible that he had.

53

The ambiguousness of it made Theodore sleepy—a pheno-menon he was familiar with. Sometimes his drowsiness, his evasion, angered him when he was trying to think some-thing out, and he paced around his room or drank coffee to combat it. And sometimes, thinking it best, he yielded to delicious little naps in mid-morning or mid-afternoon, in-duced by his chronic inability to decide anything. (Granted that he wanted to go on living, was his life worth his while or the world's? Was he contributing anything other than his paintings, which few people looked at, and the money he gave to schools and hospitals and to families like Inocenza's in Durango? Having found out that he was a good painter, would it avail him anything to try to be a better one? Should he try to take an active part in politics, even if the Mexicans made a laughing-stock of him? Shouldn't he go to see the mummies at Guanajuato, as Ramón wanted him to do, instead of saying he knew what they would look like and what his reaction would be? How much unhappier would Mexico be if it were Protestant instead of Catholic? Some-times he awoke with what seemed like brilliant answers to these and similar questions, but most of the time he did not.)

He was awakened by a knocking on the door and Con-stancia bawling, as he had asked her not to do, that it was nearly four and that she had to leave. Theodore thanked her and let his head fall back on the pillow again. Then suddenly he got up and, before his head was quite clear, went to his telephone that stood on a low table beside his desk and dialled the number of his lawyer, Roberto Martinez. Theodore told him about Ramón and asked for the name of a reliable lawyer who might help him. Sr. Martinez gave him a name and offered to ring up the man himself.

"Very well," Theodore said, "if you'll be sure to call him immediately." Theodore made certain Sr. Martinez knew which jail Ramón was in, the large one near the Zócalo, and then he hung up. It was five past four. Theodore regretted that he had waited this long. Guilty or not, Ramón was entitled to the services of a good lawyer.

The telephone rang two or three times in the next hour. One call was from Antonio Cortés, a neighbour of Theodore's in Cuernavaca, another from Mabel Van Blarcom in Coyoacán, a suburb of the city. The third was from Elissa Straeter, an unmarried American woman whom Theodore saw now and then at parties and whom he did not like. They all asked the same questions: was he all right; was there anything they could do; and would he like to visit them? Theodore was very fond of Mabel Van Blarcom and her Dutch husband, but he did not care to visit anybody now. Elissa, who was often drunk but did not sound drunk now, told him, in her invariably calm, polite tone, of a party scheduled for 4th March, during Carnaval week, in Pedregal, an exclusive residential district just north of the city.

"I can imagine you can't think about a party now," Elissa said in a sympathetic drone, "but maybe by the time a month rolls around—it's Johnny Doolittle's party, and he told me to ask anyone I wished, which doesn't mean of course that you have to *escort* me, but we'd all love to see you there. *I* would."

Theodore thanked her and said he would remember and try to come.

He went downstairs and mixed a strong whisky and water with an intention of drinking it and trying to sleep again, but he felt no nearer sleep after he had finished it, and he picked up the telephone and called the prison.

"May I speak to Capitán Sauzas?" he asked.

Much clicking and interference on the line. He could hear both ends of a conversation concerning the presence of bicycles in an area reserved for traffic officers' motor-cycles. One of the men was very angry with the other.

"Capitán Sauzas is not here," the voice said finally.

He was probably sleeping, Theodore thought. "May I speak to Ramón Otero?"

"Who?"

"Ramón Otero. O-t-e-r-o. He is being held there for questioning in the Ballesteros—the Ballesteros murder," Theodore stammered nervously, knowing already that it was hopeless.

"Prisoners are not allowed the use of the telephone, señor," said the man with a smile in his voice.

"Can you tell me what is happening to him? I'll be very glad to wait while you find out."

"No, señor, we cannot give out that information."

Theodore looked up his lawyer's home telephone number —it was nearly seven now—and called it. Sr. Martinez assured him that the lawyer he had found had gone at once to the prison, but he had not heard from him since. Theodore got the office and home telephone numbers of the criminal lawyer, a Sr. Pablo Castillo Z., and called them both, but neither the office, which did not answer, nor his home, where a maid answered, gave him any information.

Theodore opened a can of fish for Leo, fed him in the kitchen, then went to bed. He felt too tired to sleep, and there was something nightmarish about the light in the room with the blinds drawn against the slow dusk. His body felt too heavy to move, yet his brain spun lightly round and round, coming to grips with nothing.

CHAPTER FIVE

Sr. Castillo Z. telephoned at nine-fifteen the next morning and woke Theodore up.

"Well," he said on a note of triumph, "your friend is released. They questioned him all night. I haven't even been to bed yet. But he is free."

"Then they think he's innocent?"

"Why, yes. So do I. The evidence is not enough——"

"They proved what time he went to his own house after dinner?"

"No—not exactly. But what they have is sufficient to show that Ramón Otero did not do it. Señor Otero thinks he was home by ten-thirty. Now the doctor does not think she was killed before eleven. Eleven is the earliest."

Or ten minutes to eleven, Theodore thought, remembering his watch had said one-fifty when the doctor gave his two-to-three-hour opinion. And Ramón only *thought* he was home by ten-thirty. "How is Señor Otero?" Theodore asked.

"Ugh! Exhausted, señor! No sleep for two nights in a row. I can assure you, a guilty man would have broken down. But your friend protested his innocence to the last. You did not think he was *guilty*, señor!"

"Where is he now?"

"He will be allowed to go home this morning. They have sent for his partner, Señor——"

"Baldin."

"Yes. He is going to see that he gets home. Ah—shall I send the bill to your address, señor, or to Señor Otero?"

"You may send it to me," Theodore said.

After he had hung up, Theodore sat on the edge of his bed

thinking. A criminal lawyer, no matter how clever, couldn't have got a guilty man away from the police that fast, Theodore supposed. So he had to believe then that Ramón wasn't guilty. Perhaps. Things were not always logical in Mexico. In America, they might have spent a week rounding up Ramón's friends and acquaintances and trying to establish when and where he had made every move before and after the time of the murder. Only then would they have come to a decision. But in Mexico——

Theodore made another attempt at unpacking, but his mind wandered back to Ramón. He could not feel positive that Ramón hadn't done it. With policemen, Ramón could turn his heart and his face to stone, if he wanted to. Theodore began to think it was possible that he had fooled the police.

At ten-thirty he tried again to reach Sauzas by telephone. This time, after a ten-minute wait, he got him.

"Have you definite proof that he is not guilty?" Theodore asked.

"Proof?" Sauzas hesitated. "No, except that he does not behave like a guilty man, señor. He behaves like a man who has lost his wife. We believe that the murderer got in by the ruse of delivering flowers or bringing flowers, and that he had a small boy buy them for him so the flower seller would not remember him. We are trying to find this boy in the neighbourhood, but the flower seller does not remember enough about the boy."

"So—there are no new clues at all?"

"No, señor. But now our work begins, eh? You will stay in your house, señor, until further notice, if you please."

"You mean I can't go out anywhere in the city?"

"Well—yes. But don't attempt to leave the city. We shall be wanting to question you again."

"Very well. And, Señor Capitán—I should like to be

informed of any new thing you find out. Will you do that?"

"Very well, señor."

Theodore debated for a moment, then called Ramón's number. The telephone rang about ten times, but Theodore waited patiently.

Finally, he heard a confusion of two voices and then Ramón's partner, Arturo Baldin, said: *"Bueno?"*

"Bueno, Arturo. How are you? This is Theodore Schiebelhut."

"How are you, Don Teodoro? I hope well."

"Thank you. I wanted to ask about Ramón."

"Ah, he is very tired, señor. I am trying to get him to go to sleep," said Arturo in his kindly, paternal voice.

"Yes. I can understand. Is there anything I can——" Theodore hesitated, on an emotional fence as to putting himself out for Ramón.

"I don't think so, Don Teodoro. We have some sleeping-pills. They should have an effect soon."

In the background, Ramón murmured something.

Theodore had wanted to talk to Ramón. Suddenly he did not. "I'm glad you're there to look after him, Arturo."

"It's hard to keep him quiet, because he wants to go out to see—Who is it, Ramón?—Josefina."

But he doesn't want to see me, Theodore thought. "No, it's best he stays quiet," Theodore said.

They hung up cordially.

Inocenza arrived at three in the afternoon. She had seen the papers and was full of questions, sympathy, condolences from all her family in Durango, until Theodore finally said, gently: "Please, Inocenza—would you be quiet?"

"But you do *not* think Don Ramón *killed* her, señor!" She was very fond of Ramón.

"He was released this morning."

"Oh!" she said with relief. "Thanks be to God! He is not guilty!"

"No," said Theodore. "Let me help you with your things. What's all this?"

"My family sends a duck with their good wishes. And my Aunt Maria made a counterpane for you. That is this," she said, slapping a string-tied bundle on the floor. "Inside the wrapping is very pretty, but I didn't want it to get dirty on the plane. Ah, the plane, señor! The soup went this way, that way! I was afraid for my life, especially when I thought of the Señorita Lelia—*la pobrecita*. No, don't carry anything, it is not fitting for you to carry my suitcase. Would you like tea or anything, señor?"

"No, thank you, Inocenza. I am just very glad you are back." He walked to the window that looked on to the patio and lighted a cigarette. It was good to have her in the house again, to hear her hurrying footsteps and her humming and singing in the kitchen, though she would probably be careful not to hum today. Inocenza had been very fond of Lelia, too, and not at all jealous, as Ramón had suggested a few times. Sometimes Ramón tried to pique him by telling him that Inocenza was his 'real wife'. It was true she got her way most of the time, but what servant didn't? Inocenza had been with him nearly four years. Ramón wanted a servant to be more servile than Inocenza, perhaps, yet neither Ramón nor anybody else could find one justifiable complaint about her. She stayed home at night, she ironed well and cooked well. She was also pleasant to look at, with her shining black hair always neatly done up in a great bun at the back of her neck. She wore shoes with a slight heel, which set her apart from the average flat-footed drudges one saw in the markets, and she wore a little lipstick. She was only thirty-two, and at the prime of her attractiveness, Theodore thought, though the only man she seemed to like at all was a quiet fellow called Ricardo who worked in Toluca and seldom got to the city.

Eight or nine years ago she had borne an illegitimate son, Pepe, who lived with her family in Durango. Theodore sent him little gifts and toys now and then.

For the first time since he had come home, Theodore was able to unpack his canvases, six of them rolled in a waterproof cloth, and spread them on the couch and the floor of the room in which he painted. One canvas was not absolutely dry, but it had not smeared. He avoided looking at them now, because they seemed to bring Lelia very close. He called the Mercedes-Benz garage and asked for his car to be delivered as soon as possible.

At six o'clock he went out for a walk and came back at seven. Inocenza had the table set for one, and a plate of almonds on the liquor trolley for his *apéritif*. Theodore poured a small glass of Fernet-Branca. Then Inocenza's questions began again, thick and fast, because she knew he liked to talk while he took his *apéritif* and preferred to read during his meals.

"Ah, you will be very lonely now," she said over and over, shaking her head. "And poor Don Ramón, too. Aren't you going to see him?"

"I think he needs to rest now."

"And so do you. You have circles under your eyes. You must also eat. I made a chicken soup—tomorrow we'll have the chicken—and a lamb chop and salad." She smiled a little, awaiting a sign that he was pleased.

"That's very fine, Inocenza. And where is the counterpane? I haven't seen it yet."

Inocenza ran to get it from the sofa in the living-room. Theodore had gone by it without seeing it. It was in a bright pink-and-green package.

The counterpane was made of little sewn-together squares of crochet work, a vast display of patient labour.

"It's magnificent," Theodore said, feeling it between his fingers. "You must put it on my bed at once. I'll write your

Aunt Maria and thank her. It's *very* kind of her to do all this work for me."

"She would do anything for you!"

Maria was the aunt whose two children Theodore was putting through the University of Durango.

Theodore sat down at his solitary place. A new copy of *Time* lay beside his plate, and he opened it without interest. Next week, he supposed, they would report the Ballesteros case with a photograph of Lelia's body, perhaps, and get as much fun as they could out of the fact that she had been the mistress of two men who were friends. Theodore had no appetite. He could not even begin on the lamb chop.

That evening he received a telephone call from an official of the *policía*, who told him that Lelia's body had been taken to the *agencia funereal* he had asked that it be sent to, and that the autopsy revealed the stabs had been made by a knife at least five inches long and probably longer, and the widest of the stabs was an inch and a half wide. Many of the stabs had been four inches deep.

Theodore then called Josefina and got her consent to fix the funeral for the following afternoon.

"Would you mind telling Ramón about the funeral, Josefina?" Theodore asked. "I don't think he wants to talk to me just now."

CHAPTER SIX

THE funeral was at three o'clock the next afternoon at a cemetery some twenty miles from the city. A safari of some thirty cars crept along the ugly, bus-congested Avenida Guatemala eastward, jogged and crept eastward again on the highway that eventually led to Puebla and to Veracruz, where Lelia had been born. Huge, impatient Pemex petrol and Carta Blanca beer trucks pulled into the oncoming lane and tried to get beyond the front of the safari, always failed and had to creep back between two of the funeral cars. Theodore had hired twelve cars to take Lelia's friends and neighbours and several of her relatives who had come from Veracruz and gathered at Josefina's house. Theodore himself drove his grey Mercedes-Benz with Carlos and Isabel Hidalgo in the back seat and Olga Velasquez—who had asked Theodore that morning if she might come—in the front seat beside him. In front of him for most of the way was Josefina's family's car with her husband Aristeo, their daughter Ignacia and her fiancé Rodolfo, and two other people Theodore did not know. The cemetery was a dry, flat field surrounded by a wall of white-painted brick, behind which grew cypresses of varying heights. On either side of the gates was written in fading black paint:

POSTRAOS! AQUI LA ETERNIDAD EMPIEZA
Y ES POLVO AQUI LA MUNDANAL GRANDEZA!

a legend on nearly every Mexican cemetery that still sent a shiver of awe through Theodore—even though he did not believe in an afterworld. There was no doubt, at any rate, that here worldly grandeur was dust.

63

Theodore looked around for Ramón and saw him standing, head down, in the third or fourth row of people who bordered the grave. Ramón did not take his eyes from the casket, and though Theodore could see his tears, his face seemed strangely relaxed. Beside him stood the short, comfortable figure of Arturo Baldin, who was holding his hat respectfully against his stomach.

The coffin lid was fastened. Lelia's face had of course been beyond the powers of the embalmers to repair, and Theodore —having heard earlier that she would not be exposed to view —had felt grateful to have the lid of the coffin closed. And yet when he saw the shining dark brown wooden lid with its hideously functional-ornamental fastenings, he realised that however horrible her face may have been to look at, it could not have been more painful to his eyes than this permanently closed and fastened lid. The people ranged themselves all around the grave, trampling on near-by graves, and people stood with bowed heads in three or four of the paths around the grave, too far away to see or hear anything. There were young painters, middle-aged art dealers, a few officials from the Bellas Artes, shopkeepers, Lelia's pharmacist, a couple of cousins from Guadalajara, whom Josefina introduced to Theodore. And there were flowers everywhere—wreaths leaning three deep around her tombstone, flowers in hands, in arms, roses and lilies and chrysanthemums and gladiolas and great yard-long garlands of red and white and purple bougainvilleas carried by some families who Josefina said had come up from Cuernavaca. There was little José and his family of many brothers and sisters. A man of about sixty with walrus moustaches, grey and drooping, stood with his hat pressed over his diaphragm and resembled, Theodore thought, a composite of retired Presidents of France. The priest was an anxious-looking, spare man with yellowish hands. His face held a worldly anxiety. He pattered on about Lelia's glorious career in the arts, cut short so cruelly and

64

without warning. Perhaps he had known Lelia, perhaps not. Lelia had not gone to church very regularly. Josefina glanced once at Theodore and shook her head slowly, as if to say that the priest was not what he might have been, but what could they do?

And it really didn't matter, Theodore thought. His proximity to Lelia's body now did not seem to matter. He merely felt quiet and solemn as he did sometimes when visiting church or when hearing sacred music. He realised that for moments he had not thought of the question that had tortured him for the past sixty hours, even when he slept: who had killed her? He let his eyes pass over all the people he could see in front of him and by turning his head a little; he tried to see if any face set off a train of thought. But none did. Theodore looked up at a cruising *zopilote* which was paying no heed to the dead in the cemetery but was inspecting the adjacent field, where the carrion might lie unburied.

Theodore woke up a little at the sound of the priest's handful of soil clattering on to the coffin top. The familiar Latin went on and on as the gravediggers sprang to work. For a moment it seemed to Theodore that the bystanders flinched at each shovelful, but this impression changed. They stood unmoving, he thought, each with his own thoughts, and perhaps not even thoughts of Lelia just now, much as they had liked and loved her. The wreaths and the flowers rained down on the fresh grave until they were higher than the tombstone, which stood near-by, awaiting its final place. A choice of Josefina, it was a flat square of nearly white stone surmounted by an angel on one knee with arms outspread. Like the priest, it also sufficed, and Theodore even liked the outspread arms, because that had been Lelia's attitude towards life. Then the sight of the cold stone angel and its significance struck him in the heart, and his eyes filled with tears. He looked at Ramón's stern but composed face and listened to his own heart, that seemed to be flogging him to

65

act before it was too late. Rape—and mutilation. He was looking now at the guilty man, Theodore thought. Ramón, whom Mexican justice had released, at best, would never punish sufficiently. All at once, Theodore yielded to the realisation of Lelia's last horrible moments of life. He exerted his imagination to grasp what she had suffered. And with a kind of relish and satisfaction, he let himself be borne up on a sea of hatred and wrath against her slayer, who now, as he looked at Ramón, seemed to him could have been no one else.

Olga Velasquez patted his arm gently. People were stirring. The service was over.

"Look at Ramón," Olga said. "Don't you want to go and speak to him?"

Ramón had hidden his face in his hands, and Arturo was standing by, trying to comfort him.

Theodore set his teeth and could not move. A woman he did not know touched his arm and said something to him. Theodore moved in the direction of his car, a way that took him closer to Ramón. Olga came with him. Three or four people stopped him to clasp his hand and to say a few words of sympathy—rather as if he had been her husband, Theodore thought.

"I shall write you a letter very soon," said the man with the walrus moustaches, pressing Theodore's hand, and Theodore suddenly recognised him as Sanchez-Schmidt, a wealthy art collector and honorary curator of several museums.

Finally, Theodore stood hardly more than a yard away from Ramón. He did not want to speak to Ramón, but people expected him to speak to him. "Ramón?" Theodore said.

Ramón looked at him dully, out of wet eyes. "I wanted to speak to her parents. Where are they?"

Automatically, Theodore looked around, though he was not sure he could recognise them. He had seen them only once in Veracruz.

Ramón was already moving towards the large, greying man in the black overcoat and his much shorter wife, who were surrounded by people. Theodore, after a glance back at Olga and the Hidalgos, who were waiting for him, followed Ramón and Arturo Baldin. After all, he thought, he should speak to her parents, too.

"I did not do it," Ramón was saying in a desperate whisper to the solemn, resigned pair. "I do not want you to think that I did do it."

Theodore looked at Ramón to see if he were possibly drunk, but he was not. "Señora and Señor Ballesteros," Theodore interrupted Ramón. He shook their hands, bowing a little over each. "We are all devastated by this. I want you to consider me your friend. Your daughter was very dear to me." He was conscious that his Spanish was not adequate for the occasion, that something as simple as this was perhaps not fitting. He saw tears in the man's grey, brown-speckled eyes that were so embarrassingly like Lelia's.

"*Gracias,*" said the man.

"I want you to know that I'm innocent," Ramón pleaded.

"Oh, Ramón," Theodore said quickly, "I don't think they——"

"I have to be believed!" Ramón said, shaking off Arturo's hand on his arm.

"He is more upset than any of us," Arturo said gently to the parents, and Lelia's father nodded, obviously wanting to be gone.

"Lelia was very fond of me," Ramón said. "I was falsely accused. You understand that, don't you?"

"Yes, of course," said Lelia's father, whose friends were now pulling at him to leave.

"We understand," said Sra. Ballesteros dully, as if who had murdered her daughter did not matter at all, at least not at this moment, only the fact that she was dead. They had one other child, also a daughter, but she had married and gone to South America. Lelia had been their favourite.

Ramón stared at them, unsatisfied. "May I come to see you in Veracruz?"

With a sigh, Lelia's mother tried to muster her good manners. "We shall always be glad to see you, Ramón."

"And you believe me innocent, don't you?" Ramón asked again, clutching at Señor Ballesteros's shoulder.

"I'm sure they believe you, Ramón," Theodore said, trying to end the general embarrassment, though at that moment it occurred to him that an innocent man did not protest so much and that this thought might be in the minds of the Ballesteros, too.

"I shall come to see you in Veracruz," Ramón said. "Good-bye. *Adiós.*"

"*Adiós*, Ramón," said Sra. Ballesteros.

Ramón stared at them as if he were about to dash after them again.

The crowd had thinned out. Theodore and Arturo looked at each other.

"You're taking care of him?" Theodore asked him.

"*Sí.* As much as I can. And my wife, too. He doesn't sleep at night."

"I suppose he had a bad time at the *policía*?"

"Of course!" Arturo said, "Ramón does not know how to talk to the police. But they know how to talk to him!"

Olga Velasquez and the Hidalgos were standing near-by, looking at Ramón and talking.

"I didn't do it, whatever you might think!" Ramón said suddenly to all of them.

No one moved or said anything.

"I'll see you at the house, Teo?" Josefina asked him. She was having a gathering of Lelia's relatives and a few friends.

"I think not, Josefina, if you'll possibly excuse me," Theodore replied.

"Oh, I am sorry. I was going to ask Ramón, of course, but

he seems in no state of mind for such a thing. So I shall let it go," she said with a faint smile, and only someone who knew her as well as Theodore could have heard the coolness in her tone. "*Adiós*, Teo."

Theodore bent over her hand, then walked on with Olga and the Hidalgos.

"If he didn't do it, why does he think everybody thinks he did?" Carlos Hidalgo asked with blunt disgust. "It might be better for him to keep his mouth shut."

"Carlos——" Isabel said admonishingly.

"Well—didn't you say so yourself?" Carlos retorted, gesturing with a trembling hand, which he at once put back in his overcoat pocket. "Until he's finally driven to confess and makes a *good* confession——" Carlos gave a snort. "He annoys everybody! Just wait! He'll think of a few little facts that'll clinch it—sooner or later. He'll be driven to it. I don't know what he's waiting for."

"And if he's innocent?" Olga asked, somewhat indignantly.

"He does not act innocent. He loved her. They quarrelled. It's quite understandable what happened," Carlos said.

It was not understandable, Theodore thought, and such a murder did not go with love. Theodore listened as he drove, and said nothing. Ramón's behaviour did look suspicious, unless one knew Ramón well and knew his frightful awareness of sin and guilt. Theodore wanted to be fair. Ramón's behaviour under normal circumstances was self-flagellating and odd enough from the ordinary person's point of view. Ramón had resisted many temptations in his youth—and to Ramón temptation itself was a sin. He had had a job as bell-hop when he was about sixteen, and he had told Theodore once, jokingly, of some of the women who had made advances to him. He was more serious and more honest than most young men so attractive would have been, and it was another thing that Theodore admired in Ramón that he took his handsomeness for granted and never tried to exploit it in the least. Then at twenty-six he had fallen in love for the first time, with a woman who did not want to marry. There was a problem, a big one, for Ramón. He had developed a pattern of 'sin' and 'atonement' in the years with Lelia, a pattern of self-torture. Most young men would have transferred their affections to a woman who would marry them. Or he might have gone to Buenos Aires, where an uncle had promised him a job in his firm. "That's where he talks of going when he says he won't see me any more," Lelia had said. "But when I suggested it last night, he became furious. Sometimes I'm afraid of him, Teo. . . ." Lelia had had bruises on her arm when she had said that, Theodore remembered, and he could not forget it.

The Hidalgos got out in the Avenida Madero—Carlos seemed to be in need of a drink—and Theodore drove on with Olga towards his house. She asked him to come in and have tea with her, but Theodore declined.

"You are not going to try to see Ramón?" she asked.

"I don't know."

"You do believe he is innocent, don't you, Teodoro?"

"I really don't know, Doña Olga. Sometimes yes—sometimes no."

"I understand, Teo." She looked at him thoughtfully through her little black veil. Even at a funeral, she could look chic. "Come to see me, if you are lonely, Teo."

Theodore let himself into his house with his keys. The house was silent. Inocenza had gone out for something, or was visiting Constancia. She had not wanted to go to the funeral because she thought they brought bad luck, and she had pleaded with Theodore to forgive her.

The telephone rang and roused Theodore from a day-dream on the living-room sofa.

"*Bueno*, Teo. Ramón. Can I see you?" Ramón asked in a tense, desperate voice.

"Yes, of course. Now?"

70

"I have some people to see first. It'll take me quite a while."

"How long is that?"

"That depends. Two or three hours."

"All right. I'll be here."

Ramón hung up.

Theodore wondered if Ramón would care to have dinner with him, then decided not to worry about it. There was no telling at what hour Ramón would appear.

Inocenza came in with the afternoon papers. In both of them there was more than half a page of black-bordered death notices of Lelia.

LELIA EUGENIA BALLESTEROS 1927–1957. Pray that her soul abide in eternal peace.

The death of LELIA EUGENIA BALLESTEROS leaves a void in the hearts of her many friends that can never be filled on earth.

Alejandro Nuñez, baker, wishes his beloved friend LELIA BALLESTEROS a serene voyage into eternity.

They were all colophoned with black crosses or rows of black crosses. There was a small square representing the regret of Xavier Sanchez-Schmidt, the art dealer. And one from a club of some sort in Veracruz.

The doorbell rang, and Theodore jumped up from his chair. "It's probably Ramón, and if so you can set another place, Inocenza."

A young man stood in front of the iron gates. Theodore hesitated, then continued across the patio.

"Yes?" Theodore said.

"*Buenas tardes.* Señor Schiebelhut?" the young man said with a faint smile. "I have something I think belongs to you." He indicated a flattened paper bag that he was holding securely under one arm.

"What is it?"

71

"A muffler." His eyebrows rose expectantly. "Didn't you lose one?"

"No." Theodore shook his head.

"I think you did. Try to remember. A few days ago?"

"I haven't lost a muffler. Where did you find it?"

The young man's face looked disappointed. "Here." He moistened his lips. "On the sidewalk here. A good muffler. I thought it might be yours. *Adiós*, señor." He turned quickly and walked away.

Another pedlar's trick, Theodore thought. If he'd looked at the muffler, the boy might have said: 'Well, I'll let you have it anyway for ten pesos. You can see it's worth twice that.' Theodore opened his gates and looked in both directions for Ramón. Ramón was not in sight but the young man with the paper bag was crossing the street near the corner, and he looked back over his shoulder at Theodore. His cheap, baggy black trousers hung on his bony hips like trousers on a scarecrow, and for an instant Theodore was reminded of the stick figures he often drew with his fountain-pen at the bottom of postcards and letters to Lelia.

CHAPTER SEVEN

RAMÓN did not want a drink, and he refused to take off his overcoat. He sat on the edge of the sofa, his hands gripping his knees, trembling. It was nearly midnight. "I've been to see Eduardo Parral and Carlos. I said I was innocent, but I don't know if they believe me. How can you tell if someone believes you?" He spoke with the tremulous rush of hysteria. "And you, Teo? Do you believe I am innocent?"

"I believe you, Ramón." Theodore did not know what Ramón might have done if he had told the truth, that he did not know what to believe. He wondered what Eduardo had made of it. Eduardo was a young hard-working painter, a good-natured fellow who perhaps had been infatuated with Lelia himself, though he had always got on well enough with Ramón and him. Theodore could not imagine Eduardo losing his temper, but what would Eduardo have made of all this protesting? Theodore went to his bar trolley, poured two whiskies, and carried one to Ramón. "This will do you good. You haven't had anything to drink, have you?"

"No. No, thank you, Teo. No whisky."

"Tea?"

"No." Ramón rubbed his hands on his thighs.

"What did Carlos say to you?" Theodore asked.

"He was very quiet. I don't know what he said. Then he had a couple of strong whiskies, and he told me to shut up. He said it was a disgrace to the memory of Lelia. Imagine! Then Isabel tried to calm him down and apologise for him, because he must have been drinking before I came and he was certainly out of his head when I left."

"Well—Carlos liked her, too."

73

Ramón laughed. "*Her?* Carlos likes any pretty face. But he has no right to tell *me* to shut up. I went to see him as a friend. I think I'll cross him off my list of friends. Teaching at the Universidad has made him an adolescent again. He's not a man, he's a little boy who depends on his wife to wipe his nose! And he tells *me* to shut up!"

Theodore was silent a moment. "I find Carlos annoying sometimes myself. It's too bad you went to see him, Ramón. You didn't have to. I realise—we all realise—the police questioning was very disturbing to you. They accused you, insulted you, so you think you have to make sure nobody thinks you're guilty." Theodore smiled a little.

Ramón looked at him angrily. "You seem to think it's a laughing matter. Look at you. Not a bit upset, are you? I'll bet you didn't shed a tear about Lelia!"

"All I meant to say was that I understand how you feel, Ramón. Arturo said you weren't sleeping well. If you need some more sleeping-pills, I have some."

"I don't want any sleeping-pills."

What did he want, Theodore wondered. Did he expect them to fall on each other's shoulders and weep about Lelia and what she had meant to them? He extended his packet of American cigarettes, but Ramón shook his head. "Are you staying at your house or with Arturo?"

"At mine. Arturo spent the night last night."

Theodore winced at the thought of Ramón's apartment in his present state of mind. The apartment consisted of one high-ceilinged room with a kitchenette in the corner. The toilet was down the hall. The room had a few bright pictures of Lelia's in it, and if Ramón was in good spirits it was not gloomy, but the gloom set in as soon as Ramón was gloomy, and one saw the grey wall out the window, the horrible light at the top of the ceiling, and the shabby, second-hand furniture.

"You're not disturbed at all, are you?" Ramón asked, blow-

74

ing smoke from his tiny Carmencita cigarette out of his nose.

"Some things one doesn't show in front of people, Ramón," Theodore replied, putting himself on guard.

"Am I people? Your best friend, you used to say?"

"I still consider you my friend. I hope the lawyer was of some help to you."

"Oh, yes. The lawyer. He stood around and listened until they were through with me."

"You weren't there very long, anyway, Ramón."

Ramón looked at him through his pink lids, a bitter smile on his lips.

Theodore wondered what he might say that would erase the hostility from Ramón's face. Ramón was afraid, Theodore thought. That was why he went around protesting to everybody that he hadn't killed Lelia. He was afraid, because many times, in his anger at Lelia, he must have imagined doing just what the murderer had done—or perhaps Ramón himself had done. Theodore wanted to ask Ramón quietly, now while he could look at him, whether he had done it, but he was afraid to ask him. Theodore glanced at the stairs. Inocenza had waited up for a while to see Ramón, but finally she had gone up to her room, and perhaps now she was asleep.

"I am so glad to see that nothing bothers you, Don Teodoro. You never wanted to marry her, did you?"

"I never wanted to marry anybody. That doesn't mean I loved Lelia any less," Theodore replied.

"Lelia was just a charming girl you met on your travels. A beautiful Latin girl with a talent for painting."

"Lelia was more to me than that. You don't know what you're saying now."

Ramón's trembling had subsided, though he had not touched his drink. "Maybe you can imagine her even closer to you now that she's gone. Everything's in one's own mind, you always say. You're not like the rest of us, are you, Teo."

Theodore did not want to get into a discussion of the

75

Catholic versus the Protestant conscience or, what was worse, the Catholic conscience versus Ramón's idea of 'Existentialist's conscience', which was no conscience at all to Ramón. Just because he did not torture himself, as Ramón did, for having an affair out of wedlock!

"Always taking trips away from her," Ramón continued, as if to himself.

"Often with you both. I was in love with her, too, Ramón."

"I believe you, Teo. It was just a funny kind of love. You used to urge me to marry her and her to marry me. Remember?"

"But that was when I'd just met you both, Ramón. Before I realised Lelia didn't want to marry. I considered myself something of an intruder then. I didn't realise. And I'm sorry I intruded on your privacy by suggesting that you marry each other. It wasn't any of my business."

"No, it was not. But you *wanted* us to get married, didn't you?" Ramón asked, pointing a finger at him.

"I thought you were enough suited and that you were in love with each other." Theodore looked at his little glass of whisky, which he was holding in his hand as if he were frozen. He felt that he was blushing. It was as if Ramón had looked in on a private fantasy, a foolish, romantic one. By feeling well disposed towards their marrying, Theodore had used to imagine that he would 'win' in the situation, and that by absenting himself from Lelia he could keep her memories of him without the blemishes that married life would put on them. He had used to imagine that if Lelia chose Ramón, she would end by not liking Ramón as much as she would have liked him, as a husband. And there had been the Christian "to give is more blessed than to receive" working its effect, too, no doubt. In all these senses, Theodore had used to imagine 'winning'. He would have been desolate if Ramón had married Lelia, yet in a perverse way would probably have enjoyed his desolation.

76

Theodore's French clock on the mantel struck twelve in little 'tings'.

"Why didn't you ever ask her to marry you, Teo? She might have accepted."

"I had two reasons. The first is, it would have hurt you. The second is that I doubt my loyalty—I would doubt it for a wife. I used to fall in love every month when I was younger, depending on what I was working on. A new picture, a new style, and there was another girl to go with it. Something like that might have happened if I'd married Lelia. As it was, I— I went on being in love with her for three years. It was pleasant for both of us, I think." He frowned and tossed his whisky down in one gulp. "I don't want to talk about that now. I'm tired, Ramón, and so are you."

Ramón stood up suddenly. "Then I won't keep you up. We are all tired. So we'll tuck ourselves in our little beds." Ramón looked at him from his full height, and there was still the contempt in his face which both annoyed Theodore and hurt him.

"Ramón, let's say you loved her more, loved her a longer time—that you would have made her a good husband—but I loved her, too, Ramón." He put his hand on Ramón's shoulder, expecting Ramón to jerk away, but when Ramón was motionless, Theodore's fingers tightened. "My friend, I'm sorry it couldn't be."

"What?" Ramón asked impatiently.

Theodore took his hand away. "Shall I come out with you? Do you want to get a *libre*?"

"Thank you, I'll walk a way."

Theodore went out and opened the gate for him. He started to say that Inocenza sent her regards, then decided not to. "Try to rest, Ramón."

"Oh yes," Ramón said mockingly, and then he disappeared into the darkness.

CHAPTER EIGHT

A WEEK passed. Sauzas telephoned Theodore one afternoon and asked him to come to the prison to look at six 'suspects' he had gathered. Theodore had not seen any of the men before, to his knowledge, though one, a wretched, scrofulous fellow of thirty-five, had been guilty of another brutal rape and murder.

Theodore tried to paint, but did so badly he stopped. As was usual with him, he was having a delayed reaction, and he felt more depressed in the third week after the murder than he had in the first. He slept badly, and got up often in the night to write something in his diary and to read what he had written in the past. He looked also for names of people that Lelia might have dropped in talking to him, and found not a single one, because he did not usually enter that kind of detail in his diary.

He phoned the Hidalgos one evening with an idea of going to see them. Carlos answered and said he had to work all evening.

"What about tomorrow?" Theodore asked. "Could you both come for dinner?"

"All this week is bad, Teo," Carlos said. "I'll give you a ring next——"

"One thing I wanted to ask, Carlos. Nothing else has occurred to you? About Lelia? Some name she mentioned, some fear—anything?"

"Teo, I'm as much in the dark as you."

"You were at least here in January, and I wasn't."

"But I didn't see her."

"Not even when she did the *Lysistrata* sets for you?"

"One set. It was nothing at all. She came out to the Universidad one afternoon———" Carlos broke off.

"All right," Theodore said, with a sigh.

They agreed to get in touch the following week.

To add to Theodore's nervousness, two or three times when he answered the telephone he got no response from the other end of the line. Theodore mentioned this to Sauzas, who showed a mild but persistent interest in it. Had Theodore heard any noises in the background? Who had put the telephone down first? Theodore had, though the second time it happened he thought he had waited about three minutes. Why hadn't he waited longer? Well, there hadn't seemed to be any purpose in waiting longer! The telephone calls might not have anything to do with the murder, after all. Could it be Ramón? Ramón was acting very strangely, not going to work, just sitting in his apartment or else dashing across town to call on someone he or Theodore knew, or Lelia had known, and assure them of his innocence. Sauzas was keeping a close watch on Ramón.

Theodore had an idea that the telephone caller might be Elissa Straeter, because she had played this telephone trick a few times before, calling again a moment later and speaking to him. This happened only when she had been drinking. Now and then, when he saw her at a party, she flirted with him, told him he was the only man she was attracted to in Mexico, but Theodore was repelled by her, and always had been. Since he had been a little abrupt with her when she had called to express sympathy after Lelia's death and to invite him to a party, he thought she might be retaliating in this way. Or she might have been too drunk to say a word. Theodore had said: "Elissa? . . . Elissa?" once into the telephone, but, feeling very silly, he had stopped. It would have been difficult to explain to Sauzas, perhaps, but Theodore knew as surely as he existed that Elissa Straeter had neither killed Lelia nor hired anyone else to kill her. She was from

79

one of the 'good' families of America, and politeness and gentleness were so deeply instilled in her they were really part of her blood, along with the alcohol. "Oh, of *cou-rse*" and "*Thank* you" were her most frequent phrases. He had once seen a drink spilled down her dress by someone, accidentally, and Elissa had said in her drunken, gentle voice: "Oh, I'm *so* sorry." Theodore could not have borne Sauzas dashing off on the tangent that Elissa had a motive if she was in love with him, so he said nothing about her. She was one of those women, not the first in Theodore's life, whose attentions were too embarrassing to acknowledge. Every man, even the ugliest, must have them, Theodore thought, such was the variety of sexual conditioning.

One morning, when Theodore was in his studio trying to work, Inocenza came in with the first mail. There was a bill from the lawyer Castillo, a bulletin from the Art Institute at San Miguel de Allende, and a postcard which showed a coloured picture of an airport with a hangar flying an American flag. Theodore turned it over and read:

Monday

Amados míos,

I am doing a little painting and having a good time with Inés, who is driving me all around Florida. Beautiful country and wonderful climate. Returning in two weeks. Love to you both,

Your Lelia

It was postmarked February 18 from Tampa, Florida. Inés was a cousin of Lelia's, who was married to an American and lived in Orlando.

"What is it?" asked Inocenza, who was watching him.

Theodore shook his head, too dazed to say anything for a moment. "A joke—somebody's joke." He handed her the card. Inocenza could not read very fluently, but the card was typewritten and in Spanish. And, curiously, it was just what Lelia might have written, but Lelia would have signed it 'L.' with a pen and put in a couple of X's, probably.

"From Señorita *Lelia*?"

"It was written only a week ago, Inocenza! And mailed from North America!"

"Name of God! It is from her spirit!" Inocenza exclaimed, and clapped her hand over her mouth while her brain struggled to convince her that this was not true.

"No, it is somebody's joke," Theodore said angrily, starting for the telephone in his bedroom.

He could not reach Sauzas, but he said firmly that it was *"muy, muy importante"*, and he was told that Sauzas would be radioed at once, as he was somewhere in a police car. Theodore walked around his bedroom, staring at the postcard and wondering if the typewriter could be traced, and if it were a Spanish typewriter, because a *tilde* was missing over one of the n's. Or the writer might have been clever enough to leave off the accents to make it appear to be written on an American typewriter. But Theodore had a feeling that the person who had written the postcard was in Mexico, D.F. It was the joke of someone who wanted to watch the reaction.

Carlos Hidalgo? One of his wild practical jokes had been to invite people to a party at a wrong address—later, laughing hilariously, he had picked them up and taken them to the right address, his new apartment—but Theodore could not believe Carlos would stoop to such a thing as this.

Sauzas telephoned within a quarter of an hour, and Theodore read him the postcard.

"Do you have any idea who sent it?"

"Absolutemente no!"

"Ah-hah," Sauzas said thoughtfully. "Señor Schiebelhut, I am now very near the house of Ramón Otero. I wonder if you could meet me there in a few minutes?"

"Well—yes. In the house?"

"On the street. On the corner to the right of the entrance as you face it. In about ten minutes. Can you do that?"

"It may take me fifteen. I'll come as quickly as I can."

"With the postcard, of course!"

CHAPTER NINE

SAUZAS was on the corner when Theodore arrived, walking up and down restlessly and smoking. Theodore got out of his *libre*—he would have taken his car, but it was impossible to park here—and crossed the street, dodging bicyclists and trucks because he was against the light. He took out the postcard, that he had carefully put in the inside pocket of his jacket.

"*Buenas*," Sauzas said casually, and held the card close to his eyes, reading it. He turned it over, removed the cigarette from his mouth and smelled the card "Do you know anybody in Florida now?"

"No. Lelia has a cousin there, Inés Jackson, who lives in Orlando. I've never met her. Her name was mentioned in the newspapers as one of the surviving relatives."

"Hm-m. Lelia was on good terms with her?"

"Yes, as far as I know. Not close, but——"

"Okay, *vamonos*," Sauzas said, and with his rolling gait started off for Ramón's door.

The narrow door of Ramón's apartment house was open, and two barefoot little girls were playing a game with bottle tops on the dirty tiles. Sauzas pushed the bell under Ramón's name, though Theodore remembered the bell never worked, and they began to climb the stairs. On the first floor, one went along a passage to a broader flight of stone stairs and climbed again for three flights. They walked down the corridor to a tall grey door and knocked.

No answer.

"Ramón? You had better open! Capitán Sauzas!"

They heard Ramón's carpet-slippered feet approaching

the door. The door opened, and Ramón's haggard, unshaven face showed a slight surprise at the sight of Theodore. He was in limp, pink-striped pyjamas. Sauzas pushed the door open and went in.

Ramón had evidently been lying in bed. The bedding was tousled, and there was an ash-tray on the bed and another on the floor beside the bed. A pair of trousers had been flung over a chair. The room reached up to a meaninglessly high ceiling, as if, like so many apartments in this section of the city, it had been partitioned from some enormous gubernatorial chamber that had once been elegant. In the corner near the kitchenette, Ramón's little pale blue parakeet worked indefatigably at its cage door, which kept falling with irregular *clang-clangs*. Theodore could never bear to watch it.

"We have here an interesting postcard," Sauzas said to Ramón. "Would you like to see it?"

Ramón had sat down on the messy bed. He took the postcard, and Theodore saw his scalp move as he read it. "Who wrote this?"

"We don't know. We wanted to ask if you knew anything about it."

Ramón looked at Theodore accusingly. "One of your American friends?"

"He says he doesn't know anybody who is in Florida now."

"You see the date, February eighteenth. You don't know anybody who could have done this trick, Ramón? If we find out who did it, we may find the murderer," Sauzas said.

Ramón stared with his pink, purple-circled eyes down at the floor, then closed his eyes tightly and swayed to one side, down to his pillow. He had lost weight, Theodore could see from his face and his shoulders. Theodore was really shocked at the way he looked.

"Ramón, sit up!" Sauzas moved towards him, and Theodore turned away, unable to stop it and unable to watch it.

Theodore heard a sound as if Sauzas had slapped his face. On a drop-leaf table, propped up against a rather Russian-looking mosaic icon of Christ on the cross, was a snapshot of Lelia in a bathing-suit at Acapulco. Theodore could barely remember having seen the picture before. It was cracked at the corners and curved, as if Ramón had been carrying it in his wallet. Christ seemed to be looking right down at her.

"Ramón! Do you know anybody who was going to Florida?"

Theodore turned round as he heard Sauzas sigh. Sauzas looked at Theodore and opened his arms helplessly.

"He has been this way for two weeks. Like pulling teeth to get him to tell you what day it is. Not that he knows." Sauzas took off his hat and dropped it in the seat of a straight chair. "Ramón, do you want to help us find the killer or not?"

"I killed her," Ramón said against his pillow.

"What? You killed her?" Sauzas moved towards Ramón. "You killed her, eh, Ramón?"

"Yes."

"Tell us about it, Ramón. Where is the knife?"

"Behind the stove," Ramón mumbled.

Sauzas pulled him up roughly by the shoulder. "What stove? Her stove?"

"Yes."

Theodore felt a pain in his throat and realised he had not been breathing. "You *dog*, Ramón!" He started towards Ramón, and Sauzas's arm struck him across the chest.

"We'll soon find out, Señor Schiebelhut," Sauzas said. "No need to fight now. I must make a telephone call."

Ramón looked up at Theodore, red-eyed and defiant.

"Extension eight four seven," Sauzas said. "*Bueno, Enrique? . . . Enrique, por favor.*" He got a cigarette and a matchbox and lighted the cigarette with one hand.

Theodore felt suddenly too revolted to hit Ramón or to

touch him. Ramón was like something already dead, he thought. He had died during these three weeks since the murder.

"*Bueno*, Enrique. Ramón Otero says there is a knife behind the stove in the kitchen of the Ballesteros apartment . . . *Sí!*" Sauzas said, his voice breaking with excitement. "At once! At once! I am at Otero's apartment. Do you have the number? . . . Yes, as soon as possible!" He hung up and looked at both of them, smiling, walking towards them. "So you will talk now, Ramón? Tell me about it. What happened?"

Ramón with a shuddering sigh plunged his forehead against his two palms. "We had a quarrel."

"Yes? About what?"

"I wanted her—to go away with me."

"Where?"

Ramón took several seconds. "I wanted her to marry me."

"And she said no? She said she was in love with Theodore, perhaps?"

"No," said Ramón positively, "but she wouldn't marry me and so I—I killed her. Yes. I killed her." Now Ramón stared in front of him, his hands on his knees, his back stooped like a tired old man's. "I stabbed her," he said in a whisper.

"And then?" asked Sauzas, listening attentively.

"I stabbed her," Ramón repeated.

Sauzas watched him. "And did you bring the flowers?"

"I can't remember. I think I went out and got them—and brought them back. And then I went out and locked the door, I remember."

"The flowers were bought between ten-thirty and eleven-thirty. You bought them after you killed her?" Sauzas asked.

"Oh yes," Ramón said. "I am sure of it, because——"

"Go on, Ramón."

But Ramón did not go on. He stared, as if he were peering

to see something in the air in front of him. The time would fit, Theodore thought, if he bought the flowers after he killed her. And it was like Ramón to do something crazily cynical, to bring flowers after such a ghastly act and dump them on the table.

Sauzas walked restlessly up and down the room.

Theodore, impatient for the telephone to ring, moved towards the kitchenette, an uncurtained, unpartitioned unit of sink and two-ring gas-burner which sat atop a small ice-box in the corner of the room. On the gas-burner was a bowl with a spoon in it and half an inch of tomato soup drying and turning dark red at the edge. In the sink stood a Campbell's can with a jagged lid sticking up. And thumb-tacked over the sink was Lelia's cartoon of Ramón washing dishes, smiling straight out of the picture—a very handsome Mexican face with a shining head of hair—water splashing every which way. Theodore heard Sauzas's step and turned round.

Sauzas peered at the parakeet.

The bird was working more slowly now, trying as ever to brace its little claws on two of the vertical, slippery bars as it raised the door with its beak. It could pull the door up nearly three inches, far enough for it to have got out if it had been at the bottom of the cage; but by that time the claw feet were slipping downwards, the beak had to release the door and clutch at another bar, and the door dropped shut again with a little tinny *clang*. And it went to work again, energetically bracing its claws for the upward pull of the door. Theodore turned round suddenly, irritated with himself for having watched it. There was ambiguity in this, too: was the bird really trying to get out, or was the door just its favourite toy? Ambiguity was the secret of life, the very key to the universe! Why had Ramón killed Lelia? Because he loved her. Theodore had a depressing premonition that he would never hate Ramón enough for what he had done.

"Such persistence should be rewarded." Sauzas bent closer to the cage, and now Theodore looked again.

Clang . . . clang-clang. A pause of several seconds while the bird rested its tired muscles, or perhaps exerted its tiny brain to devise a better method of bracing itself. Then *clang-clang . . . clang.*

The telephone rang and Sauzas darted across the room. "Ah-hah. . . . Ah-hah," he said, his head enveloped in smoke. "Good, good. . . . Well, that fits. He washed it." His eyes slid slyly over to Ramón, who was still looking blankly in front of himself. "Fine. Yes. At the station." Sauzas hung up, frowned as he took another puff of his cigarette, and said to Theodore: "The knife was there. They had to move the stove. It was wedged behind the stove. And his thumb-print is on it." He looked at Ramón. "You washed the knife, didn't you?"

"Yes," Ramón said, nodding.

"All right, Ramón! Get dressed! You're going to prison. And this time not getting out so soon."

Ramón stood up slowly and moved towards his closet.

"What kind of a knife?" asked Theodore.

"One of the kitchen knives. The blade fits the stabs in the body. Enrique said it was a good-sized knife that had been whetted down very much," Sauzas said, his eyes on Ramón.

Theodore suddenly remembered the knife. It was like some butchers' knives, with a wide blade that tapered to a point. Lelia had had it as long as he had known her. Theodore looked at Ramón's slowly moving figure in front of the open closet. What could they do to a man like that? What punishment was just? They should mete out to him what he had done to Lelia, and in lieu of the rape castrate him.

"We shall take care of him," Sauzas said to Theodore, as if he could read his thoughts.

Ramón had pulled on a white T-shirt, and he put his pale blue jacket on over it. He had on dark trousers. He might have been dressing in his sleep. And so he walked towards them. Sauzas pulled him by the arm towards the door.

Theodore looked at the bird, then went and took its cage down from the hook. He took also the green cloth that Ramón used to cover the cage and pocketed a box of bird-seed. Ignoring Sauzas's smile at him, he followed the two out.

Ramón turned in the opposite direction to the stairs and walked down the corridor.

"Ramón!" Sauzas called.

"He is going to the toilet," Theodore said, but Sauzas still followed him a few steps suspiciously.

Ramón disappeared behind a narrow door.

"Is there a window in there?" Sauzas asked uneasily.

"I don't think so."

"If there is, he'd be dead, anyway, from this height," Sauzas said, with an indifferent lift of his black brows.

They waited, and finally from the little w.c. that Theodore knew was lightless and paperless and sometimes even water-less came a torrential, sustained sound of flushing. Then Ramón came out and they proceeded, Ramón first, then Sauzas, then Theodore. Ramón did not seem to notice that Theodore carried his bird.

"I would like to go to the Cathedral," Ramón said on the sidewalk.

"The Cathedral? At the Zócalo?"

"Just for a moment. It's not far."

Sauzas looked annoyed, yet Theodore could see his Catholic mind yielding. "Very well. Come on, but don't be all night. And don't try any funny business inside, understand?"

They began to walk. After only half a block, they could see the yellowish spires of the Cathedral of Mexico against the sky. The blocks of Ramón's neighbourhood were all huge, square and gloomy with the gloom of former grandiosity now degenerated to shoddy little shops and dilapidated apartments. An old barefoot woman with a face like a shrunken monkey's stepped into their path and demanded, for the love of God, a few centavos. Her claw-like hands slipped from Ramón's jacket and caught at Theodore's. Recoiling in his nervousness as if a snake had touched him, Theodore with the same movement reached in his pocket and brought up some loose centavos and dropped them into her little wrinkled palm. Ramón stepped off the kerb directly into the way of a *libre* that was coming around the corner at full speed, and Theodore grabbed his arm involuntarily and pulled him back.

A light sweat broke out over Theodore. Angry with himself because he had saved Ramón from the *libre*, he said between his teeth: "You've a fine nerve going into your church after what you've done!"

Ramón glanced at him with resentment and fear, but he said nothing.

A string of light globes from some fiesta or holiday still followed the outline of the domes and spires on the Cathedral's façade, light globes plain and coloured, askew in tangles of electric wires. The face of the Cathedral was beautiful, its carvings and ornaments abraded by time and rain, bullet-pocked, all mellowed to a soft yellowish dust colour. Just outside the gates, a man was hawking popcorn from a cart. Children played with tops, and men lounged in the forecourt, talking and smoking, buying Chiclets and penny candies from the small boys who flitted about selling them. Some six or eight women and girls with bright-coloured scarves tied under their chins came out of the Cathedral just as they went in. The girls were all chattering.

"Let's go to the Café Tacuba!"

"Ah, no! Too many people!"

"But the chocolate's so good! And the *waffles*!"

"Dolores! Look! My heel came off!"

Then a cascade of laughter.

The interior of the Cathedral was almost as chaotic. A mass seemed to be going on in the centre. A sprinkling of people were deep in prayer or in sleep in the dark pews. A group of tourists, whose new-looking clothes caught the eye in the general greyness, shuffled down one of the broad side aisles behind a man who was pointing into the air. Theodore looked up at the narrowing grey dome that was lit now by a circle of yellowish electric lights. The height of it and the smell of the place made him feel slightly sick.

Ramón had installed himself on his knees before a dark niche, perhaps a special one to him, because some of the other niches with saints' figures in them were lighted. Sauzas sat down at the end of a pew some three yards away from him, and Theodore took a seat across the aisle from Sauzas. Theodore wondered if Ramón were confessing the murder now, or reciting some nonsense he had learned by rote. The smell of the Cathedral irked Theodore—candle wax, incense, the hollow, stale smell of a tomb without even the virtues of coolness and privacy, the smell of old cloth and old wood, the sweaty sweetness of crumpled peso notes, and, bringing it all out and binding it like salt, the smell of human bodies and breaths. Theodore supposed that Ramón reacted like Pavlov's dog to this particular smell and its variations in other churches. *Sanctity. Genuflect. Cross yourself. Tread lightly. This is a holy place. The air has not been changed in four hundred years*—or however old the place might be. This Cathedral was nearly four hundred years old. And now to bring his barbarity in here with him and spill it all out! With the bland certainty, too, that some invisible yet all-powerful thing was going to forgive him!

Theodore squirmed on the hard wooden seat. Ramón's sins were only different in degree, after all. People came in sometimes scheming how to pick somebody's pocket. A sign on the front of the door warned people in Spanish and in English to beware of pickpockets within the Cathedral. It was impossible to get one's mind off money. Wooden alms boxes on pedestals everywhere pleaded in printed notices for money for the children, for the poor, for the upkeep of the church; and each had a huge padlock on it to keep those very poor from taking what was as much theirs as anybody else's. His disconnected thoughts surged through him like emotions, warming his cheeks and quickening his blood, as if his body were readying itself for a fight, or was already fighting.

The dozen men in white gowns in the centre of the Cathedral were reciting in Latin, murmuring fast after the leader, with an air of being pressed for time.

Ramón suddenly crossed himself and stood up. He walked towards them in the aisle, but might not have seen them. Sauzas took his arm. At the front of the Cathedral, Ramón turned, half knelt, and made the sign of the cross.

"Did you confess to that saint, Ramón?" Sauzas asked him as they crossed the court.

"Yes."

"Confessed the murder?"

"Yes," said Ramón. He walked with his head up, but his eyes looked—apparently sightlessly because they had to keep yanking him out of people's way—at some place ahead of him on the sidewalk.

Sauzas hailed a *libre* at the corner.

Ramón got in first. Now, Theodore thought, for all his good looks, Ramón looked like just any other murderer whose picture was on the front page of the tabloids. Once, Theodore remembered, he had thought he saw something fine and honest in Ramón's eyes, something that could never change.

"You don't want to come?" Sauzas asked Theodore. "You can come if you like."

"No," Theodore said.

CHAPTER TEN

RAMÓN'S confession appeared in the *Excelsior* and *El Universal*, which Inocenza bought the following morning. Theodore had told her that Ramón had confessed, and Inocenza could not believe it, but the picture of Ramón at the police station, holding the kitchen knife suspended between his two palms, apparently convinced her. Inocenza began to cry, and, for the first time in Theodore's presence, sat down on the edge of a chair in the living-room and bowed her head.

In the photograph on the third page of the *Excelsior*, Ramón looked out with stubborn, haggard intensity—like any other murderer. They would not kill him, unfortunately, but they would give him fifteen years at least, Theodore thought, perhaps in some wretched, evil-smelling jail. And it might be that Ramón's conscience would punish him more severely than death.

That afternoon, Theodore had another of the mysterious, silent telephone calls.

"Elissa?" he asked. "Elissa, if it's you—just say it's you." He thought—but he wasn't sure—that he heard a sigh. And how could one tell if a sigh were male or female? He strained his ear to hear any background noise, then put the telephone down in anger.

He called Sauzas's number, asked for Extension 847, and after a wait of five minutes or so Sauzas came to the telephone. "*Bueno.* Teodoro Schiebelhut," Theodore said. "I've just had another telephone call in which no one speaks. I thought I should tell you, so that at least we know it is not Ramón."

"Hm-m," Sauzas said in a preoccupied way.

Thedore did not know what to say next. "What're you going to do to Ramón?" he asked.

"*Do* to him? Ugh! If he is guilty, twenty years."

"*If?*"

"He is a strange one. I think he is guilty, yes, but he's now saying he sent the postcard. This I just don't believe——" Sauzas trailed off in a dubious grunt.

"That's not very important, is it? He probably thinks, since he confessed, he should confess everything."

"Yes—but I am not absolutely sure. I am going to have some psychiatrists look at him."

"If they pronounce him insane, that's not true," Theodore said quickly. "He has spells—temper, headaches—but it's not true that he's insane."

"We'll see, Señor Schiebelhut!" Sauzas interrupted. "Are you nervous? Would you like to have a guard at your house?"

"Why, no," Theodore protested. "Why?"

"No reason. Just for your sake. It would be easy to arrange, but if you think it's not necessary . . ."

Theodore felt most dissatisfied with the conversation after he had hung up. Of course, it was easy to post a guard in Mexico, they did it readily for the rich, but Theodore was not used to a system in which he was supposed to decide whether a guard should be posted or not. The police should know whether a guard was necessary, and if so simply post one.

It was Sauzas's doubt that upset him most. ". . . not absolutely sure . . ." Psychiatrists! Well, the police were being cautious, Theodore supposed. There would be justice done, even in Mexico. Ramón's fingerprint was on the knife, after all!

Once more the telephone calls came in. From Isabel Hidalgo, Olga next door—but not from Elissa Straeter, who perhaps slept until afternoon and had not seen the papers.

"A terrible surprise," Theodore said into the telephone.

"No. . . . Of course I had no idea that he had done it. . . ."

But of course he had, from the start.

Then, in the afternoon, the lawyer Castillo called. He wanted to know if Theodore wished to engage his services again for Ramón Otero.

"I think not now. He will be given a lawyer," Theodore said.

"This is very odd. I really did not think he was guilty. But—the best of us can make mistakes, *verdad*?"

"Yes," Theodore said. "Evidently."

"Evidently. Well, now he will need a very good lawyer to get him off with a light sentence."

"I'm afraid, señor—that is no concern of mine right now."

"No. I understand, señor. Ah, so—salutations to you and *adiós*."

"*Adiós*."

A good lawyer, perhaps, but Ramón could certainly not afford to hire him on his own. Theodore smiled a little bitterly at the thought that he had hired him for poor Ramón just three weeks ago. Poor Ramón! It was more bitter to remember that he had considered Ramón his best friend. In spite of their difference in temperament—Latin from Anglo-Saxon, south from north, difference of education, upbringing, religion, everything—he had thought of Ramón in a brotherly way. He had never felt jealous in regard to Lelia, nor had Ramón seemed to feel any jealousy towards him. And perhaps there had been no logical reason for Ramón's killing her. Perhaps it had been quite unpremeditated, the result of a horrible burst of anger.

This thought removed much of his resentment against Ramón, and left only a tremendous regret that anger had taken from him both the woman he loved and his friend.

In the next days, Theodore scanned the papers for news of Ramón's investigation, but the papers said only that it was 'continuing' and that psychiatrists were making tests, not that they doubted or did not doubt his guilt. When Theodore on the second day of Ramón's imprisonment tried to call Sauzas, he was unable to get him. He left a message that he would like Sauzas to call him, but the man on the other end of the telephone sounded indifferent, and Theodore doubted if Sauzas would ever get the message.

Theodore attempted a portrait of Inocenza, only the second that he had ever tried, and he found the picture neither very good nor very bad, which irritated him more than a total failure would have done. He could not get his mind off Ramón, and he was in a mood of mingled hatred and apprehension. He even imagined that the police might release Ramón. What then? Theodore realised that the block in his thinking was that he could not believe in Ramón's innocence, whatever the police might say. If the police found him guilty and insane, that would not satisfy him either, but that had not happened yet. The chances were, Theodore thought, that Ramón would be pronounced guilty, and sane enough to be held responsible for his act.

He went over to visit Olga Velasquez. She cheered him superficially, planning and chattering about her Carnaval party and the decoration of the house and the garden.

"Promise me you will come, Teodoro. I know you are still depressed, but the party is three days from now. Maybe by that time you will *like* to come to a party."

She sounded quite like Elissa Straeter. Theodore pushed his hand through his yellow hair and tried to smile.

"You think I am silly, talking of nothing but a party for days now, don't you?" she asked, with a happy laugh.

"I love you for it," Theodore said, meaning it sincerely, but wondering if he had said something vaguely improper in Spanish, because Olga looked at him with a surprised smile and her head on one side. When Theodore and Olga had first become acquainted, about three years ago, he had asked her to correct him when he made a blunder in Spanish, and she still sometimes did. But his accent was not so bad, he thought, in Spanish as it was in English. Theodore wrote his diary in English and read a great deal of English aloud to himself to try to improve. "Do you think I should make sure Ramón has a good lawyer, Olga?" Theodore asked suddenly.

She sat up a little in surprise. "You? Why should you?"

"It's the law. If a man is guilty or not—and there are differences in lawyers."

"Who says he deserves a lawyer!" Olga exclaimed impulsively. "Teo, I don't see how you can *think* of that! And you still taking care of his bird! You should give it to your cat!" She slapped her hand down on her thigh and smiled.

But Theodore did not smile. "Perhaps I'm too exhausted to hate, Olga. When a man does a crime like that—he is out of his head, at least at the moment. Later, he regrets it himself. After the first shock of it, one's hatred dies down." He looked at her uncomprehending face.

"Still, he has done it. He has to be punished. I never thought Ramón was perfectly normal, Teo. Very charming, surely, and he knows how to behave with women! But it's a look in his eye sometimes. Anyone could have seen that he had a temper like a wasp. And this—this horrible thing! Ramón deserves to pay for it, or else he'll just do it to somebody else!"

"Oh, I didn't mean that he shouldn't pay for it. I didn't mean a lawyer to get him off free," Theodore protested, and stopped, because the conversation suddenly seemed futile to him. Besides, he was not sure of his own motives. It was a curse to be able to see two sides of things, perhaps three. He himself, along with the majority of Mexicans, did not believe in capital punishment, and yet when it came to something personal, it was an eye for an eye again. "You are right, Olga. It's none of my business."

"What is happening to him now? Isn't there going to be a trial?"

"I suppose so. When they finish questioning him. They're still questioning him. It's been five days now."

Theodore got the answer half an hour later, when he went home. Sauzas telephoned him and said that Ramón was to be released. His story did not hold water. There was no trace of blood on the knife, even under a microscope, and no blood on any clothes or shoes belonging to Ramón.

"He could have thrown his clothes away," Theodore said.

"Hm-m. Well, it is my opinion and the opinion of the doctors that Ramón is just a psychological confessor—a psychological confessor," Sauzas repeated, as if to lend weight to the phrase, which had no weight at all to Theodore when he heard it. "I suggested to Ramón that he dropped the knife behind the stove accidentally when he was drying the dishes with Lelia. He admits they used the knife that evening. And when you dry a knife and start to put it somewhere—in the box on the shelf right over the stove, as it happens—there will likely be a thumb-print, if one hand is holding the dish-cloth. Do you see?—Are you there, Señor Schiebelhut?"

"Yes, I am here."

"There were, in fact, some traces of grease on the knife. But nothing else. No, señor, I think we must go back to the postcard and perhaps to the silent telephone calls you are getting. But the telephone calls will be very hard to trace. We shall have to try to trace the typewriter. The main reason I called you is because I would like to see you now. Are you free?"

"Yes," Theodore said.

"Good. In about twenty minutes, then."

CHAPTER ELEVEN

SAUZAS had not been to Theodore's house before. He looked around him appreciatively, and commented on a painted wooden *santo* that Theodore had bought in San Miguel de Allende, and looked a long while also at one of Theodore's paintings, which was of his left hand, the forefinger and thumb making a circle that enclosed the façade of an imaginary cathedral.

"You lead a pleasant life, Señor Schiebelhut. Not like Ramón Otero. Hmph!" Sauzas was reaching for his cigarettes, before he had even removed his overcoat. "A miserable man, señor."

"They're absolutely sure he's not guilty? Everybody who examined him?"

"Yes," Sauzas said, nodding. "Some more sure than others, but sure!" he added, smiling. "We have a lot of such cases in police work, but usually they are total strangers. I didn't even bother to tell you that one old man who looks too old to—to *look* at a girl, much less rape her, confessed to the crime a couple of weeks ago. He had read a few details in the newspapers. He is an old man without family, without a job—destitute!" Sauzas shrugged. "No, Ramón is not guilty. His behaviour is not that of a guilty man. Nor was it on the night of the murder. He had not seen the body before he walked in there that night."

Theodore looked at him and tried to believe, just to see how it felt to believe. Sauzas had seen many more criminals than he had. Sauzas has no reason to say Ramón was innocent if he were guilty.

"Now, Señor Schiebelhut, I think I must go more extensively into your circle of friends. I can understand your reluctance to mention their names, but I would like to get to the bottom of the postcard."

"So would I. I suppose it is barely possible that a friend or an acquaintance wrote it, Señor Capitán, but I can't believe that anyone I know could be guilty of the murder. There is a difference!"

At that moment Inocenza came in from the kitchen and busied herself at the sideboard by the dining-table.

Sauzas looked her over. "Is she married?" he asked Theodore after she had gone again, doubtless to stand behind the swinging door of the kitchen.

"No."

"Does she have many men friends?"

"Almost none. There is one friend in Toluca named Ricardo. A quiet fellow who has worked for the same man for years, I think."

Sauzas pulled a paper and pencil from his jacket pockets. "Do you know his full name?"

Theodore turned to the kitchen. "Inocenza? Would you come in, please?"

Inocenza came in, looking attentively at Sauzas. Theodore was sure she had heard the question, but he repeated it.

"Ricardo Trujillo," she replied. "His *padron* is José Cerezo, but I do not know the address by heart."

Sauzas wrote the names down. "Do you have any other— friends?" he asked, using the masculine form of the word.

Inocenza blinked modestly and smiled. "No other friends, señor."

Sauzas looked doubtfully at Theodore.

"It is true, I think," Theodore said.

Sauzas seemed to drop the subject reluctantly. "Very well. Now, señor—I have spoken to about twelve of your friends already—and in the last days I have seen a few of them again in regard to the postcard."

100

"You may go, Inocenza," Theodore said.

Inocenza turned and went.

Theodore and Sauzas sat down on the sofa, and in the next few minutes Theodore racked his brains for more names and at last mentioned Elissa Straeter, too. He went upstairs to get his address book from his desk. Sauzas shouted up the stair-well:

"Señor! If you perhaps have a photograph album. That would be a help."

Theodore came back with his blue address book and his thick photograph album bound in antelope skin. Sauzas excused himself perfunctorily and spent several minutes browsing through the address book, which contained the names of people who lived in Europe and North America, too. He copied down many names and addresses.

"We must be patient, you know," Sauzas said. "With the people who have typewriters, we must make a sample to compare with the postcard."

"What did you hear from Inés Jackson in Florida?" Theodore asked.

"She does not recognise the typewriter. We sent her a photostatic copy of the postcard." Sauzas shrugged. "She wrote a very intelligent letter back. She was shocked. But she does not know who could have written it." Sauzas's head was bent over the album as he spoke. "A photograph album sometimes refreshes the memory."

Painfully true. Half the pictures at least were of Lelia, because he had bought the album since he had met her, and he had saved comparatively few old pictures from Europe, the United States, or South America. Theodore did not let his eyes rest on any of the pictures of Lelia, but Sauzas peered at them and commented on her good looks.

"And who is this? . . . And who is this?" Sauzas kept asking, and Theodore told him who everyone was, with a few exceptions of people he could not remember in group photographs.

At last Sauzas had so many names he began to be selective.

"What do the psychiatrists advise should be done with Ramón?" Theodore asked.

"Ah!" said Sauzas, as if this were a totally different subject. "*Quién sabe?* He is not insane, no, but he has a kind of obsession. He is a very religious man, is he not? Almost all the time he was in his cell, you know, he was on his knees praying."

"No. I didn't know."

"What religion is yours, señor?"

"I was brought up a Protestant."

"Um-m, naturally. Well——" Sauzas said with a deprecating shrug, as if to say Theodore would not possibly be able to understand how Ramón felt. "Some psychiatric treatment might help him, but he does not like psychiatrists."

"I know."

"Nor do I very much. Well—it is a terrible thing, you know, to live with a murder on the conscience and not to have committed it!"

Theodore said nothing, but he was not sure Ramón had not committed it. Perhaps he would never be sure. And maybe that was his fate, to be doubtful and undecided about everything. But this matter was tremendous. Compared to it, all the other unresolved questions in his mind seemed mere debating games. And he was paralysed by the conviction that any other man would know what to do in an instant and would be able to take a stand.

"You are worried about him, señor," Sauzas said.

"If he is really innocent—if he is just a man who needs help——"

"I'm not sure you could help him. Perhaps it would take a doctor after all." Sauzas's short thumb rubbed the antelope cover of the album sensually. "Or he should go back to work—since he hasn't the money for a sea voyage." Sauzas chuckled.

"Why do you think he confessed, Señor Capitán, if he did not do it?"

"Perhaps a way of getting attention. Perhaps for something else on his conscience." Sauzas looked calmly at Theodore, and it was plain that he did not much care why Ramón had confessed.

Theodore tried to think of any previous behaviour of Ramón's that might help to explain his confessing. Sauzas's presence rattled him. He sat there coolly professional, not caring about the why of anything. Theodore knew Ramón took his weekly confessions to the Church very seriously, and now he wondered if Ramón had ever invented in the confession-box sins and misdemeanours he had not been guilty of. "What did Ramón do when he found nobody believed his confession?"

"Oh! Just what they all do! He stuck to his story. He thinks we're all wrong. He prayed for our souls on the floor of his cell!" Sauzas chuckled.

Theodore tried to imagine this. All he could really imagine, or think, was that the police and the doctors had made a mistake. "As a layman, I can't understand how the doctors can be absolutely sure he is lying. Suppose, for instance, he knew the flower vendor slightly and didn't want to be remembered as buying two dozen carnations that evening. He would have had a little boy buy the flowers for him—just as he did!"

"Señor—it is the *way* he lies. Why didn't he say that about the flowers? No, señor, he couldn't think why he'd had the little boy buy them for him. He couldn't put that much together. It wasn't clear. One minute he said he bought the flowers himself, the next that he had a little boy buy them. The only thing that was clear was that he hadn't bought the flowers at all! And the postcard, señor, don't forget that.

You remember how he looked when we showed it to him—first accusing one of your American friends of sending it, which may yet be true. Just a minute, Señor Schiebelhut! There is no doubt Ramón is not the murderer. One of the psychiatrists was trained at the Johns Hopkins Institute of North America. Such a man doesn't make a mistake." He waited for a sign from Theodore that he believed him.

Theodore did not make it. "Would it be possible for me to speak to this doctor?"

"*Sí.* He is going to be here for a couple of days, I think, then he goes back to a sanatorium in Guadalajara. His name is Vicente Rojas." Sauzas looked in his wallet, pulled out a dozen papers and cards, and finally gave Theodore two telephone numbers and the name of the hotel at which Rojas was staying. "You should be able to get him at one of these places, but he is here on business and he is very busy." Then Sauzas stood up. "I must be on my way. Many thanks for your co-operation today, señor. We——" He stopped to look at Inocenza, who was coming in, and he smiled and thanked her as she held his coat for him. "*Adiós, adiós,*" Sauzas said to both of them, and Inocenza crossed the patio in front of him to open the iron gates.

Theodore stood in the living-room.

Inocenza came back smiling. "What did I say, señor? I never believed Ramón was guilty, did I?"

"No."

"I'm so happy for him!" she said, still radiantly smiling. "He was simply out of his mind from grief!"

She looked happy as a child, not at all puzzled or troubled by what might have made Ramón confess in the first place. To Inocenza it would all somehow be a mistake of the *policía.* Her side—which was Ramón and himself and herself—had won.

CHAPTER TWELVE

Dr. Vicente Rojas looked at Theodore in a friendly way through round, black-rimmed glasses. "I can understand your doubt, Señor Schiebelhut. You would like to find who did it. But you may take my word—I would stake my reputation as a doctor that he did not." He peered at Theodore again for a moment, then rather shyly cut a piece of papaw with his fork. He was about thirty, slender and dark-haired, with a large nose that projected from a lean, dry face.

Theodore conceded that the man looked intelligent, not the kind of man to make hasty judgments, but how much experience could one have as a psychiatrist at thirty or thirty-two at most?

"You are quite fond of Otero, are you not?"

Theodore picked up his black coffee. They were in the downstairs coffee-shop of the Hotel Francis on the Paseo de la Reforma. "Yes. We were very good friends."

"He needs a good friend now," Rojas remarked, looking down at the centre of the shiny black table, which resembled polished obsidian and reminded Theodore of a necklace that Lelia had often worn which had an oval obsidian pendant.

"His problems seem to be within himself." Dr. Rojas was continuing. "He is much troubled by guilt, you know." He moved his chair a little to let the man at the next table get out.

"But anybody who confesses to a crime he didn't commit is in a way insane, isn't he?"

Dr. Rojas gave a smile and a shrug. "It is certainly not normal. He does not fall into the category of the insane, quite. Others tests we gave he scored quite normally on. So this could be a temporary reaction to the shock of the murder —the murder of a woman he was in love with. And couldn't marry besides."

"Do you think that he is enacting something that he had thought of doing——" Theodore did not have to go on, because Rojas had seized upon it.

"Yes, very possibly. Not consciously thought of doing, but unconsciously. And he would like to take the blame above all. He feels so much guilt, you see, that nothing can assuage it! *Nada, nada!*"

"It's the extent that I find hard to believe. The extent of the guilt."

"Guilt is mostly below the surface—like an iceberg," Dr. Rojas said, smiling, cutting more *papaya*. He never took a full meal in the evening, he had told Theodore, just some fruit or pastry and coffee, and he liked the fresh *papaya* here. It was a quarter to eight. Dr. Rojas had said he had an appointment at eight.

"So you think he will get over this, that it's a temporary— attitude?"

"I *believe* so," Dr. Rojas said, though without certainty. "He would benefit from some psychiatric treatments. Believe me, I tried to help him without his knowing what I was doing, señor." Rojas smiled. "He resists everything which he considers 'help'. It is a sad situation. And he is not the only person in the world with such an attitude. It's because he's only thirty that I have hope. Ordinarily, the religion can be of great assistance. But not when you let it burden the mind with more guilt, eh? The Catholic Church is the greatest psychiatrist of all, taken—taken properly. And yet the Pope recently found it necessary to tell the Catholics in Spain to practise less strictly, for their mental health." Rojas's eyes widened.

Theodore nodded. He had read Herbert Matthews on the

same subject, and he wondered if that was also Dr. Rojas's source of information.

"Oh, for the undisturbed it is fine," Rojas went on, "even for the slightly disturbed. I have seen mental patients become increasingly fanatical, however, and that is not good. Don't you agree? But let us hope Otero is not such a type. He is a man in love. His beloved is dead. Romeo was also disturbed when he thought Juliet was dead. If you remember, señor," he added, smiling with pride at his erudition, "he killed himself."

"Do you think Ramón is in danger of killing himself?"

Dr. Rojas appeared to consider this. "I do not see it at present, no. But I'm not omniscient. No, señor, if we had seen any immediate danger, we would not have permitted him to leave. Besides, the Catholic Church considers suicide a great sin, you know."

Theodore looked at Rojas's alert eyes and wondered what he could ask next, what would make it all definite and sure.

"Are you going to see Otero?" Dr. Rojas asked.

"I don't know."

Rojas was silent for a minute. "He bears some grudges against you, but they are superficial. It would help him if he could have a peaceful relationship with you."

"Do you think he could? Now?"

"You could try. He might be resentful if you don't believe his fantastic stories—for a while. But this is what we are counting on to go away. He is very stubborn and proud. It may slip into a pose, his attitude of guilt. But I am expecting he will grow strong enough to turn loose of it. He is not so disturbed that he can't." Dr. Rojas smiled confidently. "I am sorry, but I think I must be leaving you. I'm expecting a caller in the lobby." He signalled for the bill.

Theodore insisted on paying, and thanked Dr. Rojas for his time. He started to ask where he might reach him in future, and then realised that he would never want to reach him in future, because he did not have that much confidence in him.

They parted cordially in the busy lobby of the hotel, amongst glittering counters of souvenirs and silver jewellery, and Theodore walked down the stairs and out on the sidewalk of the great avenue, which at this hour of late dusk, with the mildly chill breeze blowing through the tall trees that bordered it, always reminded him of Paris on an evening in early spring. It was only six blocks or so to his house, and he decided to walk. While he had been talking to the psychiatrist, he had had an impulse to ring up Ramón and to be friendly. The impulse had vanished, and Theodore reproached himself for his naïveté, for hanging on the psychiatrist's words as if they couldn't possibly be wrong. He went over again what the newspapers had said. The psychiatrists' opinions had simply been reported. No name had been given to Ramón's aberrations. They had put them down to 'emotional stress'.

Theodore reached his house and kept on walking. He walked around the corner, and stopped and stared at a display in a small shop that sold modern furniture. A starving orange-coloured dog, a ghost of a dog, slunk along the side of the building and stopped when it came to Theodore, looking up with a beseeching expression, its feet braced to run. If there had been a food shop near-by, he would have bought the dog a meat sandwich, he thought. Theodore extended his hand, and the creature started and loped away with its tail between its legs. He hadn't really been going to touch it, because he hadn't wanted to. And he wouldn't really have fed it, because he didn't believe in prolonging the life of an unwanted dog in Mexico. It was only a matter of time until the dog picked up some poisoned food left especially for it in some public market. Yet he felt he had let the dog down, from the dog's point of view, at least.

He walked on, feeling utterly depressed. If he could not

get an answer from Sauzas or the psychiatrists that seemed satisfactory—or rather, if he did not accept their answers—he would have to find his own, he thought. He would have to make up his own mind. He would have to see Ramón, distasteful as that might be. Tomorrow, he decided, he would call Ramón. But not tonight.

CHAPTER THIRTEEN

THEODORE had thought of taking Ramón a bottle of Strega, which he was very fond of, but decided not to bring any gift at all, lest Ramón take it as conciliatory, or worse, patronising. He climbed the dreary stairway slowly, listening even on the third floor for Ramón's voice among the voices and murmurs he heard from everywhere. Arturo was with Ramón again, and had answered the telephone when he called. "Yes, of *course* you can come! Please do!" Arturo had said hopefully, but there had been a dissenting mumble from Ramón in the background.

He knocked.

Footsteps came to the door, and Arturo opened it with a smile of greeting. "Welcome, Don Teodoro, welcome!" he said warmly, his round face with its usual two-day growth of beard full of joy at the sight of him.

Ramón got up from a chair. He was neatly dressed and shaven, as if he were about to go out. "Hello, Teo."

"Helo, Ramón. Well, you are looking better." He walked to Ramón and extended his hand.

Ramón shook it politely.

"He is better. He is tired, you know. But they didn't hurt him this time. Not at all," Arturo said, locking his short fingers together nervously.

Ramón looked only superficially better, Theodore saw. He was thinner, and there were hollows under his eyes. "Inocenza sends her greetings."

Ramón said nothing.

"He has not been out. Not since yesterday," Arturo said, putting away a broom in the kitchenette corner.

The room looked unusually clean and orderly.

"Damn, I forgot to bring your bird, Ramón! He's doing very well, but I didn't want you to think I'd stolen him from you."

"You have my bird?" Ramón said, astonished. "I thought that janitor stole it!"

"Didn't Sauzas tell you? I had it all the time."

Ramón smiled dazedly and passed a hand over his hair. "The janitor here has the key. I thought he gave it to those kids——" Ramón gestured with a wave of his hand at the door. "Those kids in the house here."

"No, Ramón. The bird is fine." Theodore knew that the unwashed, unruly children in the house bothered Ramón, mainly because he pitied them. But they were always playing annoying pranks on Ramón and perhaps everyone in the house.

"You see, Ramón?" Arturo said, smiling, trying to coax as much pleasure as possible for Ramón out of the fact that his bird was still alive.

"You're spending a lot of time here, Arturo," Theodore remarked. "How is the shop these days?"

"Oh." Arturo made an effacing gesture and smiled at both of them as if he did not want to talk about it.

The assistants came and went in Arturo's shop, but they were all alike, good-for-nothings who worked with a tongue-in-cheek attitude and talked about their girl friends with each other all day long. Theodore had used to drop into the shop every now and then, and Ramón would always be at work on a chair or a table leg, and Arturo was usually reading a newspaper on an old sofa that someone had brought in years ago and never called for. Arturo could do masterly work, but as a master he did not like to work. He preferred to teach Ramón, which in fact he had done, starting from scratch, when Ramón had asked him for a job three or four years ago. Ramón had had nothing but perseverance, but this Arturo appreciated, and Theodore knew that Arturo wanted to leave his shop to Ramón when he died. It had been a curious choice of work for a young man as handsome and intelligent as Ramón, Theodore had often thought. Now he recognised a martyrdom in it that he had been unaware of before.

Ramón was standing by his bed, watching him, his handsome head erect. On the low table at the head of the bed lay Ramón's old gilt-edged black Bible.

"I'm glad to hear that you weren't treated badly, Ramón," Theodore said.

"Oh, not in the least," Ramón said, with subtle sarcasm.

"I phoned several times to find out what was happening."

Ramón's eyes flinched. "Well—they just don't believe me."

Theodore wondered whether to tell Ramón that he had seen one of the psychiatrists. He decided against it. He glanced at Arturo, who was looking at him with a puzzled anxiety. From down the hall came the sound of the toilet being flushed. Theodore turned slightly, and was met by the grey wall just four feet from Ramón's single window. "What are your plans, Ramón?" Theodore asked, turning again. "Are you going back to work soon?"

"I don't know."

"Maybe I'm keeping you, Ramón. Were you going out?" Theodore asked.

"Oh no, not at all!" Arturo said. "Sit down, Don Teodoro. Sit down, if you please."

Theodore sat down on the bed, but felt at once depressed by the surroundings and the atmosphere and wished he were standing again. "And how are your daughter and granddaughter, Don Arturo?"

"Very well, thank you. Uh—the little one is cutting her first tooth!" Arturo put a forefinger up to his own teeth. Then he straightened and pulled his waistcoat down. "Well,

I must be going. No, no, you are not running me off, Don Teodoro. I'm supposed to see a customer at twelve o'clock, and it's nearly that now."

Ramón seemed about to protest, then accepted it with resignation—though Theodore was not sure he was not going to announce his leaving with Arturo until he said good-bye at the door and closed it after the man.

"I'm glad you have such a good friend," Theodore said, with a smile.

Ramón looked at him blankly.

"Don't you appreciate friends, Ramón?"

"You were not my friend when you thought I had killed her."

"Well, Ramón—how could I have been? Would you have been my friend if you thought I had done it?"

"No."

"Well, then. I apologise, Ramón. We were both distraught. How could we not have been?"

Ramón only looked at him disappointedly.

Was this the time? Theodore could not imagine progressing with Ramón if he postponed it. "I don't believe you're the murderer, Ramón. I believe you may think you are—to that extent I believe you. I talked with one of the doctors last night. Dr. Rojas."

"Rojas," Ramón murmured, smiling. He crushed out the little cigarette that he had just lighted.

Theodore watched him as he walked slowly around the room. Ramón's walk seemed different, the way his hands hung at his sides, the way he held his head, somewhat higher than usual. "Well, Ramón, what do you intend to do?"

Ramón continued to walk slowly. "Why do you worry about me? Don't trouble yourself. The city'll be the same, the people the same, the buildings, the *policía*, as if nothing has happened. You'll be the same—but I didn't expect it of you, Teo, that you'd be the same affectionate, kind, naïve

Teo—whom I have to protect from a pedlar selling bogus silver jewellery on the street!" Ramón finished, laughing.

Theodore smiled, too.

Ramón sat down on his bed.

"I worry about you because I like you, and you are my friend, Ramón."

Ramón looked at him and said calmly: "But I killed her—and I'm not your friend any more."

Thodore did not move. He felt an alarming power of convincing in Ramón, an insidious thing, like being swayed from an entrenched position by a good argument. And suppose he *had* done it? In that moment of passion and rage that was supposed to extenuate a crime? Would it be possible to forgive him through understanding him? Theodore wanted to forgive him, in the abstract. But now he simply did not know what to think about Ramón. He did not feel sure about one thing or the other. Theodore went to the head of Ramón's bed and picked up his Bible. He held it out towards Ramón, who had jumped up. "If I asked you to swear that you killed her—would you swear it, Ramón?"

Ramón looked at the Bible and said: "That's not the kind of thing you swear on a Bible!"

"But would you?"

"I swear it. I don't want to touch the Bible, but I swear it," Ramón said.

"Then I don't believe you."

"What do I care what you believe or not!"

"All right, don't care!" Theodore said hotly.

Ramón suddenly gripped the Bible. "There! You see? I swear it! I killed her!" He looked defiantly at Theodore, then thrust the Bible from him.

Theodore replaced the Bible on the little table. What had he learned now? That Ramón had really killed her or that Ramón was insane?

A stubborn, angry silence filled the room.

Then Ramón said: "I can't understand you, Teo. But that's a small matter, isn't it?"

"I'm not vindictive. Maybe that will help you to understand. I don't want to think you killed her, Ramón—but even if you had, I don't think I'd be vindictive. You think that's foolish, I know. You've often thought I was foolish."

"Yes. And emotionless—comparatively speaking."

"That doesn't matter much, what you think of me. I offer you my friendship, in spite of the fact you may have killed her. I just don't know, Ramón. I want to believe that you didn't——"

"Therefore you believe I didn't. That's the way you believe in God and Christ, or anything else, just what you want to believe and nothing more!" His voice rose in nervous anger.

"I would be the same, Ramón, if I thought you'd killed her. That's what I wanted to say." Theodore was trembling. He felt he had committed himself to a pledge he could never take back. "You've always made fun of my philosophy of life —called it no philosophy at all. It has some elements of Christianity——"

"The few you choose to have!"

"I try to practise what I believe in."

"So you would forgive everybody? Every murderer, every thief?"

"No. No, I would not," Theodore said, feeling suddenly defeated and resentful because he did not deserve the defeat, and did not know how to turn it his way. "It's because I don't believe you're an evil man, Ramón. Some men are evil."

"Who is and who is not? Whoever you decide?" Ramón asked, flinging his hands out. "You must remember my threats to Lelia. I made no secret of how I felt, did I, Teo? She was a torture to me, and yet I loved her. We have had some fine, friendly talks about that, haven't we, Teo?" he asked, his voice on a strange note of remorse and hysteria.

"Yes," Theodore said.

"You remember I said once I could kill her, Teo?"

Theodore did remember, but he was silent.

"You see? You don't choose to remember!" Ramón cried triumphantly. "But it's true, Teo!"

And did it matter? Did a threat prove anything? Theodore walked a couple of steps in the room and turned again. "I think there are worse crimes than murders—especially murders of passion. There the emotions are involved. It's a momentary thing—and usually the murderer feels remorseful. He's a human being at least! But take the men who exploit their fellow men, crooked landlords, crooked politicians—who exploit thousands of people and know what they're doing and do it all their lives, with calculation, too. They're the real criminals, the men who should be ashamed before their wives and their children and their God. You're not one of those, Ramón. Not at all."

Ramón was walking about restlessly, smoking. "The answer to that one is simple, Teo. Such men have no consciences. Else they couldn't sleep. And then they'd die. And the world would be better off, I'll grant you."

Theodore also lighted a cigarette. What more could he say? Ramón might reject his friendship in his words, Theodore thought, but the friendship would remain. Theirs was that kind of friendship. Even if they did not see each other for weeks now, each would miss the other's dissonance in his life. Theodore went to Ramón, clapped him on the shoulder and smiled. "Ramón, I have an idea. If you'd like a change of scene for a few days, why don't you come and stay at my house? There's an extra bedroom and bath, and you could be completely alone if you wished—read, play the gramophone, take walks, even eat your meals alone. Or with me." He waited. "We might take a trip together a little later—to Lake Pátzcuaro or somewhere."

"No, Teo. Many thanks."

"I would like to go somewhere out of this town myself, but I feel we should be around to help Sauzas. Something new may turn up."

"Oh, nothing new will turn up," Ramón said with a sigh. He laughed suddenly, like a boy. "How could anything new turn up?"

Theodore laughed, too, with a sense of relief. "Well, Ramón, think it over. You may change your mind. I'll be going." He walked to the door. When he turned, Ramón was standing where he had been, looking at him. "*Adiós*, Ramón."

"*Adiós.*"

Theodore went quickly down the stairs. An elderly woman in black was struggling up with a *bolsa* of groceries, holding to the banister. Theodore took the centre of the stairs to let her pass. At the next landing, he almost collided with a priest in a black robe and hat. The priest looked at him quizzically, and on an impulse Theodore stopped.

"I am looking for the apartment of Ramón Otero," said the priest. "I am Padre Bernardo."

"He is two flights up. The first door on the left as you leave the stairs. Did he send for you?"

"No," said the priest, who had a weak, drooping mouth, which the sadly drooping lines of his eyebrows followed above his small brown eyes. "I am coming to pay him a visit."

"Because I am his friend—is the reason I asked," Theodore said. "Are you his priest? Does he confess to you?"

"Sometimes to me, sometimes to another."

"Did he confess the murder?"

"*Sí*," said the priest without emotion.

"And do you believe him?"

The priest gave a slow, worldly shrug and said: "*Sí*. I must believe. He tells me so."

The man had the languid, slow-witted manner that Theodore often noticed in priests. He looked as limp as his black robes. "Well—what are you going to do with him?"

"You are not a Catholic?" the priest asked, jerking his shovel-capped head back a little.

"No, I happen not to be. I ask because I'm a friend of——"

"Well—I shall comfort him. I shall do the duty of a priest," he said matter-of-factly, and even smiled a little.

"You know he has been exonerated by the police. He is not guilty."

The priest smiled with a superior air now. "That is no concern of mine, señor."

"You should try to convince him that he is not guilty," Theodore said quickly, but the priest looked uninterested.

"We are all guilty in the eyes of the Lord."

Theodore's anger surged suddenly into his face.

The priest was climbing the stairs.

Theodore fumed inwardly, without being able to think of a single thing to call after him. In fact, only the ludicrous phrase *l'esprit d'escalier* crossed his indignant mind. He hurried on down the stairs. A worthless lot! *What* comfort would he be to Ramón? To reassure him that the fires of hell would be hotter than any he had known on earth? What Ramón needed was a psychiatrist! Dashing out of the door, Theodore overturned a pyramid of oranges on the sidewalk, sending half of them into the gutter.

"Ah, look at that! Why don't you watch where you're going with your big feet!" screamed the fat old woman, who was not stirring from her pillow seat on the sidewalk.

"I am sorry. I am very sorry." It seemed to Theodore that the pyramid of oranges had been put there purposely for him to upset in order to make himself feel more asinine, but he repressed his anger and patiently collected the oranges and brought them back to the woman, though the average Mexican might not have bothered, Theodore thought. Theodore knew that he was obviously a *forastero* in Mexico, and for this reason he felt that his conduct had to be above reproach. He smiled and gave the old woman a five-peso note, for which he got quite a friendly smile in return and a "May God reward you in Heaven!" which lingered in his ears.

CHAPTER FOURTEEN

2 March 1957

TODAY painted well for the first time since Lelia's death. A composition in yellows of the view from my studio window. For the first time, a pleasant tiredness after a day's work—which lasts no longer than I can keep thinking about my day's work. There is no word from Ramón, and Sauzas says no one intends to make an attempt to treat him. The police are finished with him. They have left him to the priests —who believe everything he says.

Have the feeling people on the street are watching my house, and when I look at them for a moment, realise I must be wrong. Yet Inocenza says she has never had the telephone ring and there be no voice. Gives me the feeling someone watches to know when *I* am home and even when I am going to answer the telephone, since I. answers it at least half the time.

A few American friends in town (Ernest & Judy Riemer, Paul Shipley) & Riemers asked me to dinner, but I have no heart to see them and got out of it. Have seen in the last week only R. once, Josefina once and Olga. Josefina *wants* to believe R. is guilty just as I want to believe him innocent. "If he is innocent, he is wicked to have put us through all this," says J. with passion. My efforts to persuade her not to judge R. she laughs off, says I judge him, too, and I cannot convince her that I bear R. not the slightest ill will.

Night before last: a dream Lelia was decorating

her apartment with coloured streamers for a Carnaval party. Nothing happened in the dream. It left me oddly cheerful. J. with Sanchez-Schmidt (very decent man) is arranging a sale of Lelia's paintings & drawings along with the dissolution of her apartment. I am relieved that J. does not expect or need me to help her. I offered. J. gave me the silver box that L. never polished and which I adore, in which she used to keep her jewellery and trinkets —though I was given little of the last, and not my choice: gold pin with figure 8 knot and seed pearls and one odd ear-ring. This is what comes of modestly saying I did not want anything!

Theodore kept his fingers in the place and turned back. The diary was two and a half years old. He did not write in it every day. Here and there he had made a sketch, and he had made more than he realised of Ramón, who had never agreed to sit for him. It amused Theodore to draw him in front view as a Roman with a wreath on his head, and in profile as a sharp-featured Spanish *torero*, and to find one sketch as much like him as the other. There was a pen-and-ink drawing of himself hectically feeding Leo in the kitchen, setting a broiled and split lobster before the cat with one hand and with the other pouring melted butter from a pitcher, and below it their dialogue:

LEO: Where have you been, damn you! Don't you
      know it's after midnight?
  T: I told you I'd be late coming home, and I'm
      sure Inocenza gave you a little something at
      five o'clock.
LEO: She did not.
  T: Don't lie, Leo. And here's a fine broiled
      lobster. Smell it!

LEO: R-row! If you think this makes up for waiting six hours!

T: I promise not to do it again.

LEO: You will. You're lucky I stay around at all,
because you don't deserve me.

Theodore turned back to what he had just written and
added:

Kurt Zwingli (now in Zurs) wants me to illustrate
in pen and ink a new short book of his. The MS
came yesterday. 'The Straightforward Lie'. A satire
of modern life. A young man of the kind who never
existed—like those in the exercises of old-fashioned
grammar books who stay at *pensions* in London in
order to learn the language, attend concerts and
visit musems and exhibit *Schwärmerei* for every
vital statistic—travels around the world today and
finds everybody dubious about the good and value
of everything, cynical and pessimistic. Our hero
refuses to be dampened and misses all the cynicism.
Summary cannot do it justice. I adore it.

I see rather dense but fine penwork which would
combine the static stiffness one sees in grammar-
book illustrations (ill-fitting clothes, sexless bodies,
everyone with two left feet) plus nightmarish darkness, the darkness of pessimism and resignation. If
I get myself into the proper frame of mind, I'll
attempt it. Must be done by Sept. To get in proper
state of mind, something must happen. Sauzas is
apparently making no progress.

Looked at Rouault. The solace of looking at
other people's paintings.

About midnight, when Theodore was in the living-room

reading, his telephone rang. He felt suddenly sure that it would be his silent caller, and the things he had thought of before to say went through his mind in a frightened flash. His hand was already perspiring as he rested it on the telephone. He yanked the telephone up.

"*Bueno?*"

He heard a confusion of voices at some distance from the telephone, then: "*Bueno?* Don Teodoro?"

Theodore relaxed a little. "*Sí*, Arturo."

"If you will pardon the hour, Don Teodoro, Ramón would like to see his bird," Arturo said distractedly.

"Oh. Does he want me to bring it?"

"No, he will come. Or is it too late?"

"Not at all."

"In a few minutes, then. Is that all right, Don Teodoro?"

"*Seguro que sí!*"

Arturo hung up.

Theodore turned on another light in the living-room, then climbed the stairs to the second floor, saw that Inocenza's light was out, and knocked gently at her door.

"*Sí!*" Inocenza said in a frightened voice as if she had awakened from sleep at the same instant.

"Inocenza, it's I. I would like to get Ramón's bird. I'm very sorry to disturb you."

"*Sí*, señor." He heard a bustling about, then Inocenza opened the door in her robe, barefoot, and turned and took the bird cage down from the hook.

"He telephoned. Ramón's dropping over for a moment, but there's no need for you to disturb yourself."

Inocenza smiled. Her glossy hair hung loose, and it was very beautiful falling behind her shoulders. "I would be glad to come down, if you need me, señor."

"No, no, I don't think we will. Thank you, Inocenza." The bird was silent as he carried it down the stairs, and he wondered if it was still asleep under its cloth, or if it was awake and waiting in a state of terrified suspense for what might be going to happen to it.

Theodore put a jacket on over his shirt and sweater. The house was chilly. There was kindling and some heavier wood in a leather hod beside the fireplace, and Theodore wadded some newspaper between the fire--dogs, laid kindling on it, and struck a match. A fire would be cheerful for Ramón, he thought. He put on wood as fast as the fire could take it. Then he undraped the bird cage. The bird looked at him intelligently with its head on one side, then hopped closer to the cage door and studied it as if it were contemplating a new means of attack.

Leonidas jumped silently down from a chair and approached the cage with the stealthy swagger of a lion sure of victory.

"Oh, no you don't, Leo," Theodore said, picking the cat up. He carried him to his study off the living-room, turned on a small light, and set the cat down on a couch. "Stay here and be quiet."

Theodore heard a car stop in front of the door and went immediately out to open the iron gates. Arturo was paying the *libre* driver.

"I won't be staying long, Don Teodoro," Arturo said after greeting Theodore courteously. "I just wanted to be sure that Ramón got here safely."

They crossed the patio and entered the house.

Ramón sat down on the rug beside the bird's cage. In the better light, Theodore saw that Ramón's eyes were swollen as if he had been weeping. Arturo wore his anxious smile, and looked at Theodore and shook his head as if to say he had done his best and without much success.

"Inocenza has taken good care of the bird, I think," Theodore said to Ramón. "She keeps him in her room because it gets sun and the cat never goes up there to annoy him."

Ramón might not have heard him.

124

Theodore looked with embarrassment at Arturo, then beckoned to him, and they walked to a corner of the room. "Did anything happen tonight?" Theodore whispered.

"No, señor. Nothing unusual. He went to church——"

Ramón was half-reclining beside the cage, opening the door. The bird looked at the open space for a moment, then hopped out and fluttered from the rug to the seat of the sofa. Ramón smiled at it and wiped his eyes. He looked at Theodore. "Forgive me, Teo. Forgive me."

"Of course I forgive you!" Theodore said, not knowing exactly what he meant. Theodore felt a reassuring or warning pat on the arm from Arturo.

Ramón sat up on his heels. "Forgive me," he said wearily, and held his head in both hands.

Theodore came closer to him. "Come and sit down." But Ramón did not respond to his tug at his shoulder. "Is there anything you'd like, Ramón?"

"No." Ramón took his hands down from his head and looked at his bird again.

"You've never let him out of the cage before, have you?"

"No."

Ramón had always said, the times that Theodore or Lelia had asked him to let the bird out in his apartment, that he was afraid the bird would fly up to the light fixture on the ceiling and not come down again. Theodore thought Ramón did not want to be bothered getting the bird back in the cage and, perhaps more important, did not want to give the bird that bit of pleasure. There was a curious cruelty in Ramón's attitude towards the little prisoner whom he gave no joy to and took none from, and it combined both sadism and masochism, Theodore thought, because he felt that in the bird Ramón saw himself.

Now Ramón was crawling on his knees towards the sofa, holding out his finger with a look of pathetic affection. The bird hopped along the back of the sofa, a tiny, exquisite, sky-blue thing against the terra-cotta-coloured sofa. Theodore felt that Ramón was trying to prove something by the fact that the bird would or would not come to him.

"Bird, bird!" Ramón whispered, and made a little noise with his lips to encourage the bird to come to him. *"Pájaro, pájaro!—Pájaro!"*

Theodore and Arturo watched. Ramón moved very slowly forward on his knees. The bird eyed him suspiciously and hopped farther away on the sofa back.

"You can't expect him to come to you if you've never practised with him, Ramón," Theodore said.

Ramón sank back defeatedly on his heels.

Theodore patted his shoulder. "You need sleep, Ramón. You're very welcome to stay here tonight." He saw Arturo nod in hearty agreement.

Ramón plunged forward, his head in the seat of the sofa, weeping in silent but gasping sobs.

"He is very bad tonight," Arturo whispered. "Every night he is like this—almost—but usually it's not so bad as this. Every night he asks me if I can forgive him. He begs forgiveness in the church." Arturo's face was turned up, bewildered, to Theodore. "I have asked him to stay in my house. We could make room for him, but he will not come. Teodoro!" Arturo touched his arm and whispered quickly: "Don't tell him something is for his own good. Don't tell him something will help him. Do you understand?"

Theodore was already nodding. He understood.

"He takes it the wrong way always!" Arturo added.

Theodore took a deep breath. Then he walked towards Ramón and forcibly lifted him and sat him on the sofa. He began to unbutton Ramón's jacket and shirt, then he loosened his tie. "You're going to stay here tonight, Ramón," Theodore said in a kindly tone. "Come on, we'll go upstairs."

Arturo helped him. Ramón came with apparent willingness, but he seemed to have little strength in his body and would have fallen on the stairs if the two men had not supported him. Theodore looked up and saw Inocenza peering down the stair-well. She came down from the third floor, dressed but with her long hair only tied back.

"Don Ramón!" she said in greeting, and stopped at the sight of his limp figure.

"He is very tired, and he is going to spend the night with us," Theodore said to her. "Could you turn the bed down in the guest-room, Inocenza? And get a pair of pyjamas from my room."

"Sí, señor!" she said, flying into the guest-room ahead of them.

Theodore abandoned the idea of a bath for him. He left Arturo to help him into the pyjamas and went into his own bathroom, got a nembutal, and poured a glass of water from the carafe by his bed. Then he went back into the guest-room, which was next door to his. Ramón was sitting on the edge of the bed, naked to the waist, his powerful shoulders drooping like a resting boxer's. Arturo was helping him off with his shoes. Ramón did lift a foot finally and removed his own sock.

"Take this, Ramón," Theodore said, holding out his palm with the orange pill on it. "Something to make you sleep."

Ramón took the pill and drank some water. When he lay down in the white pyjamas between the pale blue sheets, however, he looked up at the ceiling, and his face grew strained again as if he had begun to look fixedly at something that was always in front of him.

"He's bound to feel better in the morning," Theodore said.

"Ah, I should think. In such a ni-ice pretty room as this." Arturo looked around him, smiling.

That was what Theodore thought, too, and he started to open the curtains so that the cheerful morning sun would be the first thing Ramón saw in the morning, then decided it might shorten his hours of sleep if he did. He tipped the lamp shade on the bed table so that the light was away from Ramón's face. Inocenza was standing in the background, looking at Ramón. Theodore beckoned to her to come into the hall.

"Ramón may stay with me for a few days," he said in a low voice. "Be very nice to him. He is very depressed. We must try to make him feel more cheerful."

"*Sí*, señor," Inocenza said, nodding.

"The bird is loose downstairs. See if you can get him back in the cage, and then let Leo out of the study."

At that moment the telephone rang.

"No, don't answer it, Inocenza," Theodore said quickly. "Thank you."

Inocenza looked surprised for an instant, then frightened.

The telephone went on—*br-ring-br-ring*—*br-ring-br-ring*.

CHAPTER FIFTEEN

JOSEFINA MARTINEZ'S maid Juana opened the door for Theodore, and Theodore greeted her with a smile, a handshake, and the cheerful word that he always had for her, as if nothing had happened since he had seen her last. But Juana was not quite the same. She had been with the family thirty-three years. Lelia had been like her blood kin.

"The señora is not yet ready," Juana said. "Please sit down, Don Teodoro. She will be out in a minute."

Theodore sat down in a dark red plush armchair and waited, letting his eyes wander over the old-fashioned, bourgeois, comfortably cluttered living-room—antimacassars, flower-stands, paintings, and photographs crowding one another on the walls, and a huge spider plant that trailed the floor adding a note of jungle-like confusion. Josefina's apartment was like a fortress, impregnable to change. More had been added since he first came here, but nothing had been taken away. He remembered the smile he had exchanged with Lelia the first time he had come into the room and looked around.

It was nearly ten minutes before Josefina appeared. Theodore jumped to his feet and bowed over her hand. She wore a long, impeccably neat housecoat, her hair was arranged, her lipstick and mascara freshly applied.

"Sit down, dear Teo! Would you like some coffee?"

"No, thank you, Josefina."

"Or a drink? Whisky?"

"No, thank you, really. I'm quite all right."

"Ah," she sighed, sitting down, resting her plump hands palms-down in her lap. "So now Ramón is staying with you."

"Yes."

"Tsch-tsch. It is scandalous, Teo."

"What is scandalous?"

"Our courts of justice. Our police force and their psychiatrists." Her large dark eyes, full of feminine wisdom and quite devoid of logic, glanced around the room impatiently. "He will only take advantage of your unbelievable charity and perhaps kill you, too!"

Theodore leaned forward. "Dear Josefina, I think we both must yield to the opinions of the psychiatrists and the police. You have not seen Ramón lately. He is the victim of his own obsession. His story makes no sense, you see. That's why he was released. And now he——"

"No sense to the psychiatrists! But you and I know him, Teo. I myself have seen his temper." Her voice grew shriller. "I think he should pay. He should pay for what he has done. And he confessed. I cannot understand their releasing him. I have written to the President of the country, Teo. Would you like to see a copy of my letter?"

Theodore started to demur, or at least to postpone it, but Josefina was already on her feet, on her way to the bedroom. He tried to collect his facts again, his argument. He would lose, he knew it. But he had to pay this call. Josefina had telephoned him that morning, horrified that Ramón was under his roof.

She swept into the room again with her letter. It was on two sheets of typewriter paper, and, before he began to read, Theodore found himself glancing at the type to see if the t's were somewhat tilted and the e's out of line, which were two of the clues Sauzas had for the typewriter which had written the postcard from Florida. Then he began to read with respectful attention. It was, of course, a biased denunciation of Ramón's character, but, under the circumstances, Theodore had to forgive it. It was curious the way Josefina's passion began to persuade him that Ramón was not innocent, and then he came to his senses when Josefina stated that she had always suspected that Ramón would be capable of this. That, Theodore knew, was not true, because she had used to be very fond of Ramón, fonder perhaps than of him, because Ramón was one of her own countrymen. The rest of her letter was a rhetorical complaint against the inefficiency of the Mexican laws, the police and detective force, and a diatribe against "the modern medicine-men with degrees", the psychiatrists.

"Do you agree or not?" Josefina demanded.

"I, too, felt the same way at first. Believe me, dear Josefina."

"And how do you feel now?" Obviously she expected her letter to have convinced him that she was right.

"I repeat, I have spoken to Ramón. His story does not hold water——"

"That's what he wants you to think!" she shrieked, pointing a finger. "He has won you over, that's all!"

Juana, with the privilege of her years of service, was standing in the door of the bedroom, listening.

"No, Josefina, on the contrary, he wants us to think he is guilty," Theodore said quietly. "He is wretched and depressed because no one believes him, because not even the Church will punish him, until after he is dead, he thinks."

"You can be sure of that! God will punish him!"

"Yes, so Ramón thinks. But it is not enough for him now. As a matter of fact, Josefina, listening to Ramón, one can be almost won over to Ramón's side—that he did it." Theodore was leaning forward, speaking slowly and gesturing as if to convey with his hands what his words could not, he knew.

An awkward silence grew and grew. He could hear Josefina's excited breathing. Then a clock in her bedroom said: "*Coo-koo! Coo-koo! Coo-koo!*"

"I suppose, Josefina," Theodore said, a moment after the clock had stopped, "all I can say is that I do not believe Ramón is guilty. I think he is devastated by grief."

"Tyuh!" Josefina stared across the room, out of the window.

Theodore looked at his clasped hands. "Well, I didn't come to make you believe what I believe, Josefina. What I believe is only my opinion." And where would his passive attitude get him, he wondered. Where was his courage? What was so wrong about convincing others of what he believed, if he thought what he believed was true? And he was *ninety* per cent convinced of Ramón's innocence. . . . An oval portrait photograph in an oval wooden frame on the wall behind Josefina had been holding his eyes for several seconds. Perhaps its shape had attracted his glance because of its similarity to the oval pendant of Lelia's necklace, and realising this and that his staring at it would profit him nothing, he still stared at it as if its form would reveal some secret.

"Juana, *por favor*, a little coffee," Josefina said, raising a hand and letting it drop in her lap again. In defiance of her doctor's orders, Josefina drank at least a dozen little cups of very strong coffee every day. "If Ramón is not guilty, then who is guilty?" Josefina asked.

"I don't know." Then he reminded her of the postcard from Florida, and that anyone could have got Inés Jackson's name and the fact that she lived in Florida from the newspapers. He reminded her that Lelia's keys had never been found and that Ramón had been unable to tell the police what he had done or might have done with them. He told her also about the silent telephone calls, two of which had come while Ramón was either in prison or at Theodore's house. Josefina's eyes stretched wider as he spoke, and perhaps some element of doubt entered her mind, Theodore was not sure. He knew only that the doubt would not be enough to sway her.

When the coffee came in, Theodore gathered himself for the only statement he could make with conviction. "Josefina, Ramón and I have always been good friends. Since I am

132

more inclined to believe he is innocent than that he is guilty, I still must be his friend." The words were stark in his Spanish, and he felt they did not carry much weight with Josefina.

"Only inclined? Why are you not sure? Because you know in your heart that he is guilty!"

"No, I don't. It's not in my heart, and even if it were——"

"I know one should forgive one's enemies——" She shrugged. "It is hard to do when the victim is one's own flesh and blood and the crime so horrible beyond any words. Teo, you are not a stupid man, only too naïve and too generous by far. If you think he is not guilty, then you must think he is crazy for confessing. Either way he is a dangerous man for you to have under your roof."

"I'm aware of that," said Theodore.

CHAPTER SIXTEEN

THE psychiatrist arrived at four-fifteen, a quarter of an hour later than he had promised. His name was Dr. Cervantes Loera, and he had been recommended by Theodore's medical doctor for just such a service as this. Dr. Loera was an advanced thinker, "flexible and experimental", Theodore's doctor had said. He was plump, with a black moustache and glasses, about forty-five. He had come to talk about painting with a view to buying something of Theodore's. He was to be introduced to Ramón as Sr. Cervantes.

Ramón was upstairs when Dr. Loera entered the living-room. He looked around and asked which pictures were Theodore's, as if Ramón had been present.

"I've asked him to come down," Theodore said. "Perhaps he will of his own accord. Inocenza, you may bring the tea now."

When the tea and cakes were brought in and Ramón had still not come down, Theodore went upstairs to speak to him.

"I don't care to come down, thank you, Teo," Ramón said. He was sitting in a chair by the bookshelves in the guest-room, looking at a book in his lap.

"Very well. But I may bring him up to show him a picture or so, if you don't mind."

"In here?" Ramón asked, frowning.

"Yes, Ramón. I'd like him to see these two pictures." Theodore went downstairs again.

"Then we'll go up," Dr. Loera said when Theodore had reported his conversation with Ramón.

They climbed the stairs, with their teacups, and went into Theodore's studio, where the psychiatrist passed a few minutes looking at Theodore's paintings and at the work in progress on his easel. The doctor's large, restless eyes took in everything. Theodore fretted with impatience for him to see Ramón.

"Let's just go in," Dr. Loera said.

Theodore led the way to the guest-room, whose door was open. Ramón looked up from his book with surprise.

"Señor Cervantes," Theodore said, "my friend Ramón Otero. Ramón, this is the gentleman who is interested in my paintings."

Ramón nodded and murmured something, and got up from his chair with the book.

"Are you a painter, too?" Dr. Loera asked, which Theodore thought was probably the wrong thing to say, since the newspapers had made Ramón's name quite familiar to the public.

"No, I am not," Ramón replied.

Dr. Loera strolled to a wall on which hung one of Theodore's rare but pleasant paintings of a vase with flowers. "A cheerful room, isn't it?"

Ramón nodded. He was watching the doctor and moving so that he faced him at all times. Then Ramón tossed the book down on the bed and walked out of the room and down the stairs.

Theodore looked at Dr. Loera, who shrugged. Theodore was quite tired of shrugs. "Well——"

"Well, we follow him," said Dr. Loera with a wide smile.

They went downstairs and with the utmost casualness walked to the cocktail-table, on which their tea-things stood. Ramón was at the far end of the room which served as the dining area.

"I am more interested in your abstract," the psychiatrist said. "That yellow, for instance. Are you selling that?"

"I'm not sure. It's one of my latest paintings."

"You had very good notices in a show last autumn," Dr. Loera said pleasantly. "I remember them. I also saw the show. That was the one Dosamantes was in, too, wasn't it?"

"Yes," said Theodore. Lelia had chosen the three paintings he had in the show.

"Dosamantes," Ramón murmured to himself, touching the edge of a round wooden board on which stood the remains of a huge cake.

Dr. Loera walked slowly towards Ramón, who stepped a little to one side, around the edge of the table. He pretended to look at a picture, which happened to be an old engraving, on the wall above the sideboard. Then he looked down at the wide arc of white icing on the wooden board and said: "That must have been quite a cake! A wedding cake?"

Theodore braced himself for a reaction from Ramón and said: "A baker acquaintance of ours—Alejandro Nuñez— brought it. He baked it in memory of our friend who died— Lelia Ballesteros."

Ramón stared at Theodore as if he had not heard of the cake before. The cake had had a figure of Lelia on its top in pink and white icing, and a sentimental verse written around its layers in blue icing.

"You didn't eat any of it, Teo? It was a well-meant gift, wasn't it?" Ramón asked.

"Of course, and I did eat some. But it's two weeks old now. I told you about Alejandro's bringing it, Ramón."

Ramón looked at the cake with a puzzled expression. Was he wondering where the powdered-sugar figure of Lelia had gone? Theodore had removed it one day when no one was in the house, unable to look any longer at its silly red mouth and its streaming dark blue hair that was supposed to represent Lelia's black hair.

"Señor—Teo, excuse me," Ramón said abruptly, and went to the stairs.

Dr. Loera picked up the remains of his cool cup of tea, drank it and refused a second cup.

Theodore was eager to go out where they might talk without being overheard. He walked out with the doctor and continued walking with him on the sidewalk while the doctor seemed to be arranging what he had to say.

"Now you are waiting to hear words of wisdom that I can't give you," Dr. Loera said.

"I am waiting to hear anything at all."

"I might have risked saying that I heard about the tragedy —the death of your mutual friend. But I thought if he became suspicious, it might turn him against you, señor. A most suspicious nature, certainly. Paranoid, perhaps. Not easy to deal with."

"He certainly is not. He goes from humility to arrogance, but mostly he is humble. He thinks he hasn't the right to eat food at the table!"

"Don't be so humble yourself. Treat him as if he were normal. Don't talk deliberately of subjects that depress him or set him off, but don't treat him like an invalid. That will only make him feel worse, sorrier for himself and even more guilty. He has an insatiable guilt. You understand?"

Of course Theodore understood. He wanted something else.

The doctor went on coolly. "He thinks he has wronged you, you know, by killing the woman you both loved. His feeling for you is ambivalent. He would like to hurt you because of his shame and also apologise and make amends for having hurt you."

"Will he try to hurt me?"

"Probably not physically. There are other ways. His ambivalence may keep him motionless." Dr. Loera walked in slow strides, looking down at the sidewalk. "Well, that's your immediate problem, a mere detail of the whole picture. Believe me, I would have liked to spend more time with him, señor, but I could hardly have done that without appearing to chase him around the house, you understand." The doctor had stopped on a corner. "Here I must say good-bye. Another appointment." He hailed a *libre* even as he spoke. "It was very interesting to meet your friend, señor, and also to see your paintings. *Adiós.*"

"*Adiós.*" Theodore watched him enter the *libre* and slam the door, thinking that he should have made it clear to his own doctor that he would pay Dr. Loera for his time. But he hadn't made it clear. And the bill would probably come anyway, Theodore thought. As he turned away, he caught sight of the stick-figured boy a block distant, crossing the street and glancing his way. He still carried something under his arm. He should try a different neighbourhood for his mufflers, Theodore thought. He walked back to his house, feeling the familiar vague answers, the 'ifs' and 'perhapses', settling oppressively on his mind and beginning to paralyse. He had meant to ask the psychiatrist if he thought urging Ramón to go to a Carnaval party was a good idea. He had forgotten, and now it seemed of ludicrous unimportance, like Ramón's murmuring "Dosamantes", which meant "two lovers".

Ramón was standing in the living-room when he came back. Inocenza was clearing the tea-things.

"Who was he?" Ramón asked.

"A Señor Cervantes," Theodore said. "I've never seen him before."

"Did he buy a painting?"

"I think he wants to buy the yellow one."

"For how much?"

"Six thousand pesos."

Ramón's eyes widened at the sum, but he said: "Is that all?"

"I'm not Picasso. And this is Mexico." And I'm still living, Theodore started to add, but didn't.

"I don't trust him. He doesn't look honest."

Theodore lighted a cigarette, suddenly nervous and uncomfortable. "Well, this transaction is a simple one, if it takes place. You won't ever have to see him again."

Ramón turned the gramophone on, carefully took a record from a Debussy album, and placed it on the machine. It was one of the *études* that Ramón especially liked, this and two others, that he played over and over.

"Olga's party is tomorrow night," Theodore said when the *étude* was nearly over. Ramón always removed the record when the first *étude* had finished playing, though there were several others on it. "Would you like to go?"

"A Carnaval party? Are you going?" Ramón asked.

"Yes, I thought I would. She very much wants me to come. I don't have to stay long. Inocenza is going to be there to help serve."

"And I suppose you're taking somebody?" Ramón asked incredulously.

"No one. You're under no obligation to go, Ramón." He smiled. "Come upstairs with me. I want to show you something."

Ramón went with him reluctantly.

Theodore entered his room and got a package from the bottom of his cupboard. "Costumes I bought yesterday. We have to wear a costume, you know. Mine's a kangaroo. How do you like that? With my big feet, this'll look very well, don't you think?" Theodore lifted the long cloth feet that were stiffened with cardboard soles. The head had round holes so that one could see out of it, and a projecting, smiling muzzle. "The other costume is just a clown, but one can wear any kind of mask over it. Look at the masks." Theodore opened a paper bag and pulled out a gorilla mask and another that was a kitten's face with bobbing rubber whiskers. "Take your choice. Or you don't have to come, if you don't want to."

"One disguise is as good as another." Ramón looked down at them. In the lamplight, his smooth, pale forehead was like a rectangle of marble. "They don't fool anybody for long."

CHAPTER SEVENTEEN

THE Velasquez house was not a large one, and it astounded Theodore that so many people had been able to cram themselves into it. People were dancing, even in the foyer, to the Cuban music played by a four-piece orchestra in the living-room. A few of the dancers waved at them gaily. The only light was candlelight, and there was a smell of incense, a trace of a gardenia fragrance, and the mingled perfume of many women. Ramón surveyed the crowd through his clown's face with an apparently simple-minded delight.

Theodore sought out Constancia, the only person he could recognise, and said: "Where's the Señora Velasquez?"

"Señor or Señora?" Constancia yelled.

"*Señora!*"

Constancia looked around, and then pointed. "The mouse!" she said, giggling.

Theodore took Ramón's arm and made his way towards the little grey mouse figure seated on the arm of a chair. "Olga? Good evening! It's Theodore!"

"Ah!" Olga spread her arms. "Señor Kangaroo!" She pulled out the sagging marsupial pouch of his costume. "And Ramón?"

"Not in there!" Theodore said happily. "Here he is! Your hostess, Ramón!"

Ramón took her mouse's paw and bowed politely.

"Your friends the Hidalgos are here, but I don't see them now. This is Señor and Señora Carvajal—Señor Schiebelhut," Olga said, indicating the people standing near her. "Señora Guzman——"

"No-o!" protested the figure, in a falsetto. "*I* am Señora Jimenez!"

Everybody laughed.

"Well, it doesn't matter who we are tonight!" Olga said. "No more introductions. The drinks are in the garden, Teodoro. Go out and tell them what you want. Somebody stepped on my foot while I was dancing, and I can't move yet."

"Oh, is it bad?" Theodore asked, bending over her foot.

"No! I am just being lazy. Get a drink and come back and dance with me!"

More people danced and cavorted in the garden behind the house. Unrecognisable figures kicked feet into the air, jumped for the *papier mâché* devils suspended from the trees, and pranced and whirled like dervishes. It seemed unbelievable that such madness could keep up all night, but it would, and all over the city. This was the third of the four nights of Carnaval, and people did not admit fatigue until the day after the last night. For the past several nights the street noises of horns and singing and hurrying feet had drifted up from the pavement into Theodore's windows. This was his first sight of a party of the season, and it was as if all the preliminary excitement he had heard on the streets, all the costumes in shop windows that startled the eyes in the daytime, had gathered in this house for one great explosion.

"A drink, Ramón," Theodore said, handing Ramón a cup of punch with a straw in it.

Ramón felt for the space between the clown lips and put the straw in it.

"To Carnaval!" Theodore said.

"Carnaval!"

"Are you Eduardo?" a small figure asked, tapping Ramón on the shoulder.

"No," Ramón said, shaking his head. He shrugged as the

feminine little figure—some animal all green with a tail—went prancing away into the house.

Four girls were dancing in a ring, holding one another's hands. They began to do a graceful, complicated step that threw one foot into the centre of the ring, and which had nothing to do with the rumba that the orchestra was then playing. Ramón watched them, too. They were all in yellow, yellow rabbits with flopping ears, and their feet were shoeless, covered only by the yellow cloth feet of their costumes. They looked utterly charming to Theodore, like something come to life from an old story-book, fantastic and sexless and out of their minds. One really could not tell the sex of anyone except possibly by height and by the size of feet. And a couple of tall men were in women's dresses.

The green girl was back. "You *must* be Eduardo! You're joking with me!" she said in a young, tragic voice, staring up at Ramón. "*Say* something to me!"

"Who are *you*?" Ramón asked her.

"Nanetta," she replied. "Who are you?"

"Pablo," Ramón said.

"And you?" She looked up at Theodore out of a donkey face.

"Francisco," Theodore said, bowing.

The girl continued to look at Ramón, though she must have known from his voice that he was not her Eduardo.

"Would you care to dance?" asked Theodore.

She spread her arms suddenly.

"Excuse me, Pablo," Theodore said, and went off with the girl towards the living-room.

It was too noisy for talking, and at any rate the girl's head was several inches below Theodore's. He began to feel happier. Ramón would be all right this evening, he thought. Something had begun to happen to him when he put on the costume. It had to do with losing his identity, even to himself a little.

142

"Do you like dancing?" the girl asked.

"Yes."

"Do you like parties?" She danced close to him, her energetic body bending and swaying to his steps. She kept up a giddy run of questions. What kind of accent was that? Was he really so tall, or was he on stilts? "There is a man on stilts here," she said. "In the garden."

Theodore looked and it was so, a man in the costume of Uncle Sam. "Are you watching out for Eduardo?"

"No," she said, laughing.

"Did you come by yourself?"

"I came with a fri-iend," she said, with mysterious intonation. "There. The African chief." She nodded towards a group in which Theodore saw a fat man in chocolate-coloured tights with a top hat, cigar and a ring through his nose. "My uncle," she said, and laughed.

Theodore laughed, too, not believing her. "Are you pretty?"

"Oh, *si-i*," she said mockingly.

But Theodore did not want to know what her face looked like, even if it was pretty. He held her closer to him, looked around for Ramón, and realised that there were at least three clown costumes exactly like Ramón's. The girl's hand tightened on the back of his neck.

Midnight came and went. Theodore took several rum highballs, losing most of them on the living-room mantel while he danced with Olga or some other female figure or the little girl called Nanetta, who stuck with him wherever he went. Somebody had pinned up his tail for him, so he no longer had to carry it draped over one arm or stumble on it dancing. And in a corner of the room, in full view of everybody who might have cared to see, Nanetta threw her arms around his neck, held him very close with her head against his and said: "I love you, Francisco." They kissed, a bump of kangaroo and donkey muzzles. Then Theodore felt a sudden shame and embarrassment at seeing Ramón watching him with folded arms from a doorway across the room. At least he thought it was Ramón.

"Is that perhaps your friend Eduardo?" Theodore asked Nanetta, pointing to the clown in the doorway.

"Ah, no-o," she said in her breathless, eager little voice. "Eduardo is taller."

Theodore could never tell if the girl mocked him or not. He went over to the clown and said: "Is it you, Ramón?"

The figure did not answer at first; then there was a nod and a "*Sí*."

"Have you danced with your hostess yet?"

"No."

Ramón had always been fond of dancing, and he danced very well. "She's standing by the mantel now," Theodore said.

The clown still leaned against the door-jamb. He uncrossed his arms and let them hang, and at that moment Theodore knew it was not Ramón. "Teo, it's Carlos!" the clown said in a tearful voice barely recognisable as Carlos Hidalgo's.

"Old fellow, what's the matter?" Theodore asked, patting his shoulder, but obviously nothing was the matter except that he had had too much to drink.

Carlos touched Theodore's shoulder, too, and lowered his clown's face. He gave a sob, a snuffle, and lifted his head.

"Would you feel better with some coffee, Carlos? I'm sure there's coffee somewhere. I'll ask Constancia."

"No!" Carlos bleated, pushing himself off from the door and staggering.

Isabel—Theodore recognised her by her size and the way she moved—was suddenly by his side, with a firm grip on his arm. "Sorry, Teo. You see, he insists on starting out with a drink at home, and then——" She broke off with an embarrassed laugh.

"How about some coffee? Shall I ask the girl?"

"No, I'll get it, thanks, Teo." She steered Carlos away with her.

As Theodore stood watching them he remembered that Carlos had never made good his promise to phone him when he had a free evening. He still wanted to talk with Carlos about the month he had been away before Lelia's murder. Obviously, their talk could not be this night. As he turned to walk back into the room, Olga came to him and said: "Teodoro, Constancia has been looking for you! You're wanted on the telephone!"

"Oh? Where? In this room?"

"Upstairs in my bedroom! The only place you can hear anything!"

Theodore went up to the first floor, looked into the wrong room first, and then found the bedroom with the telephone off the hook and lying on a blue-satin-covered bed. *"Bueno?"* he said. He heard a hum of many voices.

"Bueno?" said a woman's melodious voice.

"Bueno. This is Theodore."

"Theodore! Elissa. How are you?"

"Very well. And you?"

"I am at the party I told you about. In Pedregal. Do you think you could come over? I could send a car for you." Her slurring voice made a lazy, scalloping pattern in his ear.

"Well, I'm not sure, Elissa, because——"

Nanetta's little green figure appeared in the doorway as suddenly as a sprite's, poised on one foot, her hands on the door-jamb.

"I've already sent the car for you, so you don't *have* to decide, Theodore. If you don't want to come, just tell the car to go away again. The party here is just beginning! I do hope to see you."

"How did you know I was here?" Theodore asked, nervous because Nanetta was clinging to him.

"Oh, I have my spies," Elissa said with a soft laught. "*A toute à l'heure*, Theodore," she said, pronouncing his name the French way, and hung up.

Nanetta's arms were around his neck again, her faintly perfumed donkey head against his. And she said not a word. They sat or fell down on the bed, and Theodore noticed at the same time that she had closed the door. It was ridiculous in the costumes—to lie embracing someone whose face you couldn't see, didn't know, and yet it was extraordinarily pleasant. Francisco and Nanetta. He kissed her green cloth neck, holding her tightly to feel some little warmth from her skin. Her hands caressed his back frantically.

Then the door opened with a sharp click.

"Nanetta! What the devil are you doing? Get up! Get out, you little——"

"I wasn't doing anything!" the girl protested shrilly, jumping to her feet.

"And *you*, señor!" It was the African chief. His pot belly was real, and perhaps he was her uncle, or her husband.

"Don't-blame-him-he-is-nice!" the girl said in a shrieking monotone.

"No, I don't blame him, I blame *you*!" roared the black man. "A *school* for you! You need a *convent*!"

They went off down the hall, and Theodore stood for a moment, confused, as a dialogue with himself raced through his head:

'Well, they don't know who you are.' 'That isn't the point. Why did you do it at all?' 'Olga will understand. What did I do, anyway?' 'They may not know who you are, but they'll recognise your costume when you go downstairs again.' 'Oh, they'll ignore it. After all, it's Carnaval.' 'Ramón will hear about it. You've been an ass. A girl probably not more than eighteen! An ass!' Theodore stared at his reflection in Olga's narrow, full-length mirror. Then abruptly he turned and walked to the door.

146

They had not ignored it downstairs. Theodore's eye was drawn at once to the gesticulating knot of people in the corner of the living-room who stood out somehow in the general confusion. Olga's little mouse figure was among them, and when she saw him she detached herself and ran over to him. She pulled his shoulder down so that she could whisper, and said:

"Theodore, don't let him bother you. He's got a dreadful temper, and besides he's had something to drink. And that girl! She's his niece, and she's just been expelled from college somewhere. You can imagine why!"

Theodore told her that nothing had happened except the girl had tried to kiss him while he was on the telephone, and he couldn't imagine why there was any fuss, but he began to sound like Ramón, protesting too much, and stopped. The fat uncle was approaching him—Theodore thought—from far across the room, and, to Theodore's discomfort, he saw that several people were looking at him, and he imagined that he could hear them saying: "The kangaroo . . . It was the kangaroo!" But the African chief, who was holding his niece's hand, veered off to one side, heading for a hall, and the girl blew Theodore a kiss as she passed.

Theodore moved towards the garden, looking for Ramón. He was not in the garden. A dart game was going on with one of the *papier mâché* devils as a target, and it would have been perilous to cross to get to the patio. At last he saw Ramón dancing among the couples near the orchestra. He was talking to his partner, a rather tall and slender woman in a royal blue full skirt and a conventional black mask over her eyes. Then he noticed a group of three people turn their heads to look at him. Olga, of course, had a few stodgy people among her friends, but one would think that at Carnaval— Theodore watched Ramón for the first opportunity to speak to him, and at the end of a song he sidled through the crowd to reach him.

"Excuse me." He bowed to the woman. "Ramón, may I have a word with you?"

"I am not Ramón!" But it was Ramón's voice and his laugh.

"Pablo—— Come on, I *know* you are Ramón!" Theodore pulled at his arm. "I would like to go on to another party. Come with me, if you like. I know you'll be welcome."

"Where?"

"A party in Pedregal. They are sending a car here, and it may have come. Olga will excuse us. Come on."

"What happened upstairs?"

"Nothing! A silly girl. Just——"

"That is not what I heard," Ramón said ominously.

"I don't care what you heard. Do you want to come or not?"

Ramón flung Theodore's hand from his arm. "A fine thing!" Ramón said. "Drunk at a party and necking with a girl in a bedroom!"

"Well—you have the key, Ramón. You can go home when you like." He walked towards the door, his face burning with shame and anger. Hadn't the psychiatrist told him to treat Ramón as if he were normal? Theodore felt he was retreating in disgrace, however. He stopped and looked around for Olga and forced himself towards her. He explained that he was going on to another party for a while, and said that he would look in again and say good night if her party was still going on when he came home.

"Of course it will be going on!"

Theodore went out into the cool night, and saw a chauffeur getting out of a long black Cadillac. "Do you come from Señorita Straeter?" Theodore asked him.

"*Sí*, señor. Señor——" He consulted a paper in his hand. "Schiebelhut."

"Schiebelhut, *sí*!" Smiling, he opened the car door. "Teo!"

Theodore turned round and saw Ramón. "You're coming, Ramón?"

"Yes," Ramón said. "I'm sorry for what I said to you. Whether it's true or not—it's a small thing, a small sin, Teo, compared to other sins."

"Now what is all this about sins!"

Ramón held Theodore's arm in a firm grasp. "Forgive me, Teo. I'm sorry for what I said."

"I forgive you. Now get in, Ramón!"

The big car raced across the city, held Theodore tongue-tied with its speed, and shot out on the wide, dark highway towards Pedregal. Why am I going here, Theodore asked himself, and did not mind at all that he had no answer. He felt quite tired of looking for answers.

"Would you like this for a change?" he asked Ramón, pulling the cat mask out of his pouch.

Ramón put it on obediently.

They were gliding past the great wall that guarded the wealthy homes of Pedregal. The car turned in at a lighted gate of tall iron bars, like the entrance of a prison. Two soldiers with torches, and rifles on their shoulders, came up on either side of the car and threw their torch beams over both of them and the car's interior. It was the usual inspection of cars entering Pedregal.

"No secret weapons," Theodore said.

The guards waved them on, a whistle blew, and the gates clanged behind them. Now the road was very smooth, curving pleasantly between terraced, well-kept lawns on which sat the expensive houses, most of them brightly lighted tonight. Dance music swelled and faded as they rolled along, yet there was a sedate, muted atmosphere here, as if they had entered a different city. Black humps of lava, made decorative with flowers, stuck out of the lawns. Gravel began to pop under the tyres. The car stopped beside two huge glass doors, through which Theodore could see a great room full of people in costumes. On the other side of the car was a swimming-pool rimmed with blue lights and a spot-lit fountain spewing up gold-coloured water, like effervescing champagne.

"Theodore! You *did* come!"

Theodore recognised Elissa Straeter's tall, slender figure in a white satin dress, though she wore a tightly fitting green cat's mask over her head and face. "Good evening!" Theodore said. "I've brought my friend, Ramón Otero. Ramón, this is Señorita Straeter. But I think you've met before, haven't you?" They had, Theodore remembered distinctly, and Elissa said:

"*Ramón!*" in a tone of wonder, and stared at him, although nothing at all of him was visible.

"Elissa, perhaps it's better if you don't introduce us to any-one. I don't want people staring at Ramón."

"Of *course!* I understand, Theodore," Elissa said, taking his hand. "You won't even have to meet the host!" She staggered a little, either from drink or the irregularity of the flagstones. "Come on, Ramón. We'll get you a drink and you can amuse yourself looking at the costumes."

The noise blared as soon as they opened the glass doors. A few people reclined with their drinks on the floor. There were several tall, bare-legged girls in tights, most of them with curled blonde hair above their masks, American girls. Elissa pushed glasses of champagne into their hands and lifted a glass herself.

"To your health, gentlemen," she said rather formally, and Theodore knew she was as drunk as usual, perhaps more so.

The sober, efficient figures of three or four maids moved among the noisy guests, collecting glasses, passing trays of hot *canapés*, though a long table at the side of the room held elaborate salad moulds and mountains of little sandwiches.

"You see, you don't have to meet anybody, if you don't want to," Elissa said in her gentle, barely audible voice. "But

150

that's our host, Johnny Doolittle, over there, in case you don't recognise him." She pointed to a small gorilla hanging over a chair, gesticulating as he talked.

There was a moment or two, when Elissa was narrating a long, uninteresting story, when Theodore wanted to leave. He knew no one, or if he did could not recognise anyone now, and Elissa was going to keep their conversation on the same dull level for the rest of the night, he knew. Her voice came with absurd earnestness and gentility through the smiling slit of the cat's mouth.

"Ramón doesn't speak English, you know," Theodore put in by way of explaining Ramón's drifting away a moment before, out on to a terrace.

Then Theodore found himself and Elissa walking towards the swimming-pool.

"It's heated," Elissa said. "Isn't it lovely?"

A smiling boy in a white mess-jacket approached them with a tray of trembling champagne glasses. Elissa set their nearly empty glasses down on the tray and took two full glasses.

"Elissa, I must ask you something. I've been getting silent telephone calls for the last month—since Lelia's death—at least one a week. If it's you, I don't mind, naturally, but——" He explained in a rush to her. He felt as if he stood beside himself and listened to his own voice, and made his judgment of Elissa's solemnly shaking head. She looked as if she really didn't know anything about it. She had taken off her cat's mask, saying she couldn't be bothered with it any longer, and her narrow, coldly beautiful face looked at Theodore with a tipsy attentiveness.

"No, Theodore, absolutely not. The police officer who called on me asked me that, too. He also took a sample of my typewriter. Now I didn't *mind*, Theodore, of course I didn't mind. This is a serious matter. The woman was very important to you, wasn't she?"

151

"I loved her," Theodore said emphatically, and shuddered. There was a chill in the air. And the liquor was unnerving him. He heard a succession of splashes in the swimming-pool. The girls in tights were diving in, masks and all.

"They're from an American show," Elissa explained.

Now they were surrounded by people who were coming out of the house to watch the events in the swimming-pool. A xylophone was being rolled out. More lights went on, making the pool a deep yet clear blue. Theodore looked around for Ramón. The people at this party moved more slowly than those at Olga's. From the voices he heard, they were nearly all Americans. A certain gaiety was missing, and, realising this, Theodore felt more depressed and apprehensive. He noticed that the moon was full.

"So you think he's not guilty?"

"I beg your pardon?"

"Ramón. You don't think he's guilty?" she asked casually.

"No, I do not think he is."

"Well, it just seems to me that in any situation like this *someone* has an idea who did it. You don't have to tell *me*, Theodore, if it's something you've been told by the police not to tell."

"No. I'm telling you the truth. No one——" A huge splash as three girls went in. "No one knows. Not Ramón, not I, not the police. But they are still working on the case. As hard as ever."

"Oh," said Elissa thoughtfully, but still with the cold unconcern. "Well, they'll find out eventually, Theodore. They always do."

"Yes," Theodore said, without conviction.

"Let's sit down somewhere," Elissa said, reaching for his hand. She took every opportunity to touch him.

"I'd like to find Ramón. Excuse me, Elissa."

He went back into the big living-room, looked around, then went out on the terrace. People were pushing balloons over the terrace parapet, trying to get them to land on the playing fountains below. Theodore saw Ramón in conversation with a man in a purple costume in a corner of the terrace. For a moment, he hesitated about interrupting them, then went on.

"Excuse me," Theodore said to both of them. "How are you, Ramón?"

"Very well," Ramón said. "I am learning about the coffee industry from this gentleman."

The gentleman in purple, costumed like a devil, bowed slightly and said: "Tonight we need no introductions. We simply talk." He laughed affably. "Your friend is in a serious mood." He turned to Ramón. "Well, *adiós*, Pablo. I must get back to my wife—who's not really my wife, of course." His hand almost touched one of his red horns in salute, and he moved off, round-bellied, slender-legged and graceful.

"He was referring to one of our jokes," Ramón said. "He said he has several wives tonight.. Tonight the devil claims his own."

"But I dare say you approached him," Theodore said.

"You are right, *amigo!*" Ramón said gaily.

"And the only thing roasted was coffee."

"Right again!" Ramón swung his arm around Theodore's shoulder and pressed his clown's mask against Theodore's cheek in a gesture of a kiss.

They stared in fascination at a tumbling balloon poised on the crest of a spraying fountain, until the balloon fell and there was a low groan and laughter from the people watching.

"You're enjoying yourself?" Theodore asked.

"No," Ramón said, though not disagreeably.

They walked back through the living-room and out on to the driveway. Theodore saw Elissa wandering on the grass near the pool, and she saw him at almost the same instant.

153

Theodore went to her and said that he and Ramón were leaving.

"But the party's just begun! Johnny's going to serve breakfast in a little while!"

Theodore said that they had to get home. Elissa then insisted that they take her car. She would go with them and come back to the party. There was no dissuading her. She sent two servants in different directions to find her chauffeur.

In the car, Elissa spoke awhile in Spanish to Ramón—her Spanish was not bad at all—and asked depressingly polite questions. She was like a polite machine wound up to run God knew how long. She was even too polite to have an affair with anyone, Theodore thought. One could not imagine her becoming that realistic. Theodore listened to her, nodded, and replied in a fog. She asked if he was going to Cuernavaca soon—she took a certain suite at the Marik-Plaza there when she went, she said—and Theodore thought of a certain street in Cuernavaca where he liked to walk, remembered the reddish-brown Indian faces of little boys he saw there, the heavier faces of the black-haired, black-moustached men who drove the beer-trucks, the faces of old men under sombreros, and he was glad they made up the majority of the people, even in Cuernavaca.

"Well, here we are," Theodore said as the car slowed at his house.

"And how is your maid, Inocenza?" Elissa asked.

"What a good memory you have! She is fine," Theodore said as he got out of the car. "Thanks very much for your *libre* service tonight, Elissa. We very much appreciate it."

"You're not going to ask me in for a nightcap?"

Theodore had feared that. "Why, of course. Come in." He felt through the slit in his costume for his trousers pocket where his keys were. The lights were still ablaze at Olga's, and he supposed Inocenza was there.

A light was on in his living-room. Leo crouched tensely in the middle of the floor and stared at them. His tail lashed from side to side. Theodore spoke to him, told Elissa and Ramón to sit down, then went to the kitchen to get some ice and to turn the furnace up.

"A beautiful house!" Elissa sighed behind him. She had been here two or three times before.

When he returned with the ice-bucket, Leo was looking at Elissa and making a sound like a siren in his throat.

"Don't be so unfriendly, Leo," Theodore said. "He's probably been chilly all evening, and he's annoyed with me."

Elissa seated herself gracefully in a corner of his sofa with her Scotch and soda. Theodore saw her face take on the slightly pained expression that had preceded all her remarks on 'the Ballesteros affair'. He lifted his own weak drink and glanced at the clock to see the time. The clock was gone. *Robbery* registered on his brain at once, simply the word.

"The clock's gone," he said, and looked down at the cocktail-table, where he thought he remembered seeing his cigarette-lighter before he went out. That was gone, too.

Ramón turned from the bar trolley, where he was getting ice water. "You think it's been stolen?" he asked in an alarmed voice.

Theodore went to the sideboard and pulled out a drawer. His silver had not been touched. His Degas statuette stood on the console table. "Pardon, I want to look upstairs," Theodore said, and ran up the stairs two at a time.

His room door was open, and he saw that a couple of drawers were pulled out of his desk. He ran up the next flight, flung open Inocenza's room door and groped frantically for the light switch on the wall by the door. The light went on, and he looked at the bed. It was empty, its cover smooth. The room did not look at all disturbed. He turned out the light and went down the stairs.

"Is it a robbery, Theodore?" Elissa asked in the hall.

155

Ramón was behind her.

Theodore looked into the room in which he painted. The window was open about two feet. His paintings were all right, but the East Indian knife which always lay in its wooden sheath on the bookshelf was missing. "Yes," Theodore said, "and I think through the window. Perhaps from the Velasquez house. You see?" he said to Ramón, gesturing to the ivy-covered bridge above the iron gates which connected his house with the Velasquez house. "Their window's open, too," he added.

"Shouldn't we call the police?" Elissa asked. "You think it's someone at the Velasquez party?"

"He wouldn't be there now," Theodore said. "Not with a big clock. We shouldn't touch anything in the house. There may be a fingerprint." But he did not think there would be. He imagined a costumed figure, perhaps one of the people whose costumes covered their hands in mitten form, crashing the Velasquez party in all probability, crawling across the ivied bridge, and letting himself out with his loot by the door. Really a small mishap of a Carnaval evening, Theodore thought as he walked into his bedroom. It was only the fact that it might have a connection with the murder that disturbed him. His fountain-pen had been on his desk before he went out, he thought. But the notebooks and drawing-pads in the two opened drawers looked untouched. "Elissa, who knew I was going to be at the Velasquez party?"

"Well——" She looked embarrassed and faintly insulted. "I'm a slight friend of Señor Velasquez. That is, I know someone who knows him and——"

"Who?"

"Emily O'Hara. He's her lawyer, and once in a while—I mean, Emily told me the Velasquezes were having a party to-night and she went, I think. Anyway, she told me you were invited. You see, I wasn't *sure* you were there."

Theodore saw. It was another of the vague and unsatisfying answers. He went to the telephone, dialled a number, and asked without hope for Sauzas. Sauzas was not there. Theodore reported the robbery, and the police officer said that he would send someone to his house at once.

"I'm sorry this has happened, Elissa," Theodore said. "Please don't feel you have to stay. It's very late, and you must be tired."

"But I'm interested, Theodore. Perhaps there're other things missing. Did you look at your clothes?"

Theodore shook his head.

"Could you fix me another short one, Theodore? Just on the rocks?"

Theodore fixed it. Ramón had gone over to the Velasquezes to get Inocenza. Theodore had told him not to tell Inocenza what had happened, because he did not want the news spread at the party. Ramón came in with her a moment later.

"I wanted to speak to you, because there has been a robbery in the house," Theodore said. "It is not serious, but there has been one."

"A robbery!" Inocenza gasped.

"Yes. And I think the robber may have come across the bridge from the Velasquez house. Did you come back here at all this evening?"

"No, señor."

"Did you hear anything?"

"No, señor."

The police arrived, two ordinary policemen in uniform, and in a somewhat bored manner went over the house and listed the items Theodore said were missing and their value. Theodore knew he would never see them again. One almost never saw stolen things again in Mexico, and the *policía* accepted robberies—little house robberies like this—with a resigned shrug. It was no doubt their conviction that people with so much money ought to be robbed now and then, that

157

it did them no harm and did the poor possibly some good. And Theodore, too, felt rather the same way.

"You're not going to try to get any fingerprints?" he asked a policeman.

"Ah, señor, if we get your stolen goods back, they'll have changed hands a couple of times. We have to go next door now."

The announcement of his robbery before the Velasquez guests shamed Theodore. It seemed not worth it. He apologised to Olga, who appeared pleasantly intoxicated now, though she was as animated as in the early part of the evening. They all went up to the room Olga called her music-room, which had a piano and gramophone and bookshelves, and where the casement window was wide open. The ivy-covered bridge was just three feet below and a trifle to the right of the window-sill. But no one could remember if the window had been open from the start of the evening or not. Constancia thought it had been open, because she had intended to open it to help ventilate the house. Señor Velasquez liked fresh air. Only fifteen or so guests were left, and they stood about in sudden sobriety, some still masked and some not.

"Señora, we would like a list of the guests at your party," one of the policemen said to Olga.

"Oh!" Olga raised her hands as if this task dismayed her, but in the next moment she said: "Of course, of course! I think I have the list still on my desk!" And she ran into another room.

"That's hopeless," Theodore said to the policeman. "Everyone was in costume tonight, and people could have come in off the street."

The policeman laughed a little, as if to say of course it was hopeless, but he had his procedure to go through.

Olga came back with her list. But she admitted to Theodore and the police that strangers could have walked right in.

158

"It's not a very serious robbery," Theodore said kindly to her. "Not even six thousand pesos' worth, I think. It could have been far worse. Now I think I should go home."

Elissa—who had greeted the Velasquezes cordially and said a few words of regret about the robbery as if she were personally responsible—came with Theodore, and so did Ramón. The police took their cue from Theodore, as he had thought they would, having nothing else to do in the Velasquez house, and departed, too. Elissa made a speech of sympathy and climbed into her waiting car.

"Sauzas will be very interested in this," Theodore said to Ramón as they crossed the patio. "I didn't want to tell these *policía* tonight about—anything at all. I suppose I shouldn't have had them come. If there were any fingerprints, there aren't any now."

Ramón tossed his cat mask down tiredly on the sofa. He had removed his clown's head when Elissa had been here, and now it hung by strings at the back of his neck. "The world's full of evil, Teo."

"No, it isn't," Theodore said. "But I suppose it has about as much evil as good."

They went up to their rooms. Inocenza leaned over the stair rail and asked if the *policía* had found the robber. Theodore told her no.

"Is anything missing from your room?" Theodore asked.

"No, señor."

"Good. Then go to bed, Inocenza. Sleep as long as you like in the morning. If I get up earlier, I'll prepare the breakfast."

"Gracias, señor. Buenas noches."

Ramón came into Theodore's room a few minutes later in the shirt and trousers he had worn under his costume. Theodore had undressed and put on his dressing-gown in preparation for a bath.

"Well, Ramón," Theodore said cheerfully. "Aren't you

159

exhausted? What a night! All we need is a hangover tomorrow. Would you care for a last nightcap?"

"No, *gracias.*"

"I don't want any either. Just a lot of Tehuacán." He opened a bottle of *agua natural.* Inocenza saw that there were always a couple of bottles of Tehuacán in his room, and he preferred it at room temperature. He gestured to Ramón with the bottle, but Ramón shook his head.

"I don't see why you're cheerful, Theodore."

"Well—I'm not!" Theodore said, smiling. "But why show it?"

"People prey on you and take advantage of you. Even this disgusting woman tonight. Even me. And now they rob you to boot."

"Everybody gets robbed now and then, Ramón. Once or twice in his life there's——"

"Yes, exactly! That's the way things are, isn't it, Teo?" Ramón waited for an answer.

"This is no hour to be grasping for life's certainties. Not for me, anyway."

"You don't see that people prey on you?" Ramón walked towards him, taking his hands out of his pockets. "Teo, can you forgive me for what I've done to you?"

"Yes, Ramón—yes."

"You've done nothing wrong that I know of. I'm sure you've done nothing. And yet you're victimised. You did nothing wrong with Lelia. You left her free, because she wanted to be free. I understand, Teo. And if I ever criticise you, consider that I'm wrong, that I'm out of my head."

"All right, Ramón. Agreed," Theodore said as seriously as he could, because he saw that Ramón was serious.

"And I've wronged you most of all."

"You have not wronged me." Theodore set his empty glass down and went into his bathroom. He turned the water on in the bath, not looking back at Ramón but listening, fearful

160

of what might be coming next. He decided to go ahead with his bath, as if their conversation was over. The door was slightly ajar.

When he came out of his bathroom about ten minutes later, Ramón had gone. Theodore wandered to his desk and looked around again for the fountain-pen. It was then that he noticed his diary was missing. It lay always on the upper left corner of his desk, or else flat on his desk if he had closed it after writing something. But now he looked around on the floor, behind his desk, too. Who would steal a diary, and in English? And with Lelia's picture, a large portrait photograph, inside the front cover? Who but the murderer? It seemed self-evident that the robber had been the murderer.

He went to bed in a fog of shock and pain. All the story of his love for Lelia there for anybody to read. All his heart, as much of it as he could put down on paper. He imagined filthy hands turning its pages.

CHAPTER EIGHTEEN

THEODORE sat up in bed at twenty minutes past ten with a feeling of not having slept at all.

He went down quietly to the kitchen, made coffee and squeezed some oranges, drank his first cup of coffee alone, and carried a tray upstairs to Ramón's room. He knocked gently. Then he opened the door a little. Ramón's bed had been slept in apparently, but Ramón was not in it.

"Ramón?" he called to the open, empty-looking bathroom.

He had gone out, and no doubt to church. Ramón walked to the Cathedral most usually, though it was a distance of about three miles, and walked back, and the expeditions took three or four hours. Theodore poured another cup of coffee and dialled Sauzas's number. This morning he was lucky. Sauzas was in the building, and ten minutes later Sauzas called him back.

"Yes, I have heard about the robbery," Sauzas said. "I have given the night officer a bawling out for not sending some men who could take fingerprints. And those stupid police for not knowing who you were! One would think they were illiterates! But they are not—quite!"

"Maybe it's not too late for fingerprints."

"Maybe not. Don't touch anything. I'll come over myself. But I have about an hour's work here before I can leave."

"One thing more, Señor Capitán. I noticed later last night that my diary is missing. It had a large photograph of Lelia in it and—it was a personal diary, very personal. Ramón is not here now. I'd rather you wouldn't tell him about the diary."

"Ah. Hm-m. Your diary. You don't think Ramón could have taken it?"

"Absolutely not! Why do you think that?"

"I didn't *think* that. But it's not part of the usual haul of a robber, señor."

"I know. That's exactly why it's important."

"We'll talk about that when I see you. Until an hour, señor."

Ramón returned a few minutes later, and Theodore told him that Sauzas was coming, a piece of news Ramón received without interest. Ramón looked refreshed, even as if he had slept well and long enough, though he probably had not slept an hour. Theodore had noticed this before when Ramón returned from church.

"Is Inocenza up?" Ramón asked.

"I don't think so. Why?"

"Because I brought her a little present." He pulled a small dark green box out of his pocket, a box the colour of Theodore's diary cover, and showed Theodore a small gold-coloured pencil inside it, attached to a button by a springed chain. "She can wear it. For telephone messages," Ramón said. "And this is for you, Teo." He handed Theodore a longer green box. "It's from Misrachi's. A good one. Not a ball-point. I know you don't like ball-points."

Theodore opened the box and saw a dark green fountain-pen. "That's very nice of you, Ramón. Thank you." He tried the point on the inside of the box. "It's fine. And just what I needed," he added with a laugh.

Ramón went out of the room. Theodore started to ask him if he wanted coffee, then didn't. Often Ramón refused coffee in the morning, though Theodore knew Ramón liked it as well as he did. It was a kind of penance Ramón seemed to be doing, especially on the mornings when he went to church —and the mornings when he didn't go, the not going seemed a kind of penance, too, in a privative sense. And there were

163

other things. He had practically stopped smoking, though to stop entirely would probably have been easier than to limit himself to two or three cigarettes a day. He refused butter for his bread, and he never took second helpings even when Theodore knew he was very hungry. And all this without ostentation, so that it had taken Theodore some time to realise it. A fine way to expiate a murder, Theodore thought. Ramón would have to do something else, that was evident. And some part of his mind must be seeking what he should do, what good deed, what sacrifice would be enough. It was hard to be a knight, a hero, a martyr, because it was hard to find a cause that seemed worthy of one's efforts and one's life. Theodore himself knew. It was a problem that bothered him. What was the value of painting, for instance? He contributed to æsthetics and gave some people some pleasure, but wouldn't it be of more value to mankind to contribute something practical, such as ministering to the sick in Africa? He thought Ramón must be in a similar quandary—and worse, a quandary that was itself imaginary and out of control—as to justifying his existence, or seeking an atonement in proportion to his crime.

Theodore stood up, impatient with himself. Where did he ever get with his thinking? He had once aspired to be a man of action, of decision, and he had become a ludicrous opposite. He kept his fingers on his own pulse simply because he had more time to do that than most people. The only thing he could say for himself was that he did not consider selfishness among his vices. He loved his friends, and love, he thought, being in most of its forms a neurotic emotion, could nourish itself on giving alone, if it was unable to take anything, or if nothing was offered. Or as Kierkegaard put it on the religious plane: "Faith has taken all chances into account . . . if you are willing to understand that you *must* love, then is your love eternally secure."

Another thought crossed his mind: Ramón had decided,

irrevocably. He had decided on the side of hell, but at least it was a decision. It put Ramón in a position as strong as his own. Since good and bad existed only in the mind, their respective efforts, his and Ramón's, became simply a contest of wills.

Theodore went out and knocked on Ramón's closed door.

"Come in."

Ramón was seated on his bed with a straight chair up-turned in his lap. It was one of Theodore's early nineteenth-century Spanish chairs. "Very well constructed," Ramón said, and set the chair upright on the floor.

Theodore nodded. "What do you say we take a trip some-where, Ramón?"

"All right. Where?"

"It doesn't matter to me at all. Where would you like?"

"I would like to see the mummies in Guanajuato," Ramón said.

Theodore had feared that. "But you've seen the mummies, Ramón. What about something new?"

"I've seen them years ago. I'd like to see them again." Ramón's face was serious and reposeful.

"All right. And then what?"

"I think I ought to find some work, go back to Arturo if he'll have me, or take any kind of job. It's all very well for you to take a long vacation, Teo. You have money, and you can do your work anywhere." Ramón stared at the Spanish chair.

Theodore tried to think of an argument. Arturo's shop was depressing and disorderly. It was impossible for Ramón to take an interest in the cheap furniture that came in to have a leg or an arm put on it for twenty and thirty pesos. He would continue doing his penance there, and finally lose all contact with the world. Theodore wanted him to look at beautiful scenery, to wake up in clean, cheerful rooms in the morning, to eat good food and live like a human being. His house in Cuernavaca? Jalapa? Jalapa was a pretty town, and full of flowers. A cruise somewhere? But Theodore suddenly saw Ramón jumping over a ship's rail into the sea. "Well," Theodore said, "we'll go to Guanajuato. I'll speak to Sauzas."

"Sauzas?"

"Naturally, he'll want to know where we are."

Ramón smiled a little. "Yes, we must keep the police department busy, along with all the other thieves and murderers."

Theodore did not know what to reply. The Catholic Church, he supposed, was Ramón's police force. And it did nothing to punish him, at least nothing tangible. Would Padre Bernardo say: "Repent of your sin and it shall be forgiven"? or would he try to fortify Ramón to stand an eternity of hellfire? "Have you seen Padre Bernardo?"

Ramón looked at him. "How do you know Padre Bernardo?"

"I ran into him on your stairs one day. He asked what apartment you lived in—and I told him."

"And you asked him who he was?"

"He introduced himself." Theodore watched Ramón's face, his resentment struggling with embarrassment at having his privacy invaded. "Do you see him often?" Theodore asked.

"I see many priests. Not just one." And what business is it of yours, his eyes seemed to ask Theodore.

"You find them comforting?"

"Yes—No. I don't know."

"What do they tell you, Ramón?"

"They tell me I am doomed to purgatory—perhaps hell."

"Unless what?"

"Unless I repent—confess."

"And haven't you done that?"

"There isn't time to do enough. I have many sins, Theodore. This is something you don't understand, because you think there isn't such a thing as sin."

"That's not true, Ramón."

"I've heard it from your own lips! So what can you understand of me? Oh, I know you're kind, Teo, you pretend to be respectful——"

"I don't pretend. I am respectful. Some things I don't understand, such as there not being enough time for something that's beyond the realm of time. If we've argued sometimes in the past, Ramón, it's because we each have our own ideas. A man is made by his thoughts, and if he——"

"Exactly! That's why you and I have nothing in common."

"But I like you, Ramón. I like you as a friend, and we've been friends for years—haven't we?"

"Yes, I know. But I don't understand why you are my friend," Ramón said. "I think it's a holy word to you—'friend'. Either you're crazy or a liar. Or you've got something up your sleeve."

"Is it inconceivable to you that——"

"You won't give it up!" Ramón interrupted him. "It's your religion, Teo!"

"Well—I don't think I'd continue being a friend of someone unworthy, Ramón. As for its being a religion, a man's kindness to his fellows is the basis of morality, isn't it?" It wasn't what he had wanted to say. It even sounded pompous. "You're trying to find reasons yourself why you like me— intellectual reasons now. Justifications. Why don't you let our friendship prove what they are? You don't have to come with me on a trip, Ramón. You're free to do as you wish. I asked you because I'd enjoy your company. I am lonely, too —without Lelia."

"But I killed her—I killed her, Teo, over such an unimportant argument. The argument didn't seem unimportant to me at the time." His voice choked off. He shut his

167

eyes tightly, covered them with his hands and rested his elbows on his knees.

"What was the argument?"

"I wanted her to marry me. I was miserable, I thought——"

"And then what happened?"

"And then I went into the kitchen and got the knife," Ramón said, looking at Theodore. "I said I'd give her one last chance. But she thought I was joking, you see. Then after I'd begun, I didn't stop. I kept on stabbing her," he said in a soft, quick voice. "But she was saying something to me all the time and maybe she'd changed her mind, Teo."

"And then you raped her?"

"I don't remember. I think I must have just lost my mind while I was stabbing her, and I don't remember anything after that. I don't remember going home—and yet I was home."

"And then you went out and bought flowers?"

"I don't remember that either. Maybe I fainted. But I don't think so, Teo. I only remember starting to stab her. And I don't remember *stopping*." Ramón looked at him with a dazed intensity, as if a demon had him in a trance and were working him like a puppet. "I remember cutting her nose off, Teo. Imagine!"

Theodore felt for a cigarette, but he had none in his pockets.

"Imagine thinking of that every night, Teo," Ramón said into his hands. "Then you'll know why I'm insane!"

"You're not insane, Ramón," Theodore said automatically.

Ramón looked up at him. "The only ones who believe me are the priests. The priests you used to call stupid."

"I never called them stupid," Theodore said, though he probably had. Their organisation kept them from being too stupid. And as a sense of sin constituted their firmest hold, they must have been quite pleased that one of their fold had presented himself to them with a ready-made sin and such a big one, enough to imprison and terrorise him for life. Then suddenly a shame of his bitterness and a desire to feel what Ramón was feeling erased his whole train of thought. "Everyone has committed sins, Ramón, crimes and sins. It's only a matter of degree."

Ramón was shaking his head. "It's not the same. It's not the same if you don't believe. You don't believe in sin."

"Of course I believe that sin can exist. I don't believe in Original Sin in the sense that you do. I think the story of the Fall is symbolic, a way of saying that with knowledge of the world comes corruption—a fall from grace. Well, we have to live in the world. I don't believe Original Sin should be a mournful handicap all one's life. Above all, I don't believe a sense of sin makes one any better. On the contrary, it makes one worse." Theodore spoke vehemently, but he did not think his words had penetrated Ramón's brain at all. Ramón stared in front of him, and his body swayed very slightly from side to side.

"I'll never hurt another thing, Teo," Ramón said quietly. "I'll never kill anything, not the smallest thing."

"And I think your thoughts will change."

"What do you mean?"

Theodore kept his hands in his pockets, because he could feel them trembling. "I mean I don't think you will keep reliving that scene over and over."

"I don't believe you," Ramón said.

The doorbell rang.

"That's Sauzas. I'll let him in," Theodore said, and went out of the room.

Inocenza was hurrying down the stairs. Theodore told her he was expecting Sauzas.

Theodore met Sauzas in the living-room and reminded him in a whisper not to mention the theft of his diary. Then they went upstairs to Theodore's studio, and Theodore repeated his theory of how the robber had entered. He said that Inocenza had been next door at the Velasquezes' all evening. Sauzas blew powder on the window-sill, then scrutinised it with a hand lens.

After a moment, he stood up, pushed the window wider, and looked for prints on the outside of the sill. Then he smiled and raised his eyebrows. "A very tidy thief. Not a single fingerprint. It might have been scrubbed with soap and water!"

They looked down at the ivy-covered bridge between the two houses. The ivy showed no sign of having been flattened or torn, but it was a sturdy, dark green ivy. The bridge was about sixteen inches wide, and on the street side a trough of dirt extended four more inches, and beyond that the outward-bending spikes, convenient grips for anyone creeping along the bridge.

Sauzas went over the items stolen, and made Theodore look into his cupboards to see if any clothing was missing. None was, Theodore thought.

"And nothing missing from your room, Inocenza?" Sauzas asked.

"No, señor."

"You had your keys with you last evening?"

"No, Señor, because I thought I would return with Don Teodoro."

"Where were your keys?"

"Pinned in my handbag, señor. In my room."

"Are they there now?" Sauzas asked. "Did you look?"

"No, señor, I did not *look*." Inocenza blinked her eyes, then went up the stairs at a trot to her room.

A moment later, they heard a cry and she came running down.

"My keys are gone, señor!"

Theodore and Sauzas climbed the stairs and went into her room. The keys had been unpinned from the lining of her handbag, and she showed them the perforations made by the safety pin to the right of the change purse. She never carried her keys in any other place.

"Well, we'll have the locks changed immediately," Theodore said, feeling tired and defeated.

"And a guard day and night," Sauzas said. "The robber didn't take much, but he covered the whole household, eh, señor? And again took the keys and left no fingerprints."

Theodore's mind hung on the 'again'. Presumably Lelia's slayer had her keys, too. But her apartment had not been entered by anyone except the police and Josefina. They were keeping a watch on Lelia's apartment.

Sauzas called the *policía* from the telephone in Theodore's room and ordered a guard. Then he said to Theodore: "We shall watch for your stolen property among the fences, señor."

"I'm not so much interested in the items as I am in who stole them," Theodore said.

"Of course. I, too." Sauzas lighted a cigarette. "And your friend Ramón is not interested? Where is he?"

"He is in his room. He was with me all last evening." Theodore saw Sauzas smile a little and nod. "Señor Capitán, we would like to go to Guanajuato—tomorrow or the next day. For a stay of a few days. I can telephone you and tell you at what hotel we are staying."

"Guanajuato," Sauzas said thoughtfully. "For any reason, señor?"

"No. Just a change of scene."

"Yes. I suppose that is possible," Sauzas said. "Does Inocenza stay here?"

"I thought so," said Theodore.

Sauzas nodded. "We shall maintain the guard. And meanwhile, I shall stay here until the guard arrives. If you'll permit me, señor, I'll wait in your studio. I can see the street from there and know when he arrives." He went into Theodore's studio.

Theodore consulted a telephone book and called a locksmith. They promised to send a man "after three o'clock", which Theodore knew could mean tomorrow or the next day, but he did not call another locksmith.

Inocenza prepared lunch, and Theodore invited Sauzas to have something with them, but he declined. The guard arrived just before Theodore and Ramón sat down. He was a plain-clothes man, Sauzas told him, and he would be across the street for the next eight hours until he was relieved by another man.

"How are you, Ramón?" Sauzas asked.

"Very well, thank you."

"Did you enjoy the party last night?"

"It was very pleasant," Ramón replied.

"I shall keep you posted," Sauzas said, and took his leave.

The locksmith did come, and the locks were changed that afternoon. They decided to drive to Guanajuato the day after next, 7th March. Theodore paid a month's rent on Ramón's apartment. Inocenza was to remain at the house until Theodore sent for her, as it was his idea that they might take a house in Guanajuato or somewhere else after a few days in an hotel. Inocenza was to be in the house in the daytime, but she made an arrangement with Constancia to sleep in her room, because she was afraid to be alone in the house at night.

The guards walked up and down the block or stood across the street. Sometimes there were two guards, walking together for company.

At about nine o'clock on the morning of the seventh, Inocenza came in from the patio, where she had been watering some flowers, with a brown-paper bag in her hand. "Look, señor! Your diary, is it not?"

Theodore was in the living-room with the suitcases. The paper bag was open at the top. It was his diary. "Don't tell Ramón," he whispered to Inocenza, because the door of Ramón's room was open. "Where did you find it?"

"Between two bars of the gate. Who do you think put it there?"

"I don't know," Theodore said. And so much for the guard, he thought.

"*Ramón?*" Inocenza asked, her voice going shrill with sudden fear.

"No, Inocenza. It was stolen the other night—along with the other things. But I did not tell Ramón. That's all. And don't mention it to him now. Do you understand? I shall simply report it to Capitán Sauzas."

Inocenza nodded, but she looked uncomprehending.

Theodore waited until she had gone off about her business, then opened the diary eagerly. He could see no change in it, no pages torn or marked. Then, as he was about to close it, he noticed that the big photograph of Lelia was missing from the inside of the front cover. And he thought, too late, of possible fingerprints that his own fingers had now destroyed. When he closed the book, he saw a scratch three inches long in the green leather at one of the top corners, a scratch that might have been made by a rough stone, the point of a knife, the claw of a cat.

CHAPTER NINETEEN

THEODORE had been to Guanajuato three or four times, but
for stays of only a day and a night. It was a special town to
him, a special favourite. Other Mexican towns were as old,
had abandoned silver-mines and aqueducts, but Guanajuato
was artistically all of a piece, like a well-composed painting.
When Theodore thought of Guanajuato, he imagined an
aerial view of a town built on hills and sheltered by gigantic
mountains, a town of exquisitely faded pinks and tans and
yellows. Once he had done an imaginary painting of his
aerial view, a smallish painting, because the town, though
large enough and spread out, suggested smallness when one
was in it, a size that one could grasp comfortably with the
mind. The picture had hung in Lelia's bedroom, and
Theodore had no idea what had happened to it, or
whether anybody would ever know it was his. He had not
signed it, because a signature would have marred his composition.

Guanajuato lay off the main highway and had only one
good road of entry and exit, the turn-off from Silao that
wriggled along the narrow Cañon de Marfil. From the
bottom of the *cañon* the road would climb to a panorama of
plains and mountains without a sign of human habitation,
then drop again in the gorge that shut out the sunlight.
Mountains on the horizon were blue with distance, and like
other landscapes Theodore had seen in Mexico it seemed to
say with a majestic voice: "Here I am—a million million
times bigger and older than you. Look at me and stop fretting over your petty troubles!" It gave the melancholy solace
that Theodore felt while looking at the stars on a clear dark

night. He began to relax, as if a frown had been erased from his forehead.

They passed a pair of Indian children who were leading a goat by its chin whiskers, and Theodore waved in response to their wave.

There was a curve, and two children sprang directly into the path of the car. Theodore stamped on the brake and the cat's carrier slid off the back seat on to the floor. Ramón's forehead hit the dashboard.

"Oranges, señor? They are good! A peso the box!" the little girl stuck the box all the way through the window.

"You will get yourself *killed* that way," Theodore said to her oblivious face. "The next car may not have such good brakes!" But already he was feeling for a peso, because she would hang on to the car if he didn't, and she would go on running in front of cars, which was the only sure way of stopping them, until she was old enough to be married.

The little girl dumped the oranges unceremoniously into his lap. "*Gracias*, señor. Another box?"

"No, thank you, *niña*." Theodore was trying to get away before her little brother could poke his lizard through the window, but he was not quick enough.

"Iguana, señor! Five pesos! Make a fine belt!"

"No—no, thank you," Theodore said, leaning away from the horribly grinning face of the thing. He moved the car slowly.

"*Four* pesos!" The boy held it by its fat throat and its tail and walked along beside the car. The iguana looked straight into Theodore's eye, and, like something out of hell, it seemed to say: "Buy me and I'll fix *you*!"

"*Three* pesos!"

"I can't *use* an iguana!"

"*Two* pesos!" The boy took the lizard out of the window, but continued to run along beside the car. "Make shoes!

175

Make belt!" He was speaking in English. The iguana suddenly twisted itself violently, but the boy kept his grip.

Theodore increased his speed.

"*One* peso!—*Ho-o-o-ombre!*" came the fading, tragic cry

Theodore looked at Ramón. "Did you hurt your head, Ramón? I'm sorry."

"It was my nose," Ramón said, smiling.

GUANAJUATO CON RUIZ CORTINES!

said white-painted letters on a great flange of rock at the road's side. Another curve, a steep descent, and they were in the town suddenly, surrounded by pinkish buildings and houses and by boys of the streets who gripped the windows and would not let go.

"Need a hotel, mister?"

"Please don't open the doors!" Theodore yelled at them. He had to go more slowly now, and the boys kept up with him.

Theodore stopped at the lower plaza, and he and Ramón got out and locked the car. There were more boys, one a little tot of five or less who looked at Theodore with a threatening intensity as if he could hypnotise him into doing as he wished, and said:

"You want hotel with hot runnin' war-rter-r? Come with me and I show you! Hotel Santa Cecilia!"

"Ah, it's full up!" said an older boy in a cracking adolescent voice. "You gotta go to a *pensión*, mister!"

"We don't want a hotel," Theodore said good-naturedly, because it was the only way to get rid of them. "We are not staying here." He took Ramón by the arm.

The boys followed them a little way, still shouting, and then gave it up. It was about five o'clock, and the sun touched only the tops of the houses. Theodore walked slowly, enjoying the sensation, which he knew would vanish in a few moments, that the people were play-acting, and that the

176

whole scene had been created by one mind to produce a single effect. Every moving thing he saw seemed dramatic and purposeful. They came to the other plaza, on which stood the grand old Teatro Juarez, its façade a mess of polished, pale green stone pillars and nineteenth-century ornament. Familiarity had made even this attractive.

"The Panteon is on a hill outside of town," Ramón said.

"Yes, I know." The Panteon was the cemetery where the mummies were. "It's late to go today, don't you think? I thought we might go tomorrow."

"All right," Ramón said agreeably.

Theodore asked Ramón if he had a preference as to an hotel. Ramón said he usually went to a very modest one called La Palma.

"It may not be comfortable enough for you, Teo."

"That doesn't matter. Let's try it if you like it."

They strolled back towards the plaza where the car was and where La Palma was, too. There was the smell of charcoal fires in the air, a hunger-stimulating fragrance of roasting corn and tortillas. The street lights had gone on. The evening was beginning.

The doorway of Hotel La Palma was wide, and as they waited for someone to appear behind the bleak desk, a car rolled into the tiled lobby and passed them, on the way to the enclosed garage at the back of the hotel. Only one room was available, at eighteen pesos. It was on the third floor, and there was an elevator, but it was temporarily out of order, the man told them. When Ramón hesitated, the man said brusquely:

"Every other hotel in town is filled up. If you don't believe me, just telephone and see." He pointed to his telephone.

"Very well, we'll take it," Theodore said.

They carried their own suitcases up. The room was an empty box with a plain double bed that sagged, a straight chair, a flimsy table, a pair of coat-hangers on a peg. There was not a picture on the wall, or a waste-basket or an ash-tray. It amused Theodore.

"Probably their worst room," Ramón said apologetically. "I don't mind it at all!"

Theodore took Leo down to the plaza and let him out of his carrier. The cat was used to travelling and had explored scores of plazas in Mexico and South America. Invariably, Leo attracted attention, a few people asked what kind of cat he was and were astounded when the cat came at command, like a dog. Even policemen, approaching him perhaps with an idea of doing their duty, ended by stooping to pet Leo and to marvel at his size and his blue eyes. The army of street boys in Guanajuato were very talkative. Theodore answered their questions with good humour, but he had to rescue Leo finally from some boys who wanted to pick him up. And there was a face or two among the adolescents that looked rather delinquent. The boy who tried to steal Leo would regret it, Theodore thought.

The water in the shower—there was no bath and not even a shower curtain—ran cool and was doubly unpleasant because Theodore was already chilled. He rubbed himself briskly with the undersized towel afterwards and said nothing about the water to Ramón. The single blanket on the bed was going to be inadequate, too, and Theodore made a mental note to get the steamer rug from the boot of his car.

They had dinner at a simple restaurant across the street from the hotel, a narrow place with wall booths, a juke-box, and undersized paper napkins in dispensers on the table. Afterwards they walked through the quiet streets that were lighted by round, yellowish street lamps. Theodore felt an inexplicable well-being and happiness, the openness of spirit that often came when he was pleased with a piece of work, but which now seemed to be caused by the town itself. He carried, folded into three napkins, the chicken from two of his three *enchilados suizos* to give to Leo.

Theodore did not think of the steamer rug until he started to get into bed. They had washed in cool water, and their teeth were chattering.

"I've got to ask them for another blanket, Ramón."

But of course there was no telephone in the room, and he was in his pyjamas. Theodore would have almost, but not quite, gone downstairs in his dressing-gown to his car, which was in the hotel garage, but—— He looked at Ramón and laughed.

Ramón did not laugh. Perhaps his headache had begun to obsess his thoughts, or perhaps he wanted him to leave the room so that he could say his prayers in privacy.

Theodore put his suit on over his pyjamas. There was no light proper in the wide hallway, but a good deal of light came from people's open doors. Glancing with impersonal curiosity at the open or half-open doors, he saw people lying in bed, people undressing, yawning, scratching, a man in pyjamas tuning a guitar. Another man in slippers and dressing-gown was walking slowly, by himself, in the second-floor hallway. Downstairs, the desk was again deserted. Theodore asked one of the boys seated on a bench in the lobby if he might have another blanket.

"Ah, no, señor. The blankets are locked up, and the señor with the keys has gone home."

"I see. Thank you." He went on to the closed door of the garage at the back of the lobby. A padlock dangled from a chain. "Can you open this?" he said to the boys.

The key had to be searched for in cubby-holes behind the desk's counter. At last it was found, the door opened, a light switch found and turned on, and by climbing along some-one's front bumper Theodore reached the boot of his car and got his blanket. His car was wedged with hardly an inch to spare on any side.

"I don't want that grey car moved by anybody but me, do you understand?" Theodore said to the boys.

"If it has to be moved, call me, whatever the hour is."

"*Sí* señor."

He had the keys and the brakes were set, but he had seen cars lifted or bumped out of the way if the owner were not to be found. Again he climbed the three flights, each with its stratum of humanity preparing for bed, and at the third floor turned left and walked towards his room.

Ramón was standing by the window looking out—though the window faced on nothing.

"The blanket, Ramón!" Theodore said, spreading it over the bed. He would have proposed that they read the newspapers or look at the books he had brought, but the single dim light in the bed lamp precluded two people reading at the same time. Theodore got up his courage and put his hand on Ramón's shoulder. "Come to bed. You'll catch a cold standing there. We're seven thousand feet high, you know." And when Ramón turned with a look of willingness, he added: "And take this stupid pill." This time Theodore had the pill ready in his hand.

"No, thank you, Teo, I have no headache."

"I know from the way you look. You'll go to bed and not sleep a wink! What're you trying to prove, Ramón?"

A silence fell. Ramón brushed his teeth in the bathroom. He came out, very quietly in his flattened grey house slippers, and lay down on the bed outside the bedclothes, with his hands behind his head. He seemed to be inviting a cold, or at least adding deliberately to his physical discomfort.

"Go on, say what you are thinking, Teo," Ramón said.

Theodore was thinking of many things, but it was difficult for him to find words gentle enough to express himself. "I was thinking about a conversation we once had about religion as—organised pretending. Do you remember, Ramón?"

"I don't remember," Ramón said indifferently.

Theodore closed his hands in the pockets of his dressing-gown and shivered. "It was one evening when you and I walked around the Zócalo and then went up to the Hotel Majestic roof—for a drink and coffee." But Ramón gave no sign of remembering. "This indifference towards your physical welfare—Whom are you pleasing? Yourself or God? You must choose to live or not to live, not do something between the two, Ramón."

"I think that is my business."

"Of course it is. But—I was reminded of our conversation about religion and its aspects of organised pretence. You saw what I meant that night. You agreed, although I wasn't trying to convince you of anything."

"Ah, I remember. We were talking about rituals. There's such a thing as believing in them, Teo. You may not. I do."

"Believing in their value. I do, too. I don't believe in their intrinsic value, and you didn't either that night."

"But that was years ago. Two years, at least."

Theodore saw his eventual defeat staring at him, but he went on: "We talked about generally practised pretence, ritual, whatever you want to call it. The ritual of fasting after Carnaval may have a value, yes, but no value *per se*. It's symbolic. Your body is not symbolic, however. Its tangible, if only for a short time. Take for instance——"

"Therefore God's a pretence, too?"

Theodore hesitated. "I'm talking about the rituals surrounding Him. Rituals become baseless beliefs, and they can lead to mental unbalance."

Ramón made no comment.

"I was reading recently about some South Sea Island people who consider paranoia a normal state of mind and encourage it among themselves. Paranoia isn't accepted in our society, and anybody with it gets into trouble one way or another. It's not socially approved. But in this South Sea Island colony, people not displaying paranoia are considered abnormal and even ostracised. Wives can't exchange bowls of soup, because they're supposed to suspect it's poisoned.

Nobody questions the rationality, you see, because everybody's been brought up the same way." Theodore paused, trembling from head to foot in the chill.

"Well, what're you getting at, Teo?" Ramón asked, propping himself on one elbow.

"That we live under equally absurd rituals that nobody —or very few people dare to criticise for fear of offending the majority of people."

"But you dare."

"Certainly, I dare. If I feel like it." Theodore lighted a cigarette and moved his fingers over the flame of his lighter for a few moments to warm them. In the room next to theirs, a man and woman were arguing bitterly as to who was responsible for leaving a thermos full of hot coffee at the last hotel they had been in. "You may be surprised at what I started out to say, Ramón. That is that a certain pretension or ritual can be very strengthening to the personality or the character——"

"Always looking for the benefits!"

"—assuming it doesn't go against society, as a belief in the Christian God certainly doesn't go against ours. It doesn't even have to be a religious ritual or pretence, though. Any pretence can give one hope and fortitude, but one should first accept the fact it's a pretence, Ramón. One can still go on pretending if one chooses to."

"You speak always as if people can choose!"

"Yes, they can."

"But they can't if they believe, Teo. That's just part of your Existentialist vocabulary. Choice—decision—and it's harder for you to make a simple decision than for anybody I know!"

Theodore smiled, because Ramón did not know how difficult and absurd had been his efforts to decide to be a friend to Ramón, and to decide this, irrevocably, and with a positive yes, when he still admitted the possibility that

Ramón could be Lelia's murderer. "I was only saying, Ramón, that certain details of every religion are baseless, and people know it consciously or unconsciously, yet they cling to them because they realise how much benefit they derive from them or think they do."

"Benefits again."

"All right! Or because they're afraid not to cling to them, which I think is a bit worse! Or out of habit. *Practically* as bad."

Ramón scowled. "I think you have no respect for anything, Teo."

Theodore had an odd twinge of fear. He stood up a little taller. "That's neither here nor there. Is it? You're always annoyed when I use the word 'choice'. I know there can't be any choice once you've taken the plunge—into a religion, I mean. Maybe there's no choice even at the beginning. You fall into it the way people fall in love. Then you can put your intellect into mothballs, at least in that department. But is it sinful to recognise that the details of self-mortification, sacrifice, and rituals are organised, socially approved pretences?" He gestured and the pill went flying from his cold fingers and hit a wall. Leo jumped down from his bed in Theodore's suitcase to investigate. Theodore sighed. All this talk to get a fellow to take a little pill for his own good!

Ramón had got up. "It amuses me, Teo, how you can always find the most painless way to hitch yourself to something somebody's already made for you and suffered to make. You take what you want and discard the rest."

"I'm not hitching myself to anything."

Ramón walked stiffly towards the foot of the bed. "And only what you care to believe is the truth."

"Oh——" Theodore suddenly wanted to sit down, but there was no place except the bed. "Truth's all things to all men—like Existentialism, you'd say. It doesn't exist, that's why we keep looking for it. If you admitted the organised pretence in your religion, truthfully, you would be standing there in pain now with a headache that's of no interest to God or anyone else but yourself. You wouldn't be farther away from God or from pleasing Him, either."

"No, and I wouldn't be feeling anything, I suppose," Ramón said, sitting down on the bed. "What would you offer me instead, Teo? Nothingness? Is that what you have?"

"In my own way, I believe in God, Ramón, but, to be perfectly honest, I don't know whether I believe or pretend to believe. Maybe I'll never know and what does it really matter? It's a person's actions that count and not the rituals. There are other fields—hope, for instance. I think I pretend there, too, but it's a beneficial pretence. I hope for something unattainable and I love it just because it's unattainable. How blissful that moment when one decides to hope!" Theodore said and drew on his cigarette. "Yes, decides," he repeated, because Ramón was smiling. "I think that's what's meant by revelation, and it's not an illustration, either. On the contrary, nothing'll stick closer to you than what you've decided to believe in. Sometimes all the doctors in the world can't prise you away from it. Revelation is the realisation that one can be happy after all, if one only decides to be happy. The truth for Christians is 'Christ is risen. He died for my sins. Therefore I shall have eternal life and a reason and a right to be happy. I can be a part of this truth.' Those disjointed statements are gathered together and labelled—'truth'. But it's nothing but a time-hallowed attitude, which can as well lead to good as to bad."

Ramón let his head fall back on his pillow. "You prove only your own point, that everybody has his own truth."

Theodore carried his cigarette, which was burning his fingers, into the bathroom and dropped it into the toilet. The toilet had no seat, and inside the bowl, high above the bit of water in it, was written: GLORIA. When he came back into the bedroom, Leo was licking his paw placidly, and it occurred to Theodore that he might have eaten the pill.

"To be absolutely honest myself, Teo," Ramón said, "I don't know what the truth is, either."

It was perhaps the most hopeful thing he had heard Ramón say since Lelia's death. He got another pill from the box and poured a glass of water from the carafe on the bed table. "I'll turn out the light if you don't want to read, Ramón."

"All right, Teo."

Theodore could feel Ramón's awakeness in the dark. Ramón did not stir at all. Theodore at last fell asleep, and awakened at the gentle movement of the bed as Ramón very carefully eased himself from it. Ramón began to walk slowly up and down, touching the left side of his head occasionally, yet not gripping it, not even whispering the curses that he sometimes muttered during his headaches. Ramón described the pain as being like an iron hook caught in his brain, a piece of foreign matter, a simile that always reminded Theodore of the metal bar itself that had struck him.

CHAPTER TWENTY

"WANT a guide, mister? You American? I speak English!"

"I got a car. You want to ride? Tour of the town! Twenty-five pesos! There is my car, señor!"

"No, we want to walk, thank you," Theodore said in English. They were on the sidewalk in front of the great bullet-scarred Alhóndiga de Granaditas, the objective of Hidalgo's attack in the Revolution, the scene of Pipila's heroic sacrifice, and the most famous building of the town.

They moved on, still dogged by two or three of the self-appointed town guides. Ramón stopped to look back at the doorway, and up at the ornamented corner, perhaps the corner where Hidalgo's head had hung for months, rotting in the sun, as a warning to all those who would revolt against the Spanish.

"You want to see the Panteon, señores?" asked an adolescent voice at Theodore's elbow. "I can take you. Mummies——"

"No, thank you," Theodore said, taking out his car keys. They were going to the Panteon at last.

The boys stood in a silent semicircle, momentarily taken aback by the car. "Many streets up there, señor!" "One-way streets! You need a guide!" "Bad roads for a car, señor. My car is only twenty pesos. I take you around the whole town."

At Ramón's instructions, Theodore took a west-bound, climbing street, zigzagged through the section of one-way streets near the beautiful Street of the Priests with its windowless pink-tan walls and windowless bridge like something out of medieval Europe, and climbed finally to a straighter, west-bound road. The town dropped behind them and a fresh, sunny wind blew through the windows. Theodore was in no mood to see the mummies, but he knew he would never be in a mood to see them, and since he had to see them during this sojourn in Guanajuato, this morning seemed as good a time as any. But the world was full of bright sunlight and green, living things. He could see the tops of trees moving miles away and he could have spent the day looking at all of it.

"There it is," said Ramón, bending low to see, because the Panteon was yet higher, on a hill to their right.

Theodore saw a very long wall, whose height he could not judge, set on a small plateau. The road took them by winds and turns inexorably towards it. On the wall was written the inscription that was on the walls of the cemetery where Lelia lay:

HUMBLE THYSELF! HERE ETERNITY BEGINS
AND HERE WORLDLY GRANDEUR IS DUST!

He drove on to a small area, indicated to him by a watchman at the gates, which on two sides dropped sheer for what looked like hundreds of feet. A boy of about sixteen ran up to the window and asked if Theodore wanted him to park for him. Theodore thanked him and said no.

"Last month a car went over the edge. I am very used to American cars," the boy said in English.

There was not room to turn around, but the boy made circular gestures with an air of authority as if this was exactly what he wanted Theodore to do—try to turn around and go over the edge. Theodore put the car into a parallel position with another car, his front bumper to the cemetery wall. On the way out, he would simply have to back to a place on the road where he could turn.

They walked through the gates and a field of graves and tombs spread before them, surrounded by the wall, that was nearly three times the height of a man and as thick as a coffin was long. The walls, every square yard of them, contained vaults and were marked off in squares, each with a name and date. The ground was yellowish and bone-dry, as Theodore remembered the ground of Lelia's cemetery, as if the feet of thousands of mourners had obliterated every blade of grass. Yet the faded pastel lavenders of the tombstones' shadows, the pale green traces of moisture in the walls and the instant-coffee and jelly jars of real and artificial flowers, fresh and wilted and dead, made it look like a picture by Seurat and relieved much of its gloom for Theodore. He wandered to an empty vault and looked in. It was lined with ordinary house bricks. A casket had evidently been removed, because on the ground, leaning against the wall, was a square of stone that had fronted the catacomb: Maria Josefina Barrera 1888–1937. R.E.P.

"They rent out the vaults," Ramón said, "and if the relatives do not pay the rent, they take the body out."

Theodore nodded. He had read it somewhere before. Some of the bodies had become the famous mummies, and some must be simply thrown away somewhere, he thought, like litter.

"The mummies are this way," Ramón said, pointing to the back wall.

Theodore followed him. Near the back wall Theodore saw a square hole in a slab of cement pavement. A wooden cover lay beside it.

Ramón stopped beside the hole and motioned for Theodore to precede him down. There were faint purple shadows under Ramón's eyes, more subtle than the purple of the tombstones.

A spiral iron stairway led down from the hole. Theodore took a last look around. Two women in black bent over a grave far to his left. A young man was walking through the gate. Theodore looked down at his feet and descended. He had thought the steps would lead to a small chamber like a dungeon, and when he reached the bottom and saw dimly lighted corridors on either side he had a sensation of having been tricked, a flash of recollection perhaps due to some description of Ramón's that he had heard long ago. As his eyes grew accustomed to the dimmer light, he saw with a shock that the mummies were right beside him on his left, lining the walls of the left corridor shoulder to shoulder all the way to the end, where more stood. Some were dressed or partially dressed, but most were quite naked.

Ramón turned to look at a little grey-suited man who was coming down the stairway.

"You want to see the mummies?" the little man asked, unnecessarily.

"*Si*," Ramón replied.

The little man turned on a brighter light and stepped into the doorway of the corridor and stood sideways, thereby impeding their passage slightly.

Theodore went in, and then Ramón. More footsteps were coming down the spiral stairs, ringing faintly in the cement tunnel. Theodore watched Ramón's face for a moment, saw that he looked tense but calm, then turned his eyes to the mummies, not that he wanted to, but because he knew Ramón would notice whether he gave them proper attention. Their skins were of a pale yellow colour, like dried leather. Nearly all had dried, stiffened black hair on their heads and in the pubic region. Women's breasts hung down like collapsed bags. Theodore took shallow breaths. There was an airlessness about the place, a faint sourness—he did not know what it was, but he sensed the absence of anything breathable by the living.

The little caretaker stood with sightless-looking eyes and a small smile, absurd in his limp business suit and hat, perhaps about to launch into his lecture, unless he was too tired today. Theodore hoped he was too tired.

A young boy came into the corridor with a casual air, one

of the boys who had lingered around them at the Alhóndiga de Granaditas, Theodore thought, and he rather expected the boy to start his own improvised commentary on the mummies. Theodore walked slowly towards the end of the corridor, pausing a moment to look into the open eyeless lids of a man whose jaw was dropped as if he were snoring, revealing a few teeth. The penis was missing, Theodore noticed, but then he saw it, a dried string-like thing unrecognisable except by its location.

"The figure in the black suit is that of a French doctor," the caretaker said, pointing to one of the few clothed mummies. "Notice the fine state of preservation." He gestured to the horrible, nearly bald head which had suddenly taken on a European colour and structure to Theodore, and touched the now ludicrous fine lace of the man's shirt front carelessly, as if the dead man no longer commanded respect. "The extreme dryness of the Guanajuato climate preserves the bodies," he droned.

Ramón looked fixedly at the French doctor's face, at his stiffly hanging hands. Theodore wondered what he was trying to see or feel by peering at something which the mind had left.

Theodore turned and was face to face with the young boy, who smiled a little and stepped aside. The boy had dark hair on his upper lip, which Theodore, at that moment, found disgusting.

The caretaker called their attention to the bloated collapsed figure of a woman who had died apparently as the result of an unsuccessful Cæsarian section—he pointed wordlessly at the slit in her side and at the tiny, mummified infant which hung from her wrist by a wire around its neck. The infant was crouched up in a foetal position and resembled a big-headed monkey. Theodore looked away in revulsion and met Ramón's accusing eyes. Theodore shrugged involuntarily and gave a bitter little smile. Enough ugliness was enough! What was the purpose of it? If Ramón had ever been articulate about the *purpose* of coming here—— Theodore noticed that the boy was watching both of them.

". . . and this woman—the wife of a mayor of Guanajuato," the caretaker was murmuring, though nobody seemed to be listening to him.

Theodore made his way slowly towards the door, still flanked by the mummies, that were so close he could have stretched out both arms and touched them. He did not like the prowling boy, who had the lively eyes of a pickpocket or worse, and who seemed to be looking at him and Ramón quite as much as he looked at the mummies. No doubt he would tell the caretaker that he had sent the two men here, and claim part of the caretaker's tip.

"And this. This woman was buried alive," said the caretaker. "An epileptic."

Theodore glanced and his attention was captured. It was a rather tall, dark-haired mummy on the left near the door. Her mouth was open and twisted, as if she were screaming. Her claw-like hands were drawn up near her left shoulder, the fingers pulling against one another in a familiar gesture of despair. Even the empty sockets of her eyes were stretched open.

". . . buried during an attack," the caretaker said with a sigh.

When, Theodore wondered. Perhaps two hundred years ago, when epileptics were considered insane? He did not care to ask. The woman's long black hair seemed to writhe in agony, too. Theodore imagined her sucking the last air of the tomb into her lungs, straining with her last strength to break the cover with her bent knees, and then straining her fingers against one another as death froze her in a pantomime of the futile struggle.

"That is impressive, is it not?" Ramón asked in a low voice.

Theodore nodded. The boy watched them in a front corner of the corridor, with a pleased expression.

A light had been turned on in the opposite corridor, which was much shorter. Theodore saw a stack of human bones about fifteen feet high, neatly piled in the manner of wood faggots, resting on two or three rows of skulls, each of which faced outward, grinning and ornamental. After the mummies, these seemed unreal, not death-like, but like a comic relief. Theodore looked in his wallet and, having no singles, gave the man a five-peso note.

Ramón climbed the stairs, Theodore followed him, and then came the boy. The sunlight fell warmly and deliciously on Theodore's face. He looked up at the sun until its glare drove his eyes away.

"*Buenos días*," said the boy, smiling at Theodore. "Were you able to find a satisfactory hotel?"

"*Sí*," Theodore said curtly.

"They are all filled," the boy continued in badly pronounced English.

"We have found a place."

"Where?"

"A place," Theodore said, walking on with Ramón.

"If you are eenterested in something like the Orozco, I think I can get you some rooms there," the boy said, walking along with them.

The Orozco was Theodore's favourite hotel, but they were booked up for the next several days. "*Gracias*," Theodore said.

"But I *could* get you a room."

"*Gracias*, no." Theodore walked on with Ramón to the car, and the boy loitered outside the cemetery's gates.

Theodore backed the car and used the gates as an area to turn around in. Going down the hill, they passed the boy walking in the direction of the town.

They had, that morning, installed themselves in a *pension*

hardly more comfortable than the Hotel La Palma, but at least with more charm. All its rooms were on the ground floor around a patio in which a fountain ran and parrots swung in metal rings or climbed among blossoming bougainvilleas. It cost forty pesos a day apiece, including meals. Four blocks from the *pension*, Ramón asked Theodore to let him out, and said he would walk the rest of the way to the *pension* and meet him there in less than half an hour. Theodore stopped the car. He noticed that a church was near-by in the same street. Ramón got out, and Theodore drove on to the *pension* and parked the car in a little blind alley at one side which served as a garage. Then he walked back slowly to the church with an idea of looking at its interior, but when he reached its modest doorway, which had a piece of brown leather, cracked and worn sleek, hanging three-quarters of the way down to its threshold, he felt he would be intruding on Ramón if he went in, even if Ramón did not see him.

Theodore crossed the street and sat down at one of two sidewalk tables of a tiny bar which served soft drinks and beer. He ordered a beer. What was Ramón praying for, he wondered. What was he confessing? He prayed for his soul, of course. What else would one pray for, if one believed in an eternal soul, after looking at eighty or a hundred horrible corpses? One would think, surely this isn't all that's going to happen after I die, death can't be just this. And for many people, he thought, the mummies would be excellent propaganda for the existence of an after-life practically tantamount to proof! It reminded him of a statement made by an American scientist which he had written down in the back of his diary, simply because of its absurdity. It went something like: "Can this be *all*? Is our planet doomed to burn out in ten or twelve billion years and the universe to be nothing more than a huge cemetery with no further potentiality of life?" Well, what if it was destined to be nothing more than a huge cemetery? The arrogance of most men's minds—and this one had been a scientist—appalled Theodore. "Life," they said with reverence, and yet they saw it only in anthropoid form, or at best as life as they knew it. If the earth became a hunk of metal, or disintegrated and vanished in particles too small for scientists' eyes or even their microscopes to find, wasn't there some beauty in that, beauty in the idea, if nothing else? It seemed quite as beautiful as three billion sweating or freezing human beings creeping around on a globe.

He took out his fountain drawing pen and began to sketch the front of the church on a blank back page of a book he carried. The old red stone columns, on either side of the door, spiralled up like twisted lava. The pointed arch of the shadowed doorway looked like a human mouth, wide open in a cry of tragic agony. The picture under his pen took on a personal quality, a special individuality, like a human face, and Theodore suddenly saw the door as Ramón, screaming at a deaf and non-existent God a cry that might have been as silent as the door.

He put his pen away and his mind slowly focused on the physical again, on the fact that Ramón had been in the church at least fifteen minutes, that there was a two-peso tab under his nearly empty bottle of Carta Blanca, that he was very hungry, and that he could not by the effort of imagining make himself a Catholic for half an hour or even one minute.

Ramón came out of the church and stood for a moment with one hand on the leather door flap, as if he did not want to turn loose of it, or did not know in which direction to go. Theodore raised his arm and called "Ramón!" He took some money from his wallet, waited for change, and left a peso tip. Ramón had crossed the street. He nodded to Theodore in greeting, and they began to walk towards the *pension* in silence. After a block, Ramón said:

"You were not impressed by the mummies?"

"Of course I was."

"I think you'll find that they'll work a change in you."
Ramón walked with his head up, a little cheered as always
after he had been inside a church.

Theodore pondered this for a moment. "Have they
changed you?"

"Yes. Not today. I've seen them before. They are reminders," Ramón went on, looking straight in front of him.
"Reminders of the unimportance of the body."

"Yes. After one is dead."

"And of the shortness of death and the eternity of life."

"Eternity of life?" Theodore asked in surprise, then
realised this was exactly what he had expected.

"Did I say that?" Ramón asked, smiling. "No, I meant
the opposite. Unless, of course, one chooses to call this death
and the other life, as some do."

"And you? Do you?"

Ramón frowned, though his smile lingered. "Maybe I do.
Sometimes this life seems only like a waiting for something.
Do you know what I mean, Teo?" he asked in a cheerful
voice, glancing at Theodore.

"Yes," Theodore said dubiously. To anticipate 'life' as an
eternity in hell—what kind of perverted joy was that? Or
was he possibly hoping for purgatory or something better?
Theodore decided to say nothing more on the subject, lest he
disturb, by a clumsy question or a statement, the precarious
chess game that Ramón was playing with himself in his
mind. Ramón began to talk about the beauty of the town.

CHAPTER TWENTY-ONE

THEODORE made another effort by telephone that afternoon to get a room at the Orozco. The manager blamed the crowdedness of the city on "the end of Carnaval." He chose to speak to Theodore in English. Theodore's name was on their list, however, and perhaps in five days, perhaps less, there should be a room. Theodore then telephoned Sauzas's office in Mexico, and gave the name 'Los Papagayos', the *pension* at which he and Ramón were staying. Sauzas was not in.

At a little before five, Theodore returned from a walk that had taken him up to the Hotel Santa Cecilia, where he had made a panoramic water-colour of the town. He thumb-tacked it over his bed, a burst of red and grey in the room of muted and faded colours. His room was identical with Ramón's next-door. Each had a thin double bed with a flimsy but ornate bedstead, a straight chair, a tall brown wardrobe which had lost the same right-hand door, each had a chamber-pot of pink and white under the bed, and each a small metal crucifix over a table on which stood a water pitcher in a basin, beside a glass carafe of drinking water with an inverted glass on top of it. In the patio the parrots chattered and gave an occasional squawk, as if the five or six of them played a card game that caused them all to talk in sequence. Buckets filled slowly at the fountain with trickling sounds that rose in pitch, ended, and began again. Mops and rags slapped constantly on the blue-and-white tiles, which were impeccably clean, as if the family of father and mother and two daughters and two sons who operated the *pension* had lost their minds on the subject of scrubbing the patio.

"Concha, have you seen the mop?"

"The what?"

"The *mop!*"

"No-o."

Slop! Water dashed over the stones and hissed to silence.

A boy laughed long and lazily and with relish, making Theodore smile as he heard him. There was a happy atmosphere in the *pension,* and Theodore had nothing to complain about, not even the simple food, but he wished for Ramón's sake that the room were prettier to look at and that the toilet was not on the patio, too, behind a wooden door, because he did not want Ramón to be reminded of his apartment in Mexico.

The inevitable conversation went on:

"Juan, you didn't see the *mop?*"

"No-o. Ask Dolores."

Trickle, trickle . . .

Theodore lay on his bed, lulled by the voices, which the patio's four walls amplified and emptied of meaning, so they became as hollow as symbols.

"No-o, Maria," came a girl's voice. "You mean the mop with the long handle?"

"Ai," said the girl in calm despair.

"Look in the kitchen, Maria!"

"*Awr-r-rk!*" A parrot expressed horror at some move in the game.

And Theodore thought of the strange moment that morning when he had felt a physical attraction—perhaps for only ten seconds, but very strongly—for the girl who had shown Ramón and him their rooms. She was barely eighteen, he thought, a little plump, modest and docile and without artifice, and there could have been no other reason for his attraction except that she was female, and he could not remember ever having been attracted to such a simple kind of girl before in his life. It had been the first time since Lelia's death that such an emotion had stirred in him—and actually the same stirring might have happened if Lelia had still been alive, so transitory and purposeless it was—yet this morning there had been the feeling that if he had touched this girl, his desire would have evaporated, because of Lelia. And so it might have, but it would not always be so. And the real source of the depression that had followed his attraction was the knowledge that he would go on in a state of being physically alive, that there would be another woman some day, or women, and that he did not even want her, or them.

He would write something about it in his diary, he thought, and while he was thinking of how best to say it in English, he fell asleep. He had a dream that Lelia was sitting at the long table in her apartment, which had been transported to the blue-and-white patio of the *pension*. She wore a bright purple-and-yellow *rebozo*, or stole, which he had just made her a present of, and she was pleased and in a good humour. They were waiting for someone, and they listened for a knock at the door, but all they heard were the parrots' squawks, which made Lelia smile. Then Lelia said that at last he was getting somewhere, wasn't he? "What do you mean?" he asked. "You are about to find out who is responsible for all this," Lelia said with laughing dark eyes, "but it doesn't matter in the least, Teo, not to me. It's just a silly game—a game for the living." She looked at her door, hearing something he did not; and then Ramón opened the door suddenly and came in, in high spirits, with his arms full of rum bottles piled high as his chin, and the bottles rested on a bed of red carnations. Theodore asked him why he had not brought white, and Ramón looked bewildered, and asked him to repeat the question. . . .

Theodore heard a knock at his door, and sat up with the dream in his head. "Ramón?" he asked.

"No, señor," said a girl's high-pitched voice. "A señor outside would like to speak with you."

Theodore stood up. "One minute," he called, smoothing his hair with one hand. He opened the door, and looking past the girl he saw a young man standing in the sunlight on the sidewalk just outside the *pension's* gate. Theodore had a sudden feeling of having seen him before, a feeling that he knew him—and then he realised that it was the boy with the incipient moustache who had been with them in the corridor of mummies.

"*Buenas tardes,*" said the young man as Theodore approached him. "Señor Schiebelhut?"

"*Si,*" Theodore said

"There are two rooms available for you at the Hotel Orozco." He gave a small, jerky bow.

"I called them just two hours ago. There weren't——"

"I have just found out," the boy interrupted in his twanging, adolescent voice. "They are not available today, but tomorrow morning sure."

"I see. Thank you very much," Theodore said politely, not knowing whether to believe him.

"For nothing," the boy said, waving a hand airily, sticking out his soft, moist underlip. "I am a friend of the manager."

"Oh."

The boy lingered, perhaps awaiting a tip, standing on one leg and swinging a key-chain around his forefinger.

Theodore abruptly decided not to tip him. "Am I supposed to call to confirm the rooms?"

"I can do that for you."

"Oh no, thank you. I'll do it," Theodore said, turning away.

"Okay. *Buenas tardes,*" said the boy.

Theodore went at once to the only telephone in the *pension,* which was in the family's living-room to the right of the entrance door. He asked permission of the grandmother, who was crocheting, and then called the Orozco. The man who answered left the telephone to check on his name, as if he had never heard of him, and then returned with the information that Schiebelhut and Otero had a suite reserved for the following morning.

"Thank you," Theodore said, pleasantly surprised. "We shall be there—say by eleven?"

"*Muy bien*, señor."

Theodore hung up and crossed the patio towards Ramón's door to tell him the news. He stopped to look at a handsome blue, green and yellow parrot who was sidling up his ring with a foolish expression. The parrot hung upside down by its feet and swung himself, the picture of health, happiness and self-esteem. Just the opposite of Ramón's lonely little parakeet. Though the parakeet had no range of facial expressions, Theodore thought of him always as wide-eyed, round-mouthed—which he was not—and lost, like a face in a painting by Monch. Theodore looked into the brazen, yellow-ringed eye of the happy parrot, and saw the boy standing on one leg in front of the door. And there was something so familiar in the stance, the doorway. He thought suddenly of the boy who had spoken to him about a muffler, on the day of Lelia's funeral. The pedlar who had reminded him of his stick-figures.

For a moment, he thought he must be mistaken. But he remembered very well the standing on one leg and the way the slight body had curved in a line with the relaxed leg, even the way he tipped his head back and sideways as he spoke. He was better dressed now and more self-assured. And Theodore did not remember the moustache. Once again he tried to convince himself that he was mistaken, but his mind slid sickeningly down to certainty again. He imagined that the voice was the same, and the weak, forgettable face the same. He did not think he was mistaken. And what did it mean? Theodore thought of the silent telephone calls. And the postcard.

The boy might even be the murderer.

Theodore went into his room and shut his door. What was the boy up to, following them here to Guanajuato? He knew both their names, or had troubled to find them out. In the corridor of mummies, he had been more interested in him and Ramón than in the mummies. He looked like a young crook, slippery, quick-witted, and as if he would be able to tell a lie as naturally as breathing. Able to rob a house, to crawl along a narrow ledge and rob a house without leaving fingerprints. Able to tell a story and get into a woman's apartment before she became alarmed. He should tell Sauzas immediately, he thought.

Then the feeling returned that he could be wrong, and he decided to wait until tomorrow to tell Sauzas. If the fellow had really followed them here, he was not going to disappear suddenly. Theodore went to the cupboard where his jacket hung and automatically felt for the lump of his wallet. It was there, and even through the jacket he could tell that his money was still in it.

He went out into the patio and knocked on Ramón's door.

Ramón was lying on his bed with his arms behind his head, a book open and face-down on his chest.

"We can get rooms at the Orozco tomorrow," Theodore said. "They sound like very pretty rooms. There's been a cancellation."

CHAPTER TWENTY-TWO

IT was a comfortably sprawling hotel, built without a thought of economising space. Giant trees sheltered it from view until one was almost in front of the door, and then vines with stems as thick as a man's arm ran above the doorway and between the windows of the lower floor. The lobby was paved with sedate, well-worn tiles. A bell-boy met them and escorted them to the first floor and then to a corner suite with two entrances and a common sitting-room overlooking gardens of mangos and bougainvilleas. There was a fireplace in the sitting-room, and on a round, polished table sat a bowl in which floated a large orange cactus blossom. Clear droplets of water stood like dew on its petals. There was a smell of flowers, sunlight on wood and wool, and the pine that lay ready to be burnt in the fireplace.

"Don't you think it's pretty, Ramón?" Theodore asked.

Ramón nodded, smiling. "It's beautiful, Teo."

"Which room would you prefer?"

"That doesn't matter," Ramón replied, as Theodore had known he would.

"Take your choice. I'm going downstairs to buy the newspapers."

Theodore went down to the lobby. The Mexico, D.F., papers had not come in yet, but were due at noon. He went to the main desk and asked for a call to be put in to Mexico. The lines were very busy, they told him, and it might take ten minutes or more. Theodore had given the clerk his name and room number, and had been overheard by the middle-aged man in the grey suit, who, Theodore thought he remembered, was the manager. Theodore nodded to him and said:

"Thank you very much for the rooms. But I thought I was seventh on your list."

The manager gave a surprised smile. "Señor Schiebelhut. Yes. I think I remember that you were," he said in English. "Your rooms are satisfactory, sir?"

"Very satisfactory," Theodore said, in English, too. "I was interested to know how I got them. The young man who reserved them for me——" He hesitated. "Do you know him?"

The manager looked at him quizzically. "I was not on duty yesterday afternoon. When I came in this morning, I saw your name had been moved up." He tapped with a pencil the open register in front of him. People's names were written there on cards slipped into isinglass slots. "I would guess, señor," he said quietly, "somebody received a little gratuity and moved your name up."

"Nobody got a gratuity from me," Theodore said.

"Well—perhaps from your friend, eh? There is no harm done, but I don't make it a practice of this hotel ordinarily." He smiled in a friendly way, as if to say it was done now, and the other people on the list did not have to know anything about it.

"Not from my friend, either. I am sure of that."

"Well, señor, I can't explain it, but we are very happy to have you, and we hope you have a pleasant stay."

Theodore noticed that a bell-boy, standing by a column a few feet away, was watching them. "Thank you, señor."

His telephone call came through. Theodore asked to speak to Sauzas, as he always did. Sauzas was there, and he had only a minute's wait before Sauzas came to the telephone.

Theodore cupped the receiver with his right hand, though everybody behind the hotel desk seemed too busy to be listening. "Have you any news, Señor Capitán?"

"No, señor," Sauzas said. "I am sorry to say we have not

recovered any of your stolen property. We are still trying to trace the typewriter, of course——" His voice trailed off tiredly or indifferently.

Theodore felt suddenly depressed. "I wanted to tell you that we shall be at the Hotel Orozco in Guanajuato for a few days."

"And then?"

"I don't know yet. Perhaps to my house in Cuernavaca. I'll let you know, of course."

"*Muy bien.* Señor, we are working. That is all I have to report."

Theodore wandered around the lobby for a few minutes, then on an impulse went back to the telephones on the desk and called Inocenza.

She was in, and so delighted to hear from him that Theodore felt immediately better. She asked about Ramón and then the cat.

"Is the guard still in front of the house?" Theodore asked.

"*Sí,* señor."

"And you are not afraid?"

"Not in the daytime. I would not like to spend the nights here. I am very glad to go to Constancia."

"Have you had any calls when nobody speaks? Like the ones I had?"

"No, señor."

"Good. I shall call you again in a few days, Inocenza."

"Are you going to take a little house somewhere?" she asked hopefully.

"I have not decided yet. If we go to Cuernavaca, you can come with us." Even as he said it and heard Inocenza's happy reaction, Theodore knew that this was what he would do.

Then he began to feel depressed again as soon as he had hung up. He walked to a counter in the lobby and bought a guide-book of Guanajuato and one of Lake Chapala, because the book looked attractive and the lake was fairly near. But he knew Ramón would simply agree to go, if he proposed going, and that he would not propose it for that reason.

Theodore walked slowly to the staircase and began to climb it, thinking of his conversation with Sauzas and of the fact that he had not mentioned the strange boy, though he had told himself yesterday that he would tell Sauzas about him today. In the cool clarity of this morning, at ten o'clock at least, it had not seemed important or definite enough to tell Sauzas. But detectives thought that anything was important, Theodore reminded himself. He stopped on the stairs and turned. He was three-quarters of the way up, and now he looked down on the entire lobby. He wondered if he should go down to the telephone again and call Sauzas now, when he was sure he could reach him.

The boy came into the lobby through the main door, walking slowly with a hand in his pocket and a newspaper in the other hand. He went directly to the desk, and Theodore saw a clerk give him a key. Then the bell-boy who had been staring at Theodore—the one who had taken the boy's gratuity, Theodore supposed—slid closer to the boy along the front edge of the desk, whispered something, and nodded in Theodore's direction. The boy looked up, saw Theodore, and smiled and nodded in greeting. Then the boy pulled a packet of cigarettes out of his pocket, lighted one and tossed the match in the direction of a big pot of sand beside a pillar. He looked cocky, like a street boy on an expensive holiday. Theodore thought of a woman at once, a wealthy woman who might be keeping him. But what woman would have him? On the other hand, who could account for tastes?

Now the boy was approaching the stairs. Theodore leaned casually against the banister, and though he intended not to stare at the boy as he climbed towards him, Theodore could not take his eyes from his small, slight figure. But the boy did not look at him until he was perhaps six feet away, and then he smiled, a one-sided, self-conscious smile.

"*Buenos días,* Señor Schiebelhut. You like your rooms?" He spoke in English, with the staccato, flat-vowelled accent of Mexicans who have picked up their English in the streets.

"*Sí,*" Theodore said. "*Gracias.*"

The boy nodded, and licked his thin lips. The sight of his tongue near the soft moustache was peculiarly disgusting to Theodore. "And your——"

"*Hablemos en español,*" Theodore said matter-of-factly. "I don't think I know your name."

"Salvador. Salvador Bejar, at your service." The Spanish courtesy rolled off his tongue automatically. He frowned a little, and the frown and the wary eyes under it looked false. "You are the Señor Schiebelhut whose friend was recently killed, are you not?"

"*Sí.*"

"And your friend is the gentleman who confessed."

"He is not guilty," Theodore said calmly.

"But—well——" He shrugged and squeezed the newspaper. "I wanted to ask if the police have found the murderer yet."

"No."

"All I know is what I read in the newspaper," he said with a flickering smile. "Not much. They have no new clues?"

"Oh yes, lots of new clues."

"Important ones? What are they?" Now his frown was meant to be one of polite attention.

"I don't think they are to be let out. Not if they're not in the newspaper."

The boy nodded. "She was a very pretty woman—judging from the photographs."

Theodore said nothing. The boy's shirt was brand new, he saw from the way the collar stood out in a corner on either side of his neck, and it was of fine, cream-coloured silk. "Why are you interested?" Theodore asked in a polite tone. "Did you know her?"

"Oh no! Well—you are her friend. You know all the people she knew—I suppose."

"I doubt that. She had too many friends for me to keep track of."

The boy smirked, and looked at Theodore with an intense and greedy curiosity. He looked as if he did not quite dare utter something that was bursting in him to be said. "Are you—— You are going to stay here a few days?"

"Yes. Are you?"

"I think so," the boy replied, with a quick nod, smiling. "Maybe we'll see each other in the dining-room. Let me know if I can be of service to you in any way, because I should be honoured," he said, a clumsy combination of his own words and a traditional courtesy of the language. He shifted his weight from foot to foot on the step. "So they have no clues. I'm sorry."

"Oh, they have a few such as—such as that my house was robbed a few days ago. A few things were stolen, including the house keys."

Theodore saw the boy's eyes waver and grow swimmy, though the eyes still tried to look straight into his face. "It was not put into the papers. The police got a fingerprint which may be useful."

"A fingerprint!" the boy said with a self-conscious laugh, or perhaps it was a laugh of amusement. "You mean, that's the only clue?"

"Yes, but it's a good one," Theodore said, excited by the eagerness in the young man's face, which seemed to him guilt. He turned to go on up the stairs, and the fellow came with him.

"I hope you recover what you lost. Are you going to have lunch in the hotel?"

"No, I think we are going into the town," Theodore said, nodding good-bye as he turned towards his room.

"*Adiós*," murmured the boy, and awkwardly turned, as if he had to force himself to move in an opposite direction from Theodore, and went on towards the next stairs.

Ramón was unpacking his suitcase in one of the rooms. Leo greeted Theodore on an everyday note and continued his quiet examination of the rooms. Perhaps Lelia's words in the dream had a meaning after all. Perhaps they were getting somewhere. He wanted to blurt it out to Ramón. But Ramón would not want to believe it. Ramón would have to have every fact laid out before him before he believed anything, and as yet there were no facts at all.

Theodore lit a cigarette, walked up and down the sitting-room a few times, then went quietly out to telephone Sauzas.

He called from one of the booths, from which he could see the clerks and bell-boys and the switchboard, the only place where he might be overheard, he thought. He got Sauzas. He told him the boy's name, described him, and said he had first seen him loitering around his house in Mexico on the day of Lelia's funeral. The money he might have got from pawning the stolen goods, Theodore suggested, would be enough for him to buy new clothes and to live well for a month or so. And he told Sauzas of the boy's interest in Lelia's murderer. To Theodore's disappointment, Sauzas did not sound enthusiastic about investigating the young man.

"Well—he may be the robber," Sauzas said. "If he is staying in the hotel a few days—— Well, I can come up to-morrow morning, Señor Schiebelhut. Don't do anything to arouse his suspicion, or he may not be there when I get there. And I have my reasons for preferring to question him myself rather than the local police."

"Very good, Señor Capitán." Theodore hung up well satisfied.

He bought the papers, and again there was no item on the Ballesteros case. But on the editorial page of the *Excelsior* a professor of law had written a long and impassioned article advocating the return of the death penalty to Mexican jurisdiction, and among the cases he cited was the Ballesteros case, for 'wanton brutality, sadism, and barbaric fury'. Another case mentioned was that of an elderly priest, slain within his church by a man who had then stolen a few valuables from the holy edifice. That had, of course, roused the passions of the Catholic populace, and rightly, and yet the killer had been given only ten years, even though it was not his only murder. Theodore removed the page, though it meant removing the front page, which was on the other side, because he did not want Ramón to see it. Ramón would agree with the professor, Theodore supposed, unless he thought that to live with a murder on one's conscience was more painful than to die at once and so meet the fires of hell sooner. Theodore read what he wanted to of the paper and, on second thought, decided to throw the whole thing away.

At one-thirty Theodore and Ramón drank a *tequila limonada* in the garden, while Leo wandered about among the trees; then Theodore took the cat back upstairs and rejoined Ramón in the dining-room. Theodore looked around for Salvador Bejar, but he did not see him. Perhaps he came in fashionably late.

Then, as they were awaiting their dessert, the obvious occurred to him, and he suddenly stood up and excused himself.

Theodore ran up the steps. What a fool he had been, when he had seen that the bell-boy was a friend of Salvador Bejar's! He took the key out of his pocket and opened the door.

At first glance, he noticed nothing unusual. Then he saw a little trail of blood drops, wavering, but leading across the carpet to the door.

"Who's here?" Theodore called.

Leo stood rigidly, staring at him from across the room with his ears horizontal.

Theodore walked through all the rooms. No drawers were pulled out, nothing taken from his suitcase that he could see from a glance into it, but he noted on returning to the sitting-room that his Rolleiflex was gone from the round table. He looked down at the blood, unwilling to touch it, but he could see from its brightness that it was very fresh. Perhaps twelve drops, eight or ten inches apart. He looked hastily into the cupboards, even under the beds, then he went to the telephone.

"Señor Bejar, *por favor*. Salvador Bejar." Without thinking it out, Theodore had decided to speak to the boy, tell him he knew he had broken into his room, and offer not to inform the police if the boy would give back what he had stolen.

"Señor Bejar has checked out, señor."

"Checked out? Are you sure?"

"*Seguro*, señor. Only half an hour ago," said the woman's voice.

"*Gracias*." Theodore put the telephone down and walked around the room. He stopped and looked at Leo's four brown feet, pressed them so that the claws came out like an eagle's arching talons, but there was no blood and no thread on them. The boy was leaving town, he thought, and if he stopped him at the bus station or the railway station, he would have to call in police help. He had another idea, and he went out and ran down the stairs.

The slim young bell-boy was carrying two suitcases across the lobby towards the door. Theodore intercepted him by stepping right in front of him.

"One moment, please," Theodore said.

"I am busy, señor!" the boy said.

"I'll tip you, too. Where is your friend Salvador Bejar?"

"I dunno. He left."

"For where?"

"I dunno, señor."

"I think you know," Theodore said quietly. "I'll give you a hundred pesos if you tell me."

The boy shook his head impatiently, and got past Theodore with his bags.

Theodore followed him out, and watched the boy load the bags into the boot of a large American car. "Come here," Theodore said as the boy turned round.

With an air of irritation, the boy came over.

"This is important. A hundred pesos if you tell me where he went."

"I dunno!" the boy said, spreading his hands.

"Did he go by bus or train?"

"He left in a car—a hired car." The boy's eyes flickered around Theodore's hands as if he expected them to move immediately to produce his tip.

Theodore did reach for his wallet in his inside pocket and handed the boy the hundred pesos. "Now where did he go? Didn't he tell you? Another hundred if you tell me where he went—or even make a good guess."

The boy looked down at the money in his hand.

"And I will not report you to the management. Come on. You will never see Salvador Bejar again, will you?"

The Americans were waiting for the boy to come back and help them, but the boy took Theodore by the sleeve, and said: "Come over here."

They stepped around a corner of the hotel.

"He said he was going to Mexico, señor. It's the truth." The boy's dark brown eyes looked at him directly, and with all the truth they possessed, Theodore supposed.

"Thank you." He handed the boy the second hundred and replaced his wallet in his pocket as he walked away. He was heading for a telephone-booth when Ramón came out of the dining-room and saw him.

"What're you doing, Teo? What's the matter?"

"Nothing, Ramón. I have to make a telephone call now," Theodore said, walking on to the booth.

"But what's *happened*?" Ramón asked, alarmed and anxious.

Theodore hesitated. Ramón seemed like a child out of control. There was no telling what he might be thinking—something worse than the truth, probably. "Let's go upstairs. I can make the telephone call from there."

They trotted up the steps. The blood would at least prove that there had been an intruder, Theodore thought. And after he had told Ramón about Salvador Bejar, he would call Sauzas, who would have the *policía* stop every car coming into the city of Mexico. If he could not reach Sauzas personally, he would send a long wire, including the detail that the boy probably had a bad scratch on one of his hands or his face.

Ramón stopped at the sight of the blood and gave a whispered exclamation.

"Another robbery," Theodore said. "This time my camera and I don't know what else. And Leo has drawn the first blood," he added, stroking the cat's back. "I know who did this, Ramón, and who broke into my house, too. And perhaps who killed Lelia. It's the boy who was with us in the cemetery—when we saw the mummies. Remember, Ramón? The fellow who came to me at the *pension* yesterday to tell me we could get rooms here. He followed us here from Mexico, in fact."

Ramón frowned. "What boy?"

"You remember the young man with us in the corridor of mummies, don't you?—— Well, he was there, take my word for it. There was one other person besides us and the caretaker. Don't you remember that, Ramón?" Theodore asked in a desperately pleading tone, but Ramón still looked at him as if he were out of his mind, or as if Theodore were trying to hoax him into believing something clearly untrue.

"Well, Ramón, I didn't rob my own room and sprinkle blood on the floor, now did I?" Theodore picked up the telephone and asked for long-distance to Mexico.

"Do you know what you're doing, Teo?" Ramón asked. "Did you *see* the boy come in here? You were with me all the while."

"I did not see him even when I brought Leo up from the garden, but I *know*——" He stopped to give Sauzas's telephone number; then there was a pause. He and Ramón looked at each other.

Then Ramón with an offended air turned and walked into his bedroom.

Theodore told Sauzas about the robbery of his room, and described the clothing the boy had been wearing when he last saw him. Sauzas asked if Ramón had also been robbed.

"Are you missing anything, Ramón?" Theodore asked.

Ramón was standing in the doorway of his bedroom, listening. "I think I am missing my address book," he said indifferently. "I think it was lying on the chest of drawers."

"His address book, he thinks, Señor Capitán. These things are not important, but I wish you would have the roads into Mexico watched so that we can find the boy. No doubt it's too late now to stop him in Guanajuato. Señor Capitán, I don't think I told you that the day I saw him in Mexico he rang my door-bell. He asked me if I had lost a muffler."

"A muffler?" asked Sauzas.

"Yes. He had it in a paper bag under his arm. He talked in a sly way, I thought, and I—— What's the matter, Ramón?" Theodore asked suddenly, because Ramón's eyes were boring through him, with hatred or incredulity.

"Go on, Señor Schiebelhut," said Sauzas.

"That's all. I told him I hadn't lost any muffler. He said he found it in front of my house—and then he dashed off. I never saw the muffler, and I don't know what he was up to."

"I see. Well, the roads will be watched, Señor Schiebelhut,

every one of them into the city. I think I shall also alert the Guadalajara police in case he has gone in that direction."

"Good. Thank you, Señor Capitán. . . . Yes, I would like very much to see them. . . . Tomorrow evening, then. We'll leave tomorrow morning. . . . Understood. As soon as we arrive. *Adiós!*" Theodore hung up and looked at Ramón.

"The muffler you mentioned," Ramón said. "*I* didn't tell you that, Teo?"

"Why, no. If you had———" Suspicion rose in him suddenly, like panic. "What do you know about it?"

"A fellow asked me the same thing. I must have told you, and you're just repeating it," Ramón said, frowning.

"When did a fellow ask you?"

"I don't know exactly when. It was before the postcard came, I think."

"And what did the fellow look like? Where did you see him?"

"In front of my apartment house one day. I was going out—and he walked along beside me. I thought he was trying to sell me a muffler."

"Did you see the muffler?"

"No. He had it in a paper bag. It happened just as you told it to Sauzas. I told him I hadn't lost one and I wasn't interested, and he went away."

"What did he look like?"

"Shorter than I———"

"Slim? About twenty or twenty-one?"

"Maybe. I don't remember."

"It's the same boy. It must be. Now why does he want to get rid of the muffler, I wonder?" Theodore said, wandering across the room. "Whose muffler?"

"It's like a dream, Teo," Ramón said, with a frightened edge in his voice. "Do you think we both could have dreamed it?"

"No, Ramón. The fellow knows us. Maybe he knew Lelia.

He stole my diary, and he knows a bit of English, too. . . .
We have an appointment tomorrow night with Sauzas to
look at some photographs. Criminals' photographs," Theodore said. "So this is our last day in Guanajuato. We ought
to get an early start tomorrow."

CHAPTER TWENTY-THREE

Theodore drove fast around the mountain curves, and he noticed that Ramón sat up two or three times in alarm. At least it was a reaction, Theodore thought, even a self-preservative one. In Morelia, he proposed lunch, but Ramón said he was not hungry, and Theodore drove on, eager to reach the capital.

"The boy may be a robber, Teo, but it doesn't mean he's a murderer," Ramón said.

"We shall see."

"I know what the police will do if they catch him. They'll keep him alone and question him and beat him until he'll say anything just to get relief!"

Theodore did not reply, only lighted a cigarette from the one he had been smoking.

"And they'll take his confession against mine, no doubt," Ramón continued. "They speak of a man's word in the law courts, and when he gives it, they don't want it. They want something they can see and touch—bloodstains—witnesses——"

"I hope you will see this boy, Ramón. You can see and touch him, all right!"

"Yes! And I suppose that makes him guilty? In your mind it seems to! A youth twenty years old!"

"I said I could believe him capable of it. They'll have to question him, naturally. So meanwhile, why don't you consider my judgment suspended?"

Ramón gave a laugh. "Because it's not! And since they've decided Ramón Otero is a madman or the next thing to it, nothing I do or say can help the boy." Ramón folded his arms. "But I can try!"

Theodore slackened his speed, because he thought it contributed to Ramón's tension. Just as he had foreseen, Ramón would have to have every fact laid out for him before he believed the boy was guilty. And Theodore began to be afraid that not every fact would be available, in the form of something one could see and touch, and so Ramón's illusion might continue in spite of everything. If the boy merely confessed, Ramón would still not believe him.

Night was falling. Theodore saw the red lights of a Mexico, D.F., radio tower in the distance. Then lights appeared on both sides of the road. They were at the western end of the Paseo de la Reforma.

"Here're the *policía*," Theodore said, slowing down.

A pair of police officers were stopping cars ahead, looking inside them with torches, then motioning the cars to go on. The torch swept his and Ramón's faces briefly, moved to the back seat and the floor of the car, then withdrew and signalled them to pass.

"I hope they've already caught him," Theodore said. "Maybe they have, and these men haven't been notified."

"But wouldn't he be coming in on this road?"

"I suppose he could zigzag and take another road in. Or get out and walk."

Half an hour later they were at Theodore's house, and Inocenza was greeting them like a delighted child. She brought the parakeet to Ramón. She told him she was trying to teach it to talk and asked him if he would give it a name.

"It doesn't matter. You may name him, Inocenza."

"Pepe," she said at once. "Will that be all right, señor?"

"All right," Ramón said.

Theodore was on the telephone, waiting for Sauzas to be found. "Would you put some ice in the bucket, Inocenza?" he asked her.

Then Sauzas came on, and said that they had not found

anything yet. "We are watching Morelia, of course, and tomorrow morning—Well, suppose I bring the photographs to you and maybe we can identify this fellow. . . . Very good, señor. In about fifteen minutes."

"They haven't caught him," Theodore said, hanging up.

"Caught who?" Inocenza asked.

Theodore related quickly the story of the second robbery, the missing camera and Ramón's address book and the other things they missed finally—the stud-box and the five ties from the inside of the wardrobe door. He described the boy to her and asked if she thought she had seen him in the street.

"I don't know, señor. There are so many boys."

"Did any boy ever talk to you in the street?"

"Sí, señor, but I do not talk to them. I don't even look at them." She frowned. "No, señor, I cannot remember a boy like this."

But there was Constancia, Theodore thought, more talkative than Inocenza. The boy could have found out from Constancia that they were going to Guanajuato, for instance. Theodore made himself a drink. Ramón declined one, and carried his suitcase—which he never let Inocenza carry for him—up the stairs to his room. Theodore told Inocenza that Sauzas was coming in a few minutes, and said they might all have some supper, if there was anything in the house.

"Sí, señor. Cold chicken, guacamole, macedonia of fruits——"

"Good. And be sure the heater is turned up. We'll want a good hot bath tonight."

Inocenza called them to supper before Sauzas arrived, and they had hardly been served their plates when the doorbell rang. Inocenza flew out by the kitchen door and ran down the patio. The iron gates grated open.

Theodore greeted Sauzas warmly and invited him to sit down at the table. Sauzas said he had eaten.

"But if you are dining, I shall wait," Sauzas said.

"Oh, no! Ramón, you go ahead, if you like."

But Ramón had folded his napkin and stood up.

Sauzas sat down on the sofa. "What could have happened," he said, pulling some photographs out of a manila envelope, "is that our young friend saw that cars were being stopped at the entrance of the city, paid off his driver and got out and walked in. We are watching the bus stations, too. Is he this boy?" He handed Theodore a photograph about the size of a postcard.

Theodore shook his head. "No."

"This one?"

"*Tampoco no.*"

"Take a look at these." Sauzas spread out twenty or thirty pictures on the sofa.

"This one! This is he!" Theodore said, seizing on one. It showed the boy in an open-collared shirt. There was no moustache. His smile was weak and shy in the thin, pale face.

Sauzas rapidly lighted a cigarette, looked at the back of the photograph and said: "Salvador Infante. Twenty-one. Stole approximately seventeen thousand pesos from a jewellery shop—March sixth. That's the day after your house was robbed, señor. You are sure it's the boy?"

"Absolutely sure. Look, Ramón. I want you to know what he looks like, too." He handed Ramón the photograph.

Ramón looked at it for a moment, then handed it back.

"This is the fellow who was with us when we saw the mummies, Ramón."

Ramón did not reply.

"Infante was employed as a messenger in the Palacio Real Silver Shop in the Avenida Juarez from December fifteenth until March sixth." Sauzas looked up from the photograph. "On the night of March sixth, after hours, when only the cashier was there, totalling up the cash, Salvador got in, struck the cashier—a woman—*and* incidentally killed her,

219

and got away with the money. At least we're reasonably sure it was Infante, because he never came back to work again. His parents have no idea where he is. But—we have no finger-prints from the shop. Only prints from some things in his parents' house."

"He must have found out we were going to Guanajuato," Theodore said.

"Evidently. I learned from his employer that he's a fluent talker, a fancy dresser, and likes the girls. We questioned two girl friends we were able to find, and neither knew where he was. His employer was about to fire him, because he didn't trust him. That's putting it mildly, eh?" Sauzas's smile grew wider and he chuckled. "This is the kind of fellow who'll spend all his money at once and attract attention to him-self. He can't help it. He drops clues everywhere for the police."

But they haven't caught him yet, Theodore thought. "Señor Capitán—you said the Palacio Real Silver Shop?"

"*Sí* señor. Why?"

"Ramón! *That's* the shop where I took Lelia's necklace to be repaired. You know, the obsidian necklace that had a broken link? You remember, don't you, Ramón? Just before I went to Oaxaca, Lelia said it was broken? One night when we were all there together?"

Ramón nodded. "Yes. I think I remember."

"Did you see the boy when you went into the shop, Señor Schiebelhut?" asked Sauzas.

Theodore shook his head. "I talked to an older man there about repairing it. But Lelia probably called for the necklace, and he may have seen her then. Or maybe the boy delivered the necklace. Do you remember, Ramón, if it was delivered?"

"No, I do not."

"She didn't say anything about a boy who brought the necklace to her? Try to remember, Ramón."

"I am trying. I don't think she mentioned the necklace at all."

"Was she wearing it while I was gone?" Theodore asked. "Maybe it's even still at the shop."

"No, I think she was wearing it while you were gone," Ramón said, "but I'm not sure." He gave a little shrug.

"What does it look like?" Sauzas asked.

"The obsidian pendant is flat—shaped like this," Theodore said, indicating its four-inch length with his thumb and forefinger. "The rest is long, thin obsidian pieces linked with gold links. I wonder if Josefina has it now?" Theodore said, looking at Ramón.

"I would not know," Ramón said. "You were offered some of her jewellery, but I was not."

"Excuse me," Theodore said, and went to the telephone and dialled Josefina's number. Juana answered, and then Josefina came on. Theodore greeted her and asked after her health before he put the question about the necklace.

"Ah, I know the necklace, of course!" Josefina said. "No, it was not among her jewellery, Teo. I had not thought of it before, but—I suppose I thought she was wearing it that night——"

"Perhaps it's still where I took it to be repaired," Theodore said. "Don't worry, Tía Josefina."

"Is there any news? Why do you ask this?"

"Only because I suddenly remembered it—and I liked it, you know, even though it was not very valuable. And I hoped you had it."

"You are telling me the truth, Teo? It's not that you know it was stolen from her that night?"

Theodore told her it was probably still at a repair shop in the Avenida Juarez, and that he would call her when he found out tomorrow, and this quietened her somewhat. Theodore opened his hands to Sauzas. "I shall call the shop tomorrow to make sure it's not there. Ramón, do you remember ever seeing this fellow on the street around Lelia's house?"

"As far as I'm concerned, I do not remember ever seeing him at all," Ramón replied, walking restlessly about the room. "He looks like hundreds of other young men."

"Not to me," said Theodore. "Señor Capitán, do you think now that this boy could be the killer?"

Ramón hurled a match into the fireplace.

"It is possible," Sauzas said with a lift of his brows. "But I think it takes quite a motive for such a crime. This boy is more of a petty thief. His shop murder was an accident, I'm sure. This boy is full of vanity. He likes a lot of money in his pocket—pretty things. And Lelia's apartment was not even robbed, except for the keys."

"Hm-m. Well, I have another idea. In regard to the muffler," Theodore said. "Ramón told me yesterday that he was also accosted by a fellow who offered him a muffler, Señor Capitán. Undoubtedly the same fellow."

"When?" Sauzas asked, sitting up.

"Before the arrival of the postcard from Florida. A few days after the funeral, that would be. Tell him, Ramón."

Ramón repeated the story quickly, and it was just as Theodore had told Sauzas his own encounter with the boy.

"My idea is that the fellow is after money," Theodore said. "He knows the muffler belongs to the man who did the crime. Maybe he found it on the steps of her building—or even in the apartment. Maybe he's the one who got in with the flower delivery—or the necklace delivery—and found her dead—and found the muffler——" Theodore paused.

"Go on," said Sauzas.

Theodore turned to Ramón. "And Ramón said he had not lost a muffler. You are sure of that, aren't you, Ramón?"

"I have only one muffler, the grey one. It's in my suitcase now."

"That's true," Theodore said, smiling.

"And *you*, Señor Schiebelhut," said Sauzas. "Are *you* missing a muffler?"

"Not that I can see. I looked—just a few minutes ago. I don't know how many mufflers I have exactly, so I suppose it's possible I could be missing one."

Sauzas tapped the cocktail table with his fingertips. "Well—go on with your idea."

"After finding the muffler, he took it and left, taking the keys with him possibly. The door might have been open when he arrived, if the murderer had run out. And this boy also took my keys, you remember, Señor Capitán."

"Yes," said Sauzas. "It's an interesting idea."

"I admit I'm missing a motive—possibly. The motive for Infante calling on her in the first place."

"Ah, but she was a handsome woman!" Sauzas said. "There's a possible motive. Maybe he had his eye on her, watching her house. Maybe he had seen other men calling on her."

"Not so many," Ramón put in.

"Oh, enough. Like the Capitán," Theodore said, "I also think Infante watched her house. He watched our houses, too, Ramon."

"What men, Teo?" Ramón demanded.

"Why—Sanchez-Schmidt, Eduardo Parral now and then, Ignacia and Rodolfo, Carlos Hidalgo——"

"Hidalgo?" asked Sauzas.

"Yes. Lelia sometimes painted backdrops for him. For his plays at the Universidad, you know."

"And this Eduardo?" Sauzas asked.

"He is a young painter," Theodore said. "He used to come around to Lelia's once a month or so."

"You have his address?"

"Yes. It's in Tacubaya. Just a minute." He turned with his foot on the stairs. "But is it necessary to bother him, Señor Capitán?"

"It's about the muffler," Sauzas said. "We've got to find who the muffler belongs to. And I expect to have the muffler in less than twenty-four hours. As soon as we find Infante."

Theodore climbed his stairs and got his address book from his suitcase pocket.

"You should have mentioned him to me before," Sauzas said reproachfully, when Theodore showed him Eduardo's address.

Theodore started to say something in his own defence, then realised that Sauzas would remind him that the quietest people were sometimes criminals.

"The danger," Sauzas said as he copied the address, "is that Infante is already blackmailing someone with the muffler. He may have found the owner in the month he's been looking for him, and it may be someone not on our lists."

"But he took Ramón's address book only yesterday," Theodore said. "Perhaps he's still looking for people to question about the muffler."

Sauzas began gathering up his photographs.

"Señor Capitán, I should like to talk to Infante as soon as you find him," Ramón said. "Would that be possible?"

"I should *like* you to talk to him," Sauzas said politely to Ramón, and smiled. "Now I must be going."

Theodore asked Sauzas if he could have Infante's picture, and Sauzas graciously presented it to him and said he was going to have hundreds more printed.

"Thank you, Inocenza," Sauzas said as she came forward with his coat.

"And where are you going to be tomorrow, Señor Capitán?" Theodore asked.

Sauzas said he was going to be right in the city, told Theodore his office hours for tomorrow, and promised to notify him as soon as there was anything to report.

"At any hour," Ramón added. "I would like to see Infante as soon as you find him."

"It will be done, Don Ramón," Sauzas said.

Theodore saw him to the gates, and though they spoke only of the fine night it was, Theodore could feel that Sauzas's hopes had been lifted like his own.

"Ready to turn in, Ramón?" Theodore asked as he came back into the living-room.

Ramón looked up from the photograph of the boy, and tossed it on the sofa. "No, Teo, I think I'll go out for a walk."

"Will you be gone long? It's eleven."

"Not long, Teo," Ramón said with an attempt at a smile. "No, no coat." He opened the door for himself and went out.

Inocenza lingered in the living-room as Theodore drank his coffee. "Señor, may I ask if the Señor Ramón—You have asked me not to speak to him about the Señorita Lelia, señor," she said respectfully.

Theodore took a breath. "He still does not want to believe anyone else but himself is guilty, Inocenza. But I am sure he will change. Very soon now. As soon as we find the young man with the muffler."

"Oh, yes, the muffler," Inocenza said with a confident smile.

"And who owns it," he added and had a moment of depression. Why should he think the muffler had been found by the fellow on the scene of the crime? The paper bag under his arm might have contained nothing but erotic postcards. The boy might never have entered Lelia's apartment in his life! Theodore climbed the stairs to work for a while on his cover illustration for *The Straightforward Lie*. He would work until Ramón came home, whatever hour that might be, because he was not sure that Ramón had taken his keys with him.

Theodore had been drawing in his studio less than an hour when he decided to take his bath and continue his work in his dressing-gown. As he emptied the pockets of his suit, he found his address book. He opened it and went to the telephone.

Eduardo Parral lived in a *pension*. A maid answered, and there was a long wait while she went to see if he was in. Then a young male voice said:

"*Bueno?*"

"*Bueno*, Eduardo. Teodoro Schiebelhut. How are you?"

Eduardo sounded glad to hear his voice, asked how he was and if he had heard any news, by which he clearly meant news about the investigation.

"Well, some. We do not know how important it is yet. My reason for calling you at this hour is to tell you that the investigator, the Capitán Sauzas, will probably ask you some questions tomorrow. I hope it won't disturb you, Eduardo."

"Of course, it will not, Don Teodoro!" Eduardo said in a friendly tone. "I'll be out in the afternoon, but here in the morning."

"Good. I think it's better if I leave it to Capitán Sauzas to tell you what it's about."

"Yes. Naturally," Eduardo said politely.

Theodore squeezed the telephone. "You've had no strange telephone calls or such things, Eduardo?"

"No-o." He laughed in his shy way. "Unless I count one today. A man telephoned me and asked if I had lost a muffler. In a threatening tone, too. He wouldn't say his name. He told me to think twice if I hadn't lost one, because it was my last chance. My very last!" He laughed again.

"At what time did he ring up?" Theodore asked.

"A couple of hours ago. Just after eight o'clock, in the middle of supper."

"Did it sound like a long-distance call?"

"No-o. Sounded like a local call. Why?"

"Oh——" Theodore wiped his damp forehead. "The Capitán will tell you, Eduardo. I must not say anything else."

"But what's it all about? Do you know?"

Theodore hesitated. "Did he offer to sell you the muffler?"

"No-o. Just asked me if I'd lost one. He seemed sure I had lost one, but I'm just as sure my three mufflers are safe in my drawer. I even looked later to make sure."

"Good. Very good," Theodore said with relief. "I had best not say any more, Eduardo. Give me a ring tomorrow after you have seen the Capitán, if you wish."

"Very well, Teo. How goes the painting? Are you doing anything?"

"Yes—some. And you?"

"Yes. Portraits still. After June, landscapes."

Eduardo was a methodical young man. Portraits and nothing but portraits for a solid year. And after the year of landscapes would come probably a year of still lifes. Lelia had used to tease him about his routines, but she also had respected his talent. Theodore returned to his work, and after a few minutes lost all thought of anything but his pen-line drawing of the cigarette-smoking, cynical slouch of a man who was the villain of the book, and who represented reality, fatalism, and pessimism.

When he heard a murmur of voices at his gates, he realised it was after two in the morning. Then a key turned. Theodore stood up. Another key turned in the house door, and quiet steps crossed the living-room. It was probably Ramón, Theodore thought, so why was he afraid to call his name? And those were Ramón's steps, he thought, coming up the stairs. Theodore looked through the half-open door of his studio and saw Ramón's head appear as he climbed.

"Hello, Ramón! You're late!" Theodore said.

"You're still up? I was trying not to wake you."

Theodore laid his pen down. "Come in a moment. I have something to tell you. I called up Eduardo Parral tonight and out of the blue he said a man telephoned him this evening at eight and asked him if he had lost a muffler."

"Really?" Ramón said, but with only mild interest.

"Is Eduardo's name in your address book?"

"I think so. Yes."

"So that's what he is using. He'll probably call others of your friends, and he'll surely walk into a trap, if we can set one fast enough."

Ramón looked at him a moment, then bent over the drawing. "This is the villain?"

"Yes. And the hero's going to be standing here—much smaller—looking at him." Ramón had read the book in Guanajuato, and had seemed to enjoy it.

"I like the eyes. They're just right," Ramón said. "It's a good book, Teo, and your drawings will make it famous."

There were not a great many names in Ramón's address book, Theodore was thinking. If they instructed two or three people to claim the muffler and make an appointment with Infante—— But perhaps the boy was too wary now to make his transactions in person. Infante must have been aware of the police cordon around the city. "Were you talking to someone down at the gates just now, Ramón?"

"Yes, the police guard. He came up as I was unlocking the gates and grabbed my arm before he recognised me. We should feel very well protected," Ramón added with a smile.

Theodore made no more effort that night to talk to Ramón of the implication of the muffler story. It was simply not penetrating Ramón as yet.

It gave Theodore some satisfaction the next morning to see Infante's picture in a double column on the front pages of the major newspapers under the caption "Have You Seen This Youth?" His smirking face would be seen, and perhaps remembered, even by people who were too poor to buy a paper.

The next morning, Theodore called the Palacio Real Silver Shop. They did not have a necklace left in the shop in Lelia Ballesteros's name.

CHAPTER TWENTY-FOUR

"HELLO, Teo. This is Isabel Hidalgo. . . . I am all right, thank you, and you?" She spoke in English, as she often did when she was in a gay mood, but her voice sounded anxious now. "What do you make of this story in the papers today? Do they really think Infante is the guilty one?"

"They aren't sure," Theodore replied. "He certainly has something to do with it, of that I'm quite sure."

She went on asking him questions, which Theodore answered very cautiously, not wanting to label the fellow the murderer when there was really not yet enough evidence to prove that he was. The papers said that "police authorities" had reason to think the youth was implicated in the grue-some Ballesteros murder of last February, and Theodore told her nothing more than that, except he admitted having seen the boy loitering in front of his house.

"Somebody told me your house was guarded."

"This was several weeks ago—before the guard," Theodore said. "And how is Carlos, Isabel?"

"Oh-h, just as usual, Teo, maybe a little worse." Then she lapsed into Spanish. "The work at the Universidad—the plays in addition to his classes—and now he is thinking of accepting an offer to direct a play for the round theatre in Chapultepec, and meanwhile all this makes him nervous, so he drinks one too many and even during the day, I'm afraid."

Theodore murmured something sympathetic, suggested a vacation, but Isabel told him Carlos would say it was im-possible. Isabel chattered on, and even in Spanish, in which she tried to make her words light in tone, Theodore could hear that she was quite upset and that the situation was beyond minimising any longer. Carlos had even missed a few days' work, and had not gone to the Universidad today.

"Is he there now?" Theodore asked.

"No, he's gone out."

It was a quarter past noon. Theodore wondered if Sauzas had telephoned Carlos, and Carlos had gone out because he could not face a visit on a hangover morning.

"Teo dear, could you do me a favour?"

"Of course. What?"

"Come over to the house now. I'd like you to be here when Carlos gets back. You're a good influence on him. Not that you have to give him a talking-to. I don't mean that. Just be yourself. I can fix a little lunch for you! Would you, Teo?"

It was the last thing he wanted to do, but he could not resist her pleading voice. "Yes, Isabel. How soon?"

"As soon as you can. If Ramón is with you, he's welcome, too."

He knew she would prefer that Ramón did not come, but he promised to ask Ramón, anyway.

Ramón at that moment was out, and had been gone since ten, though he had said he would be back at one for his lunch. Theodore felt sure that he had walked to the Cathedral, and *en route* looked the streets for Infante.

Theodore took a taxi. He had not been to the Hidalgos' since the fatal night, and that vision of himself, light-hearted and free, with his heavy portfolio, came back to him painfully as he rang their bell. Isabel took him into the living-room, where the many-coloured mobile hung, bigger and brighter by daylight, and suggestive of a false gaiety. Isabel did her best, but her hands were nervous, spilling a few drops of the Dubonnet as she poured it.

"One would think *I'm* the one who's been drinking!" she said with a laugh.

She expected Carlos any minute. Isabel said he always

preferred to come home for lunch, but at a quarter to two he still had not come. Isabel took something from the oven —the maid came only mornings and the maid had cooked it, she explained—and they sat down. She questioned him about Ramón, having heard of his belief in his own guilt through some of their mutual friends, and Theodore replied that he was 'progressing' and that he had never, or at least only for a few days, believed that Ramón was guilty.

"Then who do you think did it?" Isabel said, leaning towards him. "You must have some suspicions, Teo. If you tell me, I promise you it won't go any farther."

"I think I *could* trust you, Isabel," Theodore said with a smile. "But, honestly, I have no suspicions. I've never had any. There's not a person I've ever laid eyes on I would think capable of such a murder. I mean, no one I personally know —whom I could name."

Isabel nodded. "I know, I know."

"Eat while it's hot. This is very good."

Isabel jumped at the sound of the doorbell. "Excuse me, Teo." She pressed the release button. "He must have gone out without his keys."

Theodore pushed his chair back and stood up, braced already for Carlos's effusive embraces.

"Who is it?" Isabel called into the hall.

"Capitán Sauzas of the Police, at your service," Sauzas's voice called, and then he appeared at the door. "Señora Hidalgo? *Buenas tardes.* I have an appointment with your husband at two o'clock. Well, Señor Schiebelhut! How are you?" Sauzas said, coming in, smiling at Theodore as if he were an old friend.

"Very well, Señor Capitán. I didn't know you had an appointment at this time."

"But yes! I rang up this morning. So sorry to disturb your meal. The police are always disturbing something, aren't they. Is your husband here, Señora?"

"No, he is out," Isabel replied, fumbling with her napkin. "But I expect him at any moment. Is anything wrong?"

"No, no. I just have some questions. I phoned him at ten o'clock this morning. Didn't he tell you?"

"No—I was out at ten myself. Well, if he made an appointment with you, I'm sure he'll be back. Will you sit down?"

Sauzas sat down on one of the studio couches in a far corner, declined Isabel's offer of coffee, and asked them please to proceed with their meal.

Isabel sat down, but did not pretend to eat. Theodore had lit a cigarette.

"Perhaps I should be going, Isabel," Theodore said. "If the Señor Capitán——"

"But you have eaten nothing! You must have your coffee, Teo, at least." She went off to the kitchen.

Sauzas was quietly looking over some papers.

Theodore did not want to ask him about news in the hearing of Isabel.

"What time did Señor Hidalgo leave the house?" Sauzas asked her as she came back with the coffee-urn.

"Around eleven," she replied.

Sauzas looked at his watch. "Nearly half-past two. Did he say where he was going?"

"No, he didn't. You are sure you would not like coffee, señor?"

Sauzas accepted the coffee now. They chattered for a few moments about Carlos's work at the Universidad. Sauzas seemed calm and as usual. Then he said:

"Well, perhaps I can ask you one of my questions, Señora Hidalgo. Maybe a wife would know as well as a husband. Did Señor Hidalgo lose one of his mufflers recently?"

"I don't think so. Why?"

"Why is very complicated to explain," Sauzas said with a polite smile. "I can only say I have a reason for asking.

Would you know from looking at his mufflers if he is missing any?"

"I don't know. I can look, if you wish," Isabel said, standing up.

Sauzas got up, too, and followed her into the bedroom, which was down the short passage, opposite the kitchen. Isabel pulled out the bottom drawer of a bureau. The drawer held mostly woollen socks, clean but in disorder, and at the right several folded mufflers of the gay stripes and plaids that Carlos preferred.

"There are six here," Isabel said, looking through them but not removing them from the drawer.

"Quite a lot of mufflers. He is fond of mufflers?" asked Sauzas.

"Ye-es. And students give them to him as presents," Isabel said. "He has given one or two away himself."

"Lately?"

"I think he gave one away at Tres Reyes. One at New Year's too."

"You would not know if any is missing from his current stock?" asked Sauzas.

Still stooping, Isabel looked up at him. "What is this about?"

Sauzas took a breath. "A most serious matter, señora. I do not want to upset you. Please take your time and think. Perhaps you can recall a muffler your husband has not worn, say, in the last two months? Do you have a good memory?"

She hesitated. "Is this in regard to the Ballesteros case?" she asked, wide-eyed.

"Yes, señora. We are asking the same questions of everybody. Everybody who knew her at all. There's nothing to be alarmed about."

Isabel suddenly burst into sobs, and Theodore lifted her by her arms. Sauzas looked at Theodore with wondering eyes.

"Her husband has been drinking a lot lately," Theodore said quietly, thinking it was better to say this than not to try to explain her state at all. "That's perhaps why he didn't keep the appointment with you."

Sauzas lighted a cigarette. "Señora Hidalgo, pardon me," he said with a small bow that she did not see. "Did your husband receive any other telephone calls this morning? Or last night?"

Isabel daubed her eyes with Theodore's handkerchief. "I don't know, señor."

"Was he also upset last night?"

"He has been quite upset for many weeks—months."

"What is he worried about? Money? His job?"

"His job is too much for him, and he takes on too much," Isabel replied.

Sauzas looked at his wrist-watch, then said gloomily to Theodore: "I'm to see Sanchez-Schmidt at three-thirty."

"You have seen Eduardo Parral?" Theodore asked.

Sauzas nodded, and smiled a little at Theodore. "Señora Hidalgo, your husband has not said anything about a muffler in the last day? Or weeks?"

"No," Isabel said, shaking her head.

And she seemed to be speaking the truth, but Sauzas questioned her closely and begged her to try to remember if there had been any strange telephone calls whatsoever, of if she thought there had been any that her husband might not have told her about, and Isabel said none that she knew of. Sauzas asked why Carlos was not at the Universidad today, a Thursday.

"Because—he did not feel well today," Isabel said, looking wretchedly down at the floor.

"Did he say last night he was not going to work today?"

"Yes," Isabel replied readily.

"He was drinking last night?"

"Drinking and playing the gramophone," said Isabel.

"I see. Well, Señora Hidalgo," he said, "it's getting on to three and I must leave. Can I give you a number to call when your husband comes in? Just ask for this exchange and leave the message with anyone." He handed her a card.

Theodore, though he thought Isabel might have liked him to stay on, was very eager to talk with Sauzas. "I shall telephone you this evening, if I may, Isabel," he said, touching her shoulder. "I'm sorry this was so upsetting to you. It was a bad time for me to come."

"Oh, no," she protested, getting up and managing a smile as she walked with them to the door. "I had rather have seen you than anyone, Teo."

"What do you make of that?" asked Sauzas when they were on the sidewalk.

"I don't know. I really don't think she knows anything about the muffler. Do you?"

"Um-m. What's Carlos drinking for? He is young, successful—a reasonably pretty wife——"

"Carlos has always drunk too much. As long as I've known him, which is two years now."

They were walking to the corner of Insurgentes, towards the spot where Theodore had caught a taxi to Lelia's on the night of her death.

Sauzas suddenly patted Theodore's shoulder. "Can I trust you to call me later this afternoon or tonight, if Hidalgo comes home? I have the feeling his wife will *not* call me. She's the protective type."

Theodore felt a tingle of alarm. "Yes. You'll be in your office?"

"I think so. After Sanchez-Schmidt. But leave the message with anyone. Here's a *libre*. Can I drop you? I'm going to Melchor Ocampo, way up."

"No, no, thanks, Señor Capitán."

"Cheer up! I expect to hear any minute that we've found Infante. I'm going to call my office from Sanchez-Schmidt's."

Theodore only nodded and waved an adieu.

When Theodore phoned Isabel Hidalgo at seven, Carlos had still not come home. He phoned again at nine-thirty. Isabel had telephoned several of their friends, and she was quite worried.

"Do you think I should call the hospitals, Teo?"

It was a moment before the question registered on him, and then it did not seem to make sense. Carlos was more likely in a little bar with piano music, somewhere. "Have you spoken to Capitán Sauzas?" Theodore asked. "Have you told him?"

"He called an hour ago. I told him Carlos had not come home."

"And what did he say?"

"I don't know. I'm supposed to let him know," she said with a tremor in her voice. "What is all this about the muffler? *What* muffler? Have they found a muffler?"

"I don't know exactly myself. It's what the police call a lead—to something. I was also asked if I had lost a muffler."

"Well—is there something dangerous connected with it?"

"I don't even know that, Isabel. Now sooner or later you must go to sleep tonight, you know. Don't try to wait up for him. Shall I call you again before midnight to see if he's home?"

"Yes, *please* do, Teo."

Ramón was standing in the hall. "What's the matter?" he asked with a suspicious frown when Theodore had hung up.

"Carlos Hidalgo. He's drinking and he hasn't been home all day."

Ramón had been out when Theodore returned from Isabel's, and he had not yet told him of Carlos's absence or of Sauzas's visit to his house. Ramón listened to it with unconcern, and remarked that Carlos was a fool and that he had always drunk like an American. "It is too bad for Isabel,"

236

Ramón added. He had always liked Isabel better than Carlos. "There is no news yet about Infante?"

"I was just going to call Sauzas." Theodore picked up the telephone again.

Ramón stood waiting with a calm, determined expression. He lighted a Carmencita and watched Theodore as he spoke.

"No. . . . No," Theodore said in answer to Sauzas's questions about Carlos Hidalgo. "I have just spoken to his wife."

Sauzas grunted an "Umph. . . . Well, there is an unconfirmed and unconfirmable report that Infante was seen this evening in Acapulco."

"Acapulco! Seen by whom?"

"One of the boys of the town, who told the police in hopes of a reward. They said the boy who told them looked reasonably honest, but they are not sure that he is correct. A bad place for Infante to be—for us. He must still have some money and for money a thief will hide a thief, and there are plenty of those in Acapulco."

"Do you think he could be there?"

"I think it is quite possible. Acapulco is a flashy place and Infante likes that. Maybe he got some money for his muffler, eh?" Sauzas said with a chuckle. "Well, we have flown a batch of photographs to Acapulco. He will certainly not leave the town on any boat or from the airport. Señor Schiebelhut, does your friend Hidalgo often go on binges and not come home for days?"

"I don't think so—but I don't know, Señor Capitán. I'm to call his wife again before midnight, and I can call you, if you like."

"I am going home. But leave the message. *Adiós*, señor."

Theodore hung up, and told Ramón that Infante had been reported seen in Acapulco that evening.

Ramón nodded. "But they are not sure?"

"No. And I don't think Sauzas is going there."

Ramón asked who had seen the boy, and Theodore told

him the little he knew. Restlessly, Ramón walked into the hall, and came back. "I think I shall go there, Teo—if there is a chance."

"But it's only a rumour!"

"I have a hunch. What can I do here in his enormous city? If he's in Acapulco, I can find him in a matter of hours."

"Quicker than the police?"

"If they find him first, I'll at least be there. You understand, don't you, Teo?" he said, looking at him.

Theodore understood. Ramón saw himself intervening between Infante and the police, somehow convincing the police the fellow was innocent of Lelia's murder—whereas it was not even certain yet that Infante was going to be accused of it—and protesting again his own guilt.

Ramón walked to a black window and stood looking out. "There're no planes until tomorrow morning." He turned round. "I have about a hundred pesos, Teo, and the fare is a hundred and seventeen one way, I remember."

"There's plenty of money in the house, Ramón."

"I'll pay you back, Teo, I promise." Then he walked out of the room as if to escape the embarrassing subject of money.

Theodore closed his fountain-pen and then his diary. Perhaps before tomorrow morning they would hear that Infante had been apprehended in Mexico, D.F., or in Acapulco and that he was being brought to Mexico, D.F., and Ramón would not go. But as he closed his door, he heard Ramón on the telephone in the living-room, making a reservation on the 8 a.m. plane.

When Theodore called Isabel again at twelve-fifteen, Carlos had not come home.

CHAPTER TWENTY-FIVE

THE gentle buzz of his alarm clock awakened Theodore at six. The house was ominously silent. For a minute he lay motionless, listening for a sound from Ramón's room. Then he threw off the bedclothes and in pyjamas and bare feet went to Ramón's door and gently turned the knob, saw the undisturbed bed and the glow of a lamp.

Ramón was sitting at the writing-table with a pen in his hand.

"Excuse me, Ramón."

"No matter." He continued to write.

His shirt was the same blue one of last night. Theodore wondered if he had slept at all. "Have you called the police this morning?" Theodore asked.

"No-o."

"I'll call them. They may have found Infante."

But they had not found Infante. Theodore stood at the telephone in his room, in his dressing-gown and slippers now, smoking a Delicado and listening to the dull words of the police officer.

"Nothing from Acapulco?"

"Nothing, señor."

Theodore went down to make coffee. Inocenza did not get up until seven, and he saw no reason to awaken her. He put coffee on, gave Leo his breakfast of an American gravel-like cat cereal with milk on it, and squeezed some orange juice for Ramón and himself. Without waiting for the coffee, he carried the orange juice to Ramón's room.

"I'll call the police again before seven," Theodore said. "If you go, I'll go with you."

"Why?"

"Because I want to. I promise you I'll not be in your way."

Ramón lifted his brows as if it did not matter at all, and sealed his letter. From his old bent note-case he produced some stamps. "We must leave here at seven, then."

Inocenza was dressed and downstairs at six-thirty, making them a hasty breakfast of scrambled eggs, asking questions.

"I can't say when we'll be back," Theodore said, "but I'll telephone, Inocenza." He was then phoning for a reservation on the Acapulco plane.

"This evening, señor?"

But he could not promise that. No, he was not taking anything with him, not even a toothbrush. He did not want to be burdened. His call to police headquarters just before seven produced no more news, and he was thinking of calling Isabel Hidalgo, when Ramón appeared in the doorway of his bedroom and said:

"Well, Teo, if you are going——"

Ramón gave Inocenza an affectionate farewell, and thanked her for caring for his bird. Theodore noticed tears in Inocenza's eyes. She understood why Ramón was leaving, because Theodore had told her that Infante had been seen in Acapulco. She looked at Theodore as Ramón spoke, as if she would have liked to beg Theodore not to let him go.

"If I had thought of it earlier this morning, I would have taken my bird to Chapultepec Park and released him," Ramón said to Inocenza.

"What? He would die, señor! He wouldn't know how to find his food!"

"With the whole woods to eat from?" Ramón replied.

"Pepe would not even like the park!" Inocenza said.

"Release him today, anyway," Ramón said quietly but like a command. "Release him in the patio."

"But—the cat, señor——"

"He may be killed, but I don't want him caged any more. *Adiós*, Inocenza." He went out of the door.

Theodore also turned to go, but Inocenza snatched up from the sofa the newspapers she had bought that morning and thrust them into his hands. He started to tell her not to obey Ramón's order about the bird, then with a wave of his hand he went out. Ramón's determination to go to Acapulco was part of his destiny, whatever happened, and the senseless sacrifice of the bird, if it improved Ramón's mental state, perhaps would play its part.

Ramón had already found a taxi. During the ride to the airport they said nothing and looked at the newspapers. Infante's being seen in Acapulco provided the headline of the story, and the incidents concerning the muffler were all there—that Ramón Otero and himself and Eduardo Parral had been approached by Infante either in person or by telephone and asked if they had lost a muffler. But there was no speculation as to the significance of this. Ramón glanced through the papers and refolded them. He stopped the taxi near a mail-box, and got out to post his letter. Theodore had noticed that it was addressed to Arturo Baldin, and it crossed his mind that Ramón might have written something like a farewell letter to Arturo, that Ramón foresaw a fight to the death with the police. It also occurred to Theodore that if he stayed with Ramón he might also become a target for the pistols of the police, though he did not know now what he could possibly do about it.

Acapulco presented its brilliant, smiling crescent at midmorning, a tumbled ring of golden green hills, a fringe of hotels that seemed to sit right in the blue ocean. White flecks of sails looked perfectly still on the surface of the bay. They got out of the plane into a warm, thick atmosphere that after a few minutes made them remove their jackets and ties. A limousine took them into the town and deposited them near the main plaza on the Costera, the great main avenue that curved around the bay.

Ramón wanted to go at once to the police station to learn whether the boy had been found, but Theodore suggested a telephone call, on the grounds of saving time. He knew that Ramón would get into some kind of altercation with the police if they went there, and that they both might be detained for some time. Ramón called from a telephone on the counter of a plaza bar, his face tense, his eyes glancing over the people at the tables and the passers-by on the sidewalk.

"Does it matter who I am? I am a citizen asking a question!" Ramón said, and Theodore gestured for him to keep calm, but Ramón was not looking at him. *"Está bien! Gracias!"* He hung up, and slid a twenty-centavo piece across the counter to pay for the call. "They have not found him," he said to Theodore, swung his jacket over his shoulder, and they walked out on to the sidewalk.

The plaza was noisy with tourists and Acapulcans, sitting at sidewalk tables over early *apéritifs.* They had walked half around the plaza when Ramón said: "Teo, I am going to do a lot of walking, and I don't expect you will enjoy it. Would you like to sit and have a drink somewhere?"

"I know what he looks like better than you," Theodore said, "and I'm just as eager to find him."

They got back to the corner at which they had entered the plaza. Before them, the row of coconut palms down the centre of the Costera swayed and hissed in the gentle breeze from the ocean. A slow-moving car with an amplifier blared a cha-cha-cha tune, and over this a man's recorded voice screamed unintelligibly about a local movie.

"So many hotels," Ramón said irritably.

"He would not go to a hotel! I'm quite sure the hotels are alerted. We should go to the lowest sections of the town— wherever they are," Theodore added, because he was not familiar with the lower sections of Acapulco. "How about the Malecón? The boys on the wharf. They always know everything that's going on, you know."

"Let's try behind the Cathedral first," said Ramón, and they turned and headed for the blue-and-white Cathedral of Arabian style whose two domes could be seen at the end of the plaza, above the trees. The Cathedral's three tall doors, one in front and one on either side, stood wide open to the tropical breezes and the stares of tourists.

Ramón hesitated at a side door and said: "I'll just be a minute, Teo," and went in.

Theodore lit a cigarette and looked up the sidewalk, which presented an uninteresting vista.

Ramón came out after two or three minutes, and they continued the slightly uphill climb and walked for half an hour among the streets of small private houses that resembled those of small towns in the U.S.A., with their bench swings and front porches. Once Ramón detached himself and crossed a street to speak to two boys sitting on a porch rail. Theodore saw them shake their heads, and when Ramón turned away, one of them put a hand over his mouth foolishly to hide a grin. They went up La Quebrada, a street that led to the steep rocks from which local boys dived every night for prize money. Ramón walked to the small plaza overlooking the rocks and looked at the few figures on the stone benches. None looked like Infante.

"Down to the Malecón!" Theodore proposed, and Ramón came with him.

It was a considerable walk, and they took a different route back to the Costera. Theodore looked over the drifting, chattering groups of boys and young men they passed on the way, but he wondered if Infante—if he were still here at all after the warning in the papers—were not holed up in the house of someone he had bought off to hide him. On the other hand, Infante was not the sort to be cautious for ever.

He would want to go to another big town, and there was none near Acapulco.

The Malecón was a cement embankment where little boats and sail-boats tied up and from which people took off for an afternoon's fishing, returning at sundown to have their pictures taken beside hanging sailfish. Here there were always boys and men fishing with hand-lines, boys awaiting their girl friends, and loiterers of all kinds who came to buy marijuana and dope from certain skippers of the sail-boats and motor-launches. Ramón asked Theodore not to walk with him now, so that he could better talk to some of the boys, and Theodore sat down on an empty bench, where he was immediately approached by a barefoot child of six or less who offered to shine his shoes for a peso.

"*Dos pesos,*" Theodore said.

A blank stare, and then a grin. "Okay! Two pesos!" in English, and he fell to work.

Twenty yards away, Ramón was talking to a slim boy in a white shirt and white slacks. The boy shook his head repeatedly, and drifted on, without a glance back at Ramón.

"Take it easy, *niño!*" Theodore said. "If you get polish on my socks, you are *worth* only one peso!"

But he gave him two pesos and a fifty-centavo tip, and continued to sit on the bench, watching Ramón's dark-clad figure growing smaller, far down the Malecón. He was bound to be recognised as Ramón Otero by someone, Theodore thought, and the word would be passed around. They'd have no peace. Theodore foresaw false leads, and gratuities paid for nothing. He stared out at the beautiful, neutral Pacific, whose surface rose and fell even within the quiet bay like a powerful and tranquil breathing. His clothes were beginning to stick with perspiration. He wondered if to-night he and Ramón could not go to that quiet stretch of beach beyond Hornos and plunge into the sea naked. Or would it remind Ramón too much of the nights when Lelia had been with them here, swimming with them, too, in the darkness? Ramón would not tell him if he were disturbed by his memories, he would simply refuse to go to the spot. Theodore closed his eyes to the glaring sun and remembered a night with Lelia and Ramón on the little beach, the nervous, cool lap of the small waves and the sound of a ripe mango or coconut falling from a tree to the sand.

In the afternoon they explored Caleta Beach as well as Hornos, the afternoon beach, Ramón oblivious of the stares of the nearly naked sun-bathers as he tramped in his city clothes among them. Theodore stayed on the paved walk, from which he could see the beach as well as the people on the street. When Ramón emptied the sand from his shoes for the last time, it was 5 p.m. Theodore persuaded him to go into Hungry Herman's for a hamburger, but Ramón would not order anything but coffee. From here, Theodore made a call to Sauzas, whom he did not get, but he learned that Infante had not been found and that there were no new reports from Acapulco. Theodore told this to Ramón, and proposed that they find a hotel for the night, rest a while, and go out again in the evening, when everyone would be out of doors or at some night club. Ramón agreed to the hotel, but said he did not need to rest. His eyes, however, were already haggard, and Theodore felt sure he had not slept the past night.

"I have the feeling he is in this town, Teo," Ramón said. "Or somewhere near. There's Pie de la Cuesta, you know, and Puerto Marques. A big hotel there, too."

"Ramón, he wouldn't dare stick his head into an hotel!"

"What makes you so sure?"

"All right, ask at the Hotel Club de Pesca, and see what they tell you!" Theodore said somewhat impatiently. The Club de Pesca was a gaudy, hulking hotel, built in a curve, just the hotel Infante would choose, if he dared.

They walked towards the Club de Pesca, and Theodore

inquired for rooms in four or five hotels that they passed, all of which were filled. At the Club de Pesca, Ramón approached the desk and asked if a Señor Salvador Infante was registered there.

"Or Señor Salvador Bejar," Ramón added, and Theodore walked farther away, embarrassed.

"Infante?" came the clerk's voice. "The one they are looking for? I wish he *would* come in here, señor!"

Angry, Ramón rejoined Theodore, and they left the air-conditioned lobby and went out into the sun. "One has to ask to know!" Ramón said as resentfully as if he had been personally insulted. In Ramón's mind, the young delinquent was a persecuted child, at worst a minor offender who had paid enough for his misdemeanors by being harassed over the whole United States of Mexico.

"Let's try the other end of the Costera for an hotel," Theodore said, "otherwise we'll be walking back all the way we've come. And I for one am going to ride on something."

There was a bus-stop very near the Club de Pesca, and a bus was just sliding to the kerb. Theodore got on it, but Ramón stood where he was.

"I'll meet you on the Malecón!" Ramón called to him.

Let him exhaust himself on this nonsense, Theodore thought. But as he walked up the bus aisle, he found himself glancing as anxiously as Ramón to make sure that no face on the bus was the pale, furtive face of Infante. Theodore rode past the Malecón until the hotels became thinner, got out and, at the second hotel at which he inquired, secured a room with twin beds for the night. The dull practicality of this jolted him from his thoughts of the preceding hour, and made him feel vaguely ashamed. He resolved not to nag Ramón to sleep in a bed tonight if he preferred to walk the streets or to explore the all-night cabarets. Ramón had a purpose and he had not. That was the difference between them.

Theodore walked back to the Malecón and stood near the warehouses, watching a couple of sandalled longshoremen rolling barrel-sized coils of copper wire from the dock into a warehouse. He walked on, looking for Ramón's figure in the bright dusk.

"*Joven!*" he called to a young man approaching, who was licking an ice-stick.

The young man strolled towards Theodore, no doubt thinking he wanted to ask a direction.

"Listen—you have not possibly heard where Salvador Infante is in this town, have you?" Theodore asked.

The boy's shining brown eyes widened very slightly, innocently.

"Two hundred pesos, if you have an idea," Theodore said. "I am a friend of his, not the police."

The boy's eyes lingered momentarily on Theodore's expensive wrist-watch, and came up to meet Theodore's eyes. He shrugged. "Don't ask me, señor. I heard he was here——"

"You don't know anyone who knows? Two hundred pesos if you tell me that. I have the money with me. No questions asked."

He turned his round, dark head to look behind him. "I don't know, señor. I am sorry." And he seemed really sorry, because no one at all was around them, or watching them.

Theodore nodded. "*Gracias.*"

They walked on their separate ways. He caught sight of Ramón at last, not on the Malecón, but across the Costera from it, walking very slowly, his jacket over one shoulder. When Theodore approached him, he said he had been waiting half an hour.

"I've been hanging around here only because if you hadn't found me, you'd have called the police or something wild like that!" Ramón's eyes were wild now, and bloodshot.

"It took me a few minutes to find a hotel room, Ramón.

Here's the key. The name is on it—Hotel Tres Reyes, way down."

"I don't need a hotel, Teo."

"Keep the key, anyway. I can get in when I go back, but you may not be able to without the key."

Ramón thrust the key back at him. "Thank you, Teo," he said with gentleness in his voice, but none in his face, and walked on a few steps.

Theodore caught up with him. "Where now, Ramón?"

The problem was solved by Ramón's suddenly collapsing. People gathered round, murmuring about the sun's rays, tequila, the low altitude, but Theodore knew it was none of these things. A couple of boys, of the kind Ramón had been approaching all afternoon, helped Theodore lift his limp figure into a taxi, and one of them laid Ramón's jacket over him with a hand as slender and gentle as a girl's.

CHAPTER TWENTY-SIX

RAMÓN was able to walk into the Hotel Tres Reyes when they reached it, though he did not seem to know where he was. Theodore got him to lie down and sent for orange juice and hot tea. Obediently, Ramón sipped at both tea and the orange juice, while Theodore sat uneasily on the other bed, listening to the waves' restless swish on the beach below their terrace. They were on the second floor of the hotel. Next to them was a suite with kitchenette, occupied now by a couple with a baby that sometimes cried at night; and for this the usual price of the room would be lowered ten pesos, the manager had told Theodore. The baby was already starting to cry, and the breeze that blew through their open terrace door brought also the sounds of a refrigerator door being opened and closed, the clatter of a pan, and the cooing efforts of the woman to get the baby to hush. Theodore sighed, depressed by the transitoriness and the vagueness of his and Ramón's position now. What if Salvador Infante had already got himself killed and was floating in the Pacific at this moment, never to be found except by sharks?

Theodore took a shower with the bathroom door open, so that he could hear if Ramón stirred or left the room, Ramón was sitting up when he came in again. Theodore proposed a shower for him, but Ramón shook his head.

"It'll refresh you—for this evening," Theodore said. "You'll want to go out again, won't you?"

This inspired Ramón to move. Theodore adjusted the shower at a tepid temperature for him and advised him not to touch the taps, since they worked backward and the hot water was scalding. Ramón emerged from the shower a few moments later, his black hair wet and combed down, buttoning his blue shirt.

"What do you say to a nap?" Theodore asked. "Everybody'll be having dinner until ten or so———"

"Only in the hotels," Ramón said. "You said the boy wouldn't be in a hotel, he'd be on the streets."

There was no denying this.

Ramón put his jacket on. "Not that you have to go with me," he added.

But Theodore got up, put his own jacket on, and went with Ramón out of the door. It was ten minutes to seven. The futility of it made Theodore feel tired, and Ramón's energetic pace on the sidewalk increased his sense of flagging.

They went to the plaza, ablaze with lights now, though the sun had still not set. Here were hundreds of faces to look at, and they paused at the open-front bars and restaurants, and Ramón walked into some alone. People looked at him, and Theodore noticed some whispering and pointing. Ramón seemed as unconcerned as if he walked through a forest of trees. They continued up the Costera to the little thatch-roofed restaurant where he and Ramón and Lelia had often come to eat when they tired of their hotel food. The twelve or so tables were visible from the sidewalk, and all were occupied; but Infante was not there.

There were the back streets, scores of them, lighted as much by the occasional tiny food counters with one table and chair in front of them as by the infrequent street lamps. Somewhere they heard a guitar. Theodore looked over his shoulder, sure that they were being followed.

"Ramón," Theodore said, touching Ramón's arm to stop him. Theodore turned round to face the tall boy, who hesitated in a frightened way as if he were going to turn and run. *"Buenas tardes,"* Theodore said, walking towards him. "You have something to say?"

The boy advanced timidly. He was ugly and stupid-look-ing, about nineteen. "You were—asking on the Malecón to-day about Infante?" he asked quietly, though the sidewalk where they stood was deserted.

"*Sí*," Theodore said. "Do you know where he is?"

A blank, frightened stare. "I, no, señor. But maybe some-body else does."

"Who?" Ramón said.

"Do you want a few pesos first? Do you really know any-thing?" Theodore asked.

"I know *something*," the boy said defensively. "Maybe worth—a hundred pesos?"

Theodore hesitated, thinking that if he really knew any-thing, he would have made the price higher. "What is it? We'll pay you." He put his left hand inside his jacket, as if to draw out a wallet.

"Another man was asking for Infante on the Malecón this afternoon," the boy said quickly. "He got into a boat. I saw where the boat went."

Theodore pulled out his wallet, turning himself slightly lest the boy suddenly snatch the whole wallet from his hands. "Now what's the rest of it?" Theodore asked with the hundred-peso note ready in his hand. He replaced his wallet.

"The boat went towards Pie de la Cuesta," the boy said.

It was a village on a promontory, some twelve miles north. "You're sure the boat went there?"

"*Sí*. I don't know if it stopped there, but it went in that direction."

"And who was the man?"

A shrug. "A man. This high." He indicated a height shorter than his own.

"A *policía*?" asked Ramón.

"I don't know." The boy looked at the hundred-peso note.

"At what time?"

"Around five—maybe six," the boy said, his face serious.

Theodore thrust the money at him, and the boy took it. "Have you seen Infante?"

"I? No, señor."

"Whose boat is it that took the man?" asked Ramón.

"A man called Esteban. His boat is—I forget the name—a red boat. No sail. A motor-launch."

"Did Esteban come back? Would he be tied up at the dock now?" Theodore asked.

"I don't know, señor," said the boy with a shrug, his information at an end.

"Gracias," Theodore said automatically, and, as if dismissed, the boy turned and ran to the nearest corner and disappeared around it.

Their search for the red motor-launch proved fruitless. The two or three skippers whom they asked on the Malecón did not even acknowledge that they knew a man called Esteban with a red boat. Theodore thought from the manner of one of them that he was lying and did know of Esteban, but what could he do about it?

"I would like to go on to Pie de la Cuesta," Ramón said.

Theodore tried to dissuade him. It was a primitive place, nothing but a strip of sand with some natives' huts and two or three very simple *pensions* on it, and it would be too dark to see anything tonight, but Ramón would not be deterred. They got a taxi to take them for sixty pesos, there and back.

The long spit of land was beautiful by starlight with its earth-shaking surf, its nodding coconut palms silhouetted in black against the sea. Ramón himself walked into all the *pensions* and talk to proprietors and sweep-up boys, all of whom Theodore saw shake their heads in denial. And they stared at Ramón as he walked back to the taxi. Ramón also asked at a few huts. By candle-light and the light of dying charcoal fires, Theodore saw these ragged, barefoot people shake their heads also. Theodore had a growing feeling that the boy to whom he had paid the hundred pesos had made the story up.

CHAPTER TWENTY-SEVEN

THEODORE awakened before Ramón and lay in his bed re-
viewing the futilities of the evening before. The cha-cha-cha
night spots, so dark it would have been hard to recognise an
old friend in them, the over-sweet *tequilas limonadas* tasted
and left at at least six hotel bars, the terrace of El Mirador,
where he had almost lost Ramón in the crowd. Ramón had
paced the floor after they had come back to the hotel. The
last Theodore remembered was Ramón sitting in the armchair by the door, holding his head. Now Theodore was
afraid to stir lest he waken Ramón from the sleep that he
needed so much. It was nine-twenty. The baby next-door
was babbling out on the terrace, and the mother sang softly
in the kitchen. A faint clatter of breakfast came from the
hotel's kitchen below.

The sudden, triple impact of a falling skillet roused Theodore from a doze. Ramón groaned and lifted his head.

"Morning, Ramón," Theodore said quietly. He knew
Ramón would not want to go back to sleep, so he picked
up the telephone and asked the operator to call the *juzgado*,
the jail.

The *jefe*, whose name was Julio, would not be in until
ten, Theodore was told. Theodore asked for news of Infante.

"*Nada*, señor."

"No rumour that he is around Pie de la Cuesta?"

"No, señor," replied the young, sober voice, which sounded
as uninterested as the voices of most of the clerks Theodore
had spoken to at Sauzas's headquarters.

Theodore thanked him and hung up. He thought of calling Sauzas again, but this, too, seemed futile. While Ramón

254

was in the bathroom, he called his house in Mexico, D.F. Inocenza reported only one telephone call, from Sra. Hidalgo.

"No message," Inocenza said cheerfully.

Theodore asked about Ramón's bird.

"I released him, señor, as I was told. After an hour or so, he flew in an open window! Isn't that a miracle? I had every window in the house open and he flew in one! Tell the señor he went back in his cage himself!"

Theodore told Ramón this when he came out of the bathroom.

"Back in the cage himself!" Ramón repeated incredulously. He gave a hopeless laugh. "Pepe and I—I suppose we both want to be prisoners!" But he looked pleased, nevertheless.

By eleven, they had got shaves and some breakfast on the plaza. Theodore bought the *Excelsior* and *El Universal*, which said briefly that the "nation-wide search" for Infante still went on, with concentration in Guadalajara and Acapulco. The pompousness of the statement struck Theodore as funny; he had not seen one sign in Acapulco that an intensive search was going on.

He went into a plaza restaurant to ring up Sauzas. Ramón was going to wait for him across the Costera.

As usual, they thought Sauzas was in the building, but they had to look for him. Theodore lit a cigarette, and it was nearly gone, and he had had to tell the operator several times not to disconnect him, when Sauzas came on.

"No, there is no news, I'm sorry to say," Sauzas said in a discouraged tone, "but I have not had the report from Acapulco this morning. That means they haven't anything to report."

"Señor Capitán, do you think there is any possibility that Infante is in Acapulco after all the publicity?"

"Umph. What can I say? We can be logical and say no, and then be wrong."

"I'll try to persuade Ramón to leave. We've walked the

town over and there's nothing. Except one rumour last night that a man looking for Infante got on a red boat belonging to someone called Esteban, and they went in the direction of Pie de la Cuesta."

"Who told you?" Sauzas asked calmly, and Theodore told him "Have you seen such a red boat? Or Esteban? Did you get a description of the man who took the boat?"

"Unfortunately not, except his height, about like Ramón's," Theodore replied, and felt most amateurish about his sleuthing.

"Hm-m. Well, I can report that Arturo Baldin was also approached, by telephone, about the muffler nearly three weeks ago. He had not thought it important enough to mention to anybody——" Sauzas's voice trailed off. "And your friend Carlos Hidalgo is not back yet. We have asked in every jail here, thinking he might have been locked up for drunkenness. His wife is very distressed."

"This is two days now?"

"Yes."

Theodore did not know what to say about it.

"Señor Schiebelhut, you expect to be back in Mexico to-night?"

"I expect to, señor. I hope so."

Theodore bought some Delicados at the cash booth of the restaurant, and walked out to find Ramón. He saw him sitting on a bench, facing the sea. Just before he reached him, Ramón got up and turned round and motioned for Theodore to keep a distance.

"I'll be back in a few minutes," Ramón murmured to Theodore as he passed him. "Don't follow me." Then he crossed half the Costera, waited on the island for the light, because the traffic was fast and heavy, then continued up one side of the plaza. Clearly, he was following someone he could see in the crowd.

Theodore crossed the Costera, too. As he reached the other

side, he saw Ramón turn the next corner, to the right. Theodore approached the corner slowly. There was a camera shop on the corner, and diagonally through its two windows Theodore saw Ramón standing, looking or pretending to look into the window of the shop next door. His lips moved, then he pulled his note-case from his hip pocket, and Theodore saw a thin, nervous hand and bare wrist, the fingers impatient. Ramón took out the contents of the note-case and the fingers swept them out of Theodore's view. Theodore walked on slowly to the corner.

Ramón came towards him, motioning him back. Whoever Ramón had been talking to had disappeared in the crowd.

"I have some information," Ramón said. "Infante is on a boat called the *Pepita*, whose skipper is Miguel Gutirrez. And there's a man called Alejandro down at the Malecón who might take us to him."

"Who was that you spoke to?"

"A boy who approached me on the Costera—just before you arrived. Come on, Teo, walk faster! He said he didn't want his friends to see him talking to me, so I had to meet him on that corner."

"What did you give him?"

"All I had. Seventy pesos. He wanted a hundred. This way, Teo!"

Ramón was optimistic, but he did not know what Alejandro looked like or the name of his boat, because the boy had not tarried long enough to tell him after he got his money. The sun throbbed hotly on Theodore's forehead. Ramón paused on the embankment near an old man who was coiling a line neatly at the prow of his boat.

"*Buenos días.* You know a boatman here called Alejandro?" Ramón asked.

"Alejandro?" the old man said gruffly in a tone of surprise. He stood up and pointed. "He ties up farther down."

Theodore dragged his steps, debating whether to insist now that they take a police officer with them. Or was this another false lead, as vague and inconsequential as the Pie de la Cuesta clue?

"You don't want to come?" Ramón asked. "I'll go alone, then."

"I do want to come. If the boy is really here, I want you to see him, and I want to see you when you do!"

Six or eight boats bobbed in the water, their prows pointed to the embankment, but only two men were in sight.

"Alejandro?" Ramón called to them.

Both men, on different boats, looked at him. One pointed to a dirty, empty-looking boat. "He sleeps," the man said, cleared his throat with a long hawk like an unintelligible sentence, and spat over the side.

Ramón stooped at the boat they had indicated and pulled it closer to the embankment by its line. "Alejandro? *Alejandro*?"

The other two men were watching them, several yards away.

Theodore heard a groan from the boat's cabin, whose door was open, then a pair of dirty feet swung down from a bunk. As the prow almost touched the embankment, Ramón jumped down to the tiny quarter-deck. An unshaven face looked out at him, squinting.

"Who're you?"

"My name is Otero," Ramón said quietly. "Señor, I want to go to the boat of Miguel Gutirrez. Will you take me? I am a friend."

"Of Miguel's? I don't know you," he mumbled suspiciously, still half asleep. He noticed Theodore on the wharf, and his face took on an alert, knowing look. "I don't know where Miguel is, *hombre*. I haven't seen him in three days. I don't need the *policía* on my boat. I've done nothing wrong." He waved a hand to dismiss Ramón.

"I'm not the *policía*. I'm a friend—of Salvador Infante's. We are both his friends."

The man looked around the wharf behind them. "You are not the *policía*?"

"Do I look like the filthy *policía*?"

Still stooping under his cabin door, Alejandro beckoned Ramón closer. "I might know where Miguel is. What'll you pay me if I take you?"

"Two hundred pesos."

"Hah!" But he was considering it, mumbling something, scratching his crotch reflectively with a pinching movement. *"Do' cien pesos.* A fine proposition and I'm supposed to risk my life—— Besides, did I even say I knew where he was?"

"I'm not a *policía, hombre*! Look. I'm not armed."

The man glanced at Ramón's trouser pockets, then pressed the pockets of the jacket over Ramón's arm. He beckoned to Theodore. Theodore stepped down on the quarter-deck and submitted to the same searching. "Six hundred," Alejandro said calmly, fixing Theodore with one eye. "In advance."

"You'll get it. We want to see Infante first," Theodore said, and Alejandro shook his head, looked away and spat. "If you don't think I'll pay you at the end of the trip, let's just call it off, and there you are out six hundred pesos already!" Theodore said. "Think of that! Don't be stupid. How soon will you see six hundred pesos again?"

The man started to tell him how soon, and left off in disgust. But he was starting to move, lifting the cover off his little engine in the cabin. "Ah, that drunken brat," he mumbled.

Ramón untied the line from the ring in the wharf. As the boat began to move, Alejandro took a long look around the wharf, and even waved to someone.

They headed for the straits of the bay. Alejandro mumbled that if anyone asked them where they were going, they were going to Puerto Marques to see the fine hotel from the sea, and he chuckled tiredly and mirthlessly, rubbing his hands on his greasy shorts. They rounded one of the two projections of land that sheltered the bay, and turned south. On their right now spread the immensity of the Pacific, empty except for a tanker almost at the horizon. Theodore kept his eyes along the shore edge. Two or three little boats sailed near the land.

"How much farther?" Ramón asked.

Alejandro waved a hand, lifted his filthy cap and scratched in his greying black hair. "Long ways. Long past Marques."

"Is the boat out in the sea or tied up?"

"You will see."

"What colour is the boat?"

"Ai! Questions!" Alejandro said, as if he were talking with a child.

Alejandro nodded to shore and announced Puerto Marques. The town looked far away, set back deeply in a notch of the shore. The motor chugged on. Ramón crouched at the prow, gazing ahead at the warm, fuzzy horizon. No little boats were in sight now. Theodore glanced at Alejandro. His coarse, square face was baked a red-brown, like a brick, and had as little expression. He looked dishonest, and that was all. Theodore suspected that he would keep going for perhaps half an hour, stop and say that the *Pepita* must have gone somewhere else, demand his six hundred pesos, and possibly take them back to the Malecón, but probably not.

Alejandro turned the boat slightly shoreward and even slowed the motor. Three little sail-boats were anchored near the land. But slowly they passed all these, at too great a distance for Theodore to read their names. Then they drew so close to shore Theodore could distinguish clumps of green coconuts at the tops of some of the trees. The land looked wild and pathless. They left the three little boats far behind.

260

Then, behind a jutting of rock, Theodore saw the blue or grey end of a small boat.

"That's it?" he asked.

Alejandro nodded calmly. He gave the rocks a wide berth. The little pale blue boat sat quite still on the sea, its barren mast motionless. Alejandro stood up and cupped his hands to his mouth. "*Oiga! Miguel!*" he yelled, with a smile.

A long, silent minute passed. Then a door on the *Pepita* opened.

"*Dos amigos!*" Alejandro shouted. ". . . . *amigos,*" the shore echoed.

There was an unintelligible reply from the *Pepita,* and a man in a light blue shirt of almost the same colour as the boat, with brown face and arms, put his hands on the low rail and leaned towards them. "Alejandro? Who's with you?"

"Friends of the boy. Shut your face," said Alejandro. He idled his motor now and gazed nonchalantly around the deserted shore.

Miguel was leaning into his cabin door. He looked unsteady on his feet. Then he stepped back from the door, and Theodore saw the head and the frail shoulders of Infante, a look of surprise on his face. The boy said something to the man and made a nervous movement as if he were about to duck back into the cabin.

Ramón was standing in the prow. "Tell him I'm a friend!" he yelled to the *Pepita's* skipper. "Ramón Otero!"

"*Otero!*" The boy had heard him. "Oh no! Keep him away! What do you mean bringing him here, you sons of bitches!" A rush of curses followed.

"I'm your friend! I'm not going to harm you!" Ramón shouted.

"They're both drunk," Theodore said to Ramón.

"Alejandro!" yelled Miguel. "You with a thousand pesos! You want more? There isn't any more! It's gone!"

The boats were only a couple of yards apart now.

"Shut your face, Miguel! These two are not the *policía*! They want to see Infante! Let me have the money," he said in a lower voice to Theodore, and stuck out a thick, greasy palm.

Theodore took five hundreds and two fifties from his wallet. The ape-like hand closed over the notes and crushed them into a pocket of the shorts.

Ramón grabbed the rail of the *Pepita* and sprang towards it, wetting a foot. Theodore followed him, looking warily at Miguel, who had retreated to the prow and was standing braced, a bar of metal like a marlin-spike in his hand.

"Salvador, I'm a friend! I only want to talk to you!" Ramón yelled at the cabin door. He pulled at the door by its handles, but Infante held it from the inside, jerking it shut every time Ramón pulled.

Theodore stuck his hand in the crack of the door and wrenched it open. The boy catapulted on to the deck, like some vermin routed from a hole. "So there he is, Ramón!" Theodore said between his teeth.

The boy scowled up at them, hurling curses and threats.

"I'm not going to hurt you!" Ramón protested. "I know you're not the murderer! They've driven him out of his mind, Teo!"

"He's drunk on rum," Alejandro said indifferently, from his boat.

Salvador Infante looked from Ramón to Theodore, his frightened eyes unfocusing. "What do you want?"

"To talk with you. Now get up!" Ramón said, pulling him up by one of his thin arms.

Infante was barefoot, in oversized dungarees and a white shirt which Theodore recognised as the silk shirt he had worn in Guanajuato. He swayed in Ramón's hold, but his expression was truculent. "What do you want, I said? What do you *want*?"

"Several things. I want to see the muffler," Theodore said.

"Ah, the muffler! You have to *pay* for that! The muffler's sold, anyway!"

"Salvador, you must leave here! Get away from these men and from Acapulco!" Ramón wiped the glistening sweat from his forehead.

"Whom did you sell the muffler to, Salvador?" Theodore asked.

"Wouldn't you like to know?" Salvador Infante tried to spit, unsuccessfully. He looked very pale, as if he were going to be sick. "Where's the rum, Miguel? Hey, Miguel, the rum-m!" He was back in the cabin, groping over a bunk.

"The rum! *Seguro!*" said Miguel, coming forward with his marlin-spike and a silly smile on his face. "Do the señores like rum?"

Alejandro laughed, standing in his boat and lighting a cigarette.

The boy emerged with a rum bottle, flourished it at them and lifted it, spilling rum on his nose before his mouth found the top of the bottle. Ramón snatched it from him and threw it overboard, and at once a roar of protest went up from Salvador and Miguel. Miguel went into the cabin, mumbling that he would find another bottle.

"See the scratch on his hand, Ramón?" Theodore pointed at the hand the boy rested on the cabin roof. A pink welt with a darker line in its middle went from his wrist to his third finger. "My cat gave you that in Guanajuato, *no es vero*, Salvador?"

Salvador stared at his hand foolishly and hung his head.

Theodore seized his shirt front. "Listen! Whom did you sell the muffler to?"

"Sell the muffler? It's here," said Miguel, gesturing at the cabin he had just come out of.

"Where is it?" Theodore asked. "Show me."

Ramón grabbed at the bottle in Miguel's hand, but Miguel

pulled it indignantly out of his reach. "Stop your drinking and get him out of here! The *policia* is after him, don't you know that?"

"Hah, don't I know that!" Miguel mocked, his thick red lips slavering. "This one here——" he indicated Alejandro —"he won't tell the *policia*—because he's making too much money out of us, *verdad*, 'Jandro? But there's no more money! No more!"

And Alejandro chuckled as if he were watching a show from a distance.

"Show me the muffler, Miguel," Theodore said.

"*Money!*" Infante said in a suddenly loud voice. He picked up a fish-head from the deck and hurled it at Alejandro, missing him. "Clear out, you filthy bloodsuckers!" He repeated the word: "*Chupasangres! Chupasangres! Todos, todos chupasangres!* You have sucked *my* blood! *Pig!*" he yelled at Miguel who swung at him with the rum bottle.

Ramón caught Miguel's arm. "Let him alone!"

"Ah, you damned fool, are you protecting that scum?" Alejandro put in, spitting into the water. He picked up his line and reached for the *Pepita's* rail.

"Can you take him away from here, Alejandro?" Ramón asked, but Alejandro paid no attention. He turned to Infante. "You don't understand the police are going to accuse you of the murder of Lelia Ballesteros? I've come to help you, Salvador!" He shook Infante's thin shoulder. "Understand, Salvador? But you have no time to waste!"

Infante's head hung listlessly to one side.

"*Oiga, hombre,*" Alejandro said, pulling at Ramón's arm. "You were one of the friends of that girl? Otero. Sure! Aren't you the fellow who confessed?"

"I confessed but nobody believes me. The *policia* doesn't believe me!" Ramón said.

"Are you *loco*?" Alejandro asked in wonderment. "Hey, didn't they *say* you were crazy? Gimme some rum, Miguel." He held his hand out for the bottle.

"We're all crazy," Infante mumbled, his head hanging. "*Todos locos, todos locos——*"

"Are you the man who paid ten thousand pesos for the muffler?" Alejandro asked, peering slyly at Ramón and passing a dirty hand over the top of the bottle.

"No," Ramón said, frowning. "What muffler?" he asked Infante. "Whose muffler is it, anyway?"

Salvador Infante looked at him sideways and smiled. "I know."

"Where did you get it?" Theodore asked him.

"From the apartment."

"Lelia's apartment?" Theodore asked.

"*Sí!*" Infante said, defiantly. "*Sississi!*"

"Lelia's apartment? You're putting words in his mouth, Teo!" Ramón frowned.

"You think he was not in her apartment, *hombre*? He was bragging about it! Come here, I want to show you something." Alejandro pulled at Ramón's arm, but Ramón shook him off and walked to the boy, who was moving towards the prow, keeping himself upright by the cabin roof.

Theodore went after Infante. "Salvador! Did you also send the postcard from Florida?"

"From Florida?" Infante smiled dreamily. "Sure. From Lelia. Hah! I had a friend send it. I told him it's to a friend whose girl friend is with me." He poked his chest with his thumb. "Lelia's with *me*, I said, but she's supposed to be in Florida!"

"And the telephone calls, Salvador?" Theodore asked. "The silent calls?"

Salvador Infante looked sleepily blank. "I don't know them—don't know them."

"I'd like to talk to him alone, Teo," Ramón said.

"Come with me, señor. Come! I'll show you something."
Alejandro pulled at Theodore's arm.

"Did she let you into her apartment, Salvador? How did
you get in?" Theodore asked.

But Infante turned his face away, silent.

Alejandro said in Theodore's ear: "The door was open!
He said he brought her flowers to get in, and when he got
in—she was dead. Dead!" Alejandro's dark face took on a
faint excitement. "So he stole a few things and left," he
finished, throwing up his hands. "You don't believe me yet,
señor? Come in, I'll show you. You want to see?"

"Ramón!" Theodore called, then went after him.

Ramón was talking to Infante, who was drunkenly telling
him to shut up.

"Come with me, Ramón," Theodore said, taking Ramón's
arm. "Alejandro wants to show us something. *Come!*"

"You have made him invent all that he said, Teo," Ramón
said threateningly.

"Come into the cabin. Just for a minute."

Reluctantly, Ramón left the boy and came with him.
Theodore headed Ramón first into the cabin. In the dim
light, Theodore saw Alejandro crouched in the narrow space
between two bunks, dragging out a small suitcase.

"This stuff—— Wait. Maybe you recognise it." Alejandro
threw out some wadded shirts. "This?" He held something
up in the air.

Theodore looked, and felt a quick, crushing pain in his
chest.

"That's Lelia's!" Ramón exclaimed. He touched it, as if
to see if it were real.

It was the obsidian necklace Theodore had taken to be repaired, the one she had worn so often that it was like looking
at Lelia herself to see it—the polished oval pendant, the
slender black segments with their fine gold links. Alejandro
was dragging more things out of a pocket of the suitcase, and

266

Theodore moved closer, stumbling past Ramón to touch the piece of red ribbon, the art-gum eraser, the couple of Venus pencils he knew had lain in the painted clay bowl on her bookcase. "And her keys, Ramón—her keys," Theodore said. His fist closed over them. "Do you still think he didn't get into her apartment?"

"This?" Alejandro held up Ramón's address book, spilling a few cards from it.

But Ramón was looking at the necklace in his shaking hand.

"And this? This is the muffler." It hung down from Alejandro's lifted hand, a pale blue muffler with crimson stripes that crossed to make large squares, a flashy muffler.

Theodore did not think he had ever seen it before. He looked at both ends of it for a label or a cleaner's mark, smelt it, but it smelt of nothing but wool. "Whose is it?"

Alejandro only gave a shrug and a smile. "He found it in the apartment. And *somebody* paid."

What kind of man would wear such a muffler, Theodore wondered.

Theodore heard a scream like a woman's.

He ran out of the cabin. Ramón was at the prow, standing over Infante, pummelling him with both fists, and Miguel was trying to pull him off. The boy writhed violently to escape, but Ramón lifted him and hurled him into the corner where the prow narrowed, and there was a crack like that of a breaking skull. Miguel had a grip with both hands on Ramón's arm, and quite slowly, it seemed to Theodore, Ramón drew his arm back and then forward. There was a deep sound as Miguel plunged into the water, then the patter of droplets. Theodore stood with his fists stupidly clenched, the keys in one and the muffler in the other.

Ramón looked at him wildly, panting.

"Is he dead?" Theodore said.

With that, Ramón whirled as if he were insane and made

a snatching movement that tore the boy's shirt off and jerked his limp body into the air. Ramón swung at him before he fell.

"And this, señor? This?" Alejandro was yelling from the stern, and, turning, Theodore saw him holding up the large photograph of Lelia that had been in his diary, torn now and flapping in the breeze. *"Linda mujer,"* Alejandro commented.

Theodore felt paralysed and strangling. In the water he saw Miguel's head emerge, and saw his face with a sad, reconciled expression tilt with his first stroke towards the boat. "Ramón, is he dead?" Theodore asked, because Ramón was bending over Infante as if listening for his heart. Then as he came closer, he saw that Ramón was looking at a thin silver cross. It lay on the boy's smooth chest and shone in the sun like something white-hot.

Ramón whimpered, his face in his hands.

Theodore put his fingers over Infante's heart, loathing to touch him. He thought he felt a heart-beat, but it may have been his own pulse. Infante's bleeding mouth was drawn back from the teeth as if death had come with a convulsion. A smear of blood darkened the hair on his upper lip.

The boy groaned.

"Salvador, whose is the muffler?" Theodore asked. "Salvador——"

"Teo, you were right," Ramón gasped into his hands. "And now I have killed him!"

"He's not dead. Salvador—the muffler—who paid you for it?" He put his ear near the boy's wet mouth.

The lips were saying something about *Dios,* over and over. His eyes looked vacantly at the sky. His lips stopped moving.

Alejandro bent over with his hands on his knees, looking at Infante. "Ugh! *Un católico. Un espléndido católico!"* He chuckled, stuck out a hand that looked incapable of feeling anything and held it against the chest below the cross.

"Still alive. *Madre de Dios*, you can't kill this kind!"

Miguel stood dripping on the deck, blowing his nose out in his hand. "He's dead?" he asked, swaying, catching his balance.

"No. He's alive," Alejandro said.

Miguel took a step towards the boy with a face full of drunken fury. "Dead or not, I don't want him on my boat! I've had enough of him!" He caught Infante by the throat and banged his head, once and definitively, on the deck, in the practised movement of a fisherman who has killed a thousand fish in the same manner.

This happened in the time it took for Theodore to stand up and for Ramón to take his hands from his face. Then, as Theodore saw the figure lifted from the deck, he sprang forward and caught Miguel by the arm. "Stop it, man! What're you trying to do?"

Miguel swung out of Theodore's reach, keeping his grip on the dungarees. The body hung like a rag. "This is *my* boat and *I* say who're the passengers!" He made ready to heave him over, and Theodore hit Miguel in the jaw.

Miguel staggered back and would have fallen overboard if Alejandro had not caught him. Alejandro laughed.

Theodore turned the limp body over. More blood came from the head, giving a horrible red sheen to the black hair. He felt for pulses, for the heart. "Now he's dead," Theodore said. He looked up and saw Ramón's terrified face looking at him.

"Good," Alejandro grunted.

"*Get him off my boat!*" Miguel roared, coming at him.

Theodore clapped his arm around Ramón's shoulders, because Ramón looked as if he would let himself sway over the rail, or as if he were going to hurl himself over. One hand, like a stiff claw, Ramón held over his face. His sobs were like the sound of choking. "It couldn't be helped, Ramón—couldn't——" Theodore said stupidly, and looked just in time to see Miguel with an easy sideways swing hurl the dead boy overboard.

There was a loud, messy splash.

"Good riddance!" Alejandro said, and put a cigarette in his mouth. "He was a dirty fish!" He nodded affirmation of himself to Theodore.

Of course it was good riddance, Theodore thought. Now Miguel would have all that was left of Infante's money.

"And all his junk——" Miguel muttered, going towards the stern.

"The rum," Theodore said to Alejandro. "If there's any rum left——"

Alejandro raised a grimy finger, smiled, and went to get it.

"And *this*!" Miguel was yelling from the stern, flinging overboard a pair of trousers. "This——" An empty bottle followed the trousers. Miguel bumped his head hard on the cabin door's lintel and cursed.

"Not that!" Theodore said, running towards him. He caught Miguel's wrist. "Give me that!"

Miguel relaxed his hold on the pencils, the red ribbon, and with his other hand threw some clothes overboard.

Ramón did not want any rum, he wanted water. Miguel had none, or at any rate refused to give Theodore any.

"Off my boat, all of you!" Miguel shouted.

"Is there water on your boat, Alejandro?" Theodore asked.

Alejandro nodded that there was, and took the rum and drank.

Theodore looked at the sea off the starboard and the prow, but the surface was smooth and empty. The sea rolled gently, as if nothing had occurred.

"Disappeared!" said Alejandro, chuckling. "He sank!"

"Can you take us back to Acapulco?" Theodore asked him.

Alejandro squinted at him knowingly. "To shore, maybe. Acapulco, no. . . . Miguel, are you throwing away money?" He went to the stern and disappeared into the cabin, where

270

Theodore heard him opening cabinets, dragging things about as he searched the last corner for a possible cache of pesos.

Ramón's hand was still over his face, his body upright and rigid, though Theodore gripped his arm as if he would fall if he did not. They talked at cross-purposes, Theodore of the water on Alejandro's boat that he wanted Ramón to board, and Ramón of Lelia. Theodore did not try to hear what he said, because Ramón was talking to himself, or to her. Then Ramón took his hand down and jumped to the other boat. Theodore found some water in a large green glass bottle in the cabin. Ramón offered it first to Theodore, who declined. Then he knelt and washed his hands in the sea, and drank from the water that he poured into his palm. Theodore could hear Alejandro demanding money from Miguel, demanding two thousand pesos from the six thousand Infante had given him to hide him, or he would tell the police about all this; and at last Miguel grumblingly consented, and his grumbles grew fainter as he went into his cabin to get it.

A moment later, Alejandro came aboard and untied them from the anchored *Pepita*. "Miguel!" he said to the man slouching against the cabin. "Miguel, *adiós*! Have a long sleep and we forget what happened today! Okay, Miguel?"

Miguel nodded sleepily.

And strangely, Theodore thought, they probably would forget what had happened today.

The motor sputtered and caught. Alejandro swung the prow towards the shore, then turned a little left, murmuring something about a beach where he could put them off. There was something spry and cheerful in Alejandro's manner now, and he never once met Theodore's eyes with his own. Either murder had made him lively, or his primitive brain was going about its own process of forgetting, by seizing on its little business of running a boat.

271

Ramón said: "You may tell me I didn't kill him, Teo, but it was only the last blow that I didn't strike. He would have died from me." He was on one knee, crouched beside the gunwale, staring down at the deck. "Revenge is not sweet, Teo. It's as evil as the rest."

Theodore stood beside him, watching the shore for a spot where they might land. "Don't think about it now." He squeezed the rolled-up muffler in his hand.

"I must—because that was how I thought I killed *her*— when I was beside myself, not even knowing what I was doing! I used to be afraid that I'd strike her like that when I was angry, you know, Teo—and wake up to find her dead. And that's what I did with Infante—struck him until he was dead."

"He would have lived but for Miguel!" Theodore said forcefully, though he was not even thinking about what he said. He was wondering when Ramón would understand the significance of the muffler.

Suddenly the memory of Lelia's mutilated face came back to Theodore. He tried, but it was beyond his imagination that anyone could have done that. But, as Ramón was saying now, in a moment of anger anything was possible.

"Alejandro!" Theodore called over the sound of the motor. He took two steps and was beside him. "This muffler—— Do you know whom it belongs to? Didn't Infante tell you?"

Alejandro glanced at the muffler, then looked at Theodore, smiling. "I don't know," he said in a singing, jocular way.

"I will pay you to tell me. What've you got to lose?" Then, as Alejandro hesitated, Theodore realised that Alejandro probably didn't know, or he would have been glad to sell him the information, or he would have wanted to appropriate the muffler himself for blackmailing purposes. Theodore gave a sigh of fatigue and frustration.

Alejandro's brown shoulders shrugged. "That brat——

Infante was always saying it was his most valuable possession. That's all I know."

"And that's all Miguel knows?"

"*Quién sabe?*" Alejandro said indifferently.

The police would have to question Miguel, Theodore thought. Sauzas. Only Sauzas should question Miguel, or they would get into a terrible mess over Infante's death. Miguel would not be able to hide out now, assuming he even wanted to, with a boat. Or would he abandon his boat tonight or tomorrow, and disappear among the millions of other Mexicans who looked like him? And with how much enthusiasm would the Mexican *policía* look for him, anyway?

As Theodore had anticipated, Alejandro gouged him for more money as they neared the shore. "You've been paid enough," Theodore said curtly, not even looking at him, and Alejandro subsided in shrugs and grumbles about wealthy misers.

But he drove his boat's prow on to the sand and jumped out to give them a hand, as if they were persons of importance. "You'll find a road at the top of the cliff," he said, gesturing towards the steep, rocky hill that confronted them. "And listen, señor, I do not want any *policía* coming around to ask me questions, eh?"

"Understood," Theodore said.

"Or else I'll tell them your friend here did it," Alejandro said, with a nod at Ramón. "Understand?"

CHAPTER TWENTY-EIGHT

THE sun touched the horizon lightly, like a buoyant orange balloon. Then rapidly the sea began to swallow it. Theodore stared at it out the window of the bus, felt its last burst of heat on his face, and tried to think what he must do next. Call Sauzas, of course, and leave it to him to inform the Acapulco police of Infante's death—otherwise the police would detain them indefinitely for questioning. Alejandro and Miguel would have to be found, too, and this prospect was ghastly to Theodore. He felt exhausted, as spent as Ramón, who had leaned forward with his arms on his knees and put his head down. There was a smear of dark red blood on the roll of Ramón's shirt-sleeve, and Theodore had discovered that the right knee of his trousers bore a stiff, dark circle, conspicuous on the grey cloth. Theodore wondered if they should try to get a plane out tonight, or find a hotel to sleep in.

The bus finished the sinuous Revolcadero highway along the cliff's edge and began the steep descent to Acapulco. Already a few lights had been turned on, and Theodore heard the restless, insistent beat of the cha-cha-cha as the bus passed some open door. He would get out at the plaza, he thought, and telephone Sauzas. Now, out of habit, he looked at the people walking under the trees on the Malecón.

Suddenly he caught Ramón's arm. "Come! We're getting off!"

Ramón stood up.

The bus was slowing for a stop. They got off.

"Back this way," Theodore said. "I think I saw Sauzas."

"Sauzas? Are you sure?"

Theodore was not at all sure. It might have been a hallucination. But he thought he had seen him talking to two men beside a palm tree. "There! See him?"

Ramón did not acknowledge it, but he walked more slowly, his eyes on Sauzas; and Theodore knew Ramón would be thinking 'How little it all means', or something like that, even if they were going to put him in prison for fifteen years for the murder of a murderer.

Sauzas saw them from a distance also, and smiled a greeting. The two shirt-sleeved men with him stared at Theodore and Ramón and at the bloodstains on their clothing. "Señores! What luck!" Sauzas said. "I thought you had left for Mexico." He turned to the two men and said: "*Muchas gracias*, señores. I'd like to speak to these gentlemen now. What has *happened*?"

Theodore told him of the encounter with Infante on the boat and of what happened there. He pulled the rolled muffler from his jacket pocket. "This is it."

Sauzas's brows went up. "A bright one. Ah, now it all fits," he said quietly.

"What do you mean?" Theodore asked.

"Do you know whose this is?" asked Sauzas.

"No. I have no idea," Theodore said. "Have you?"

"Hm-m. Señor Schiebelhut, Carlos Hidalgo is not home yet, and that's why I'm here. I discovered he took ten thousand pesos from his bank—practically all the money he had. I put two and two together. The *policía* is now looking for Carlos Hidalgo."

"I see," Theodore said nervously. He had just told Sauzas that Infante had been paid ten thousand pesos for the muffler which he did not give up. "Lelia's keys—they were on the boat," Theodore went on. "They told me that when Infante arrived, he found the door open and Lelia dead. Whoever the muffler belongs to—must have just been there. Infante took the muffler and the keys and some other things and locked the door when he left. I learned also that he brought the flowers—to get in."

"Ah-hah. So Infante thought at first the muffler must belong to one or the other of you."

"Yes," Theodore said, watching Ramón's frowning face.

"Señor Schiebelhut, you're pale," said Sauzas. "Let's cross the street and have something to drink." He took Theodore's arm.

They went into a sidewalk bar with no front wall, ordered double rums, and Theodore added to the order a pot of tea and two cups.

"Señor Capitán, how can we be sure whom the muffler belongs to?" Theodore asked. "All there is is a few circumstances——"

Sauzas put his blue packet of Gitanes on the table, took one out and lighted it. "Señores—yesterday afternoon I spoke to Señora Hidalgo. I told her of the withdrawal of the ten thousand pesos, which she knew nothing about. I suggested they might have been for the purchase of the muffler, and I told her where the muffler might have been found. With that, señores, she broke down. She admitted she had begun to wonder about Carlos herself, because of his behaviour since the murder. I would say now she really believes he is guilty." Sauzas looked rather slyly from one to the other of them, as if he had just uncovered a winning card. "When I left Mexico at noon today, Carlos was not home and neither was his wife! Nobody had answered the telephone since I saw his wife yesterday afternoon at two. We went to his apartment. Nobody is there." Sauzas spread his hands in a shrug, and looked at them brightly.

Theodore still could not think it was that simple. "Isabel might have gone to her sister's. She has a sister called Nina in Coyoacán——"

"Ah!" Sauzas shifted restlessly in his chair and watched

the rums and the glasses of ice-water being set down on the table.

Ramón was staring at Sauzas with an angry, resentful expression. Then he looked at Theodore. "He thinks it was Carlos?"

"He is not sure. Nobody is sure yet," Theodore murmured, feeling strangely embarrassed. He was aware, as he poured tea for Ramón and himself, that Sauzas was smiling, amused by him.

"Carlos may well be here, looking for Infante," Sauzas said after his first sip of straight rum. "It wouldn't surprise me if he kills himself. So many cliffs to jump off in Acapulco." Sauzas turned to a small boy who had come up to the table, trying to sell the thin daily newspaper of Acapulco, shook his head, and dropped a coin in the child's palm. *"Andale!"*

Theodore was thinking of Carlos's evasiveness in the last months, of Carlos's refusal to see him the times Theodore had called him. And it had been Isabel, he remembered, who had telephoned and wanted to go to Lelia's funeral. But was it possible that Carlos had mutilated Lelia's *face*?

"Well—I must telephone Mexico and tell them about Infante," Sauzas said. "Or rather, I'll call the *policía* here and let them worry with their long-distance telephones." He winked and stood up. "With your permission, señores."

Theodore watched him walk away to the wall telephone by the bar counter. His gait looked more rolling and self-assured than ever. And it was all so casual to him, Theodore thought, all in the line of a day's work.

"He thinks it was *Carlos*, Theo?" Ramón asked.

A numb shock went over Theodore. "I don't know. But it was not Salvador. Salvador was only a blackmailer." He looked at Ramón's eyes, where a dark comprehension was gathering. Ramón's face had changed. Though lines and signs of fatigue were there, the confused frown had gone; and Theodore realised that Salavador Infante had at least jolted Ramón out of the conviction that he was her murderer. In that, it was as if the frail Salvador had lifted a mountain from Ramón.

"I see," Ramón said finally. "And I've killed someone for no reason. It's typical, typical, isn't it, Teo?"

Theodore gripped Ramón's wrist. "You have *not* killed anyone. Will you get that idea out of your head, Ramón?"

"Yes," Ramón said obediently, nodding. "I did not kill him. Just almost."

"And forget the almost. Miguel killed him. And the boy was evil, very evil, anyway. That's not a fact of importance for the *policía*, perhaps, that he was evil, but a fact for *you*. The boy himself had killed someone before."

"The boy was evil," Ramón repeated. "That is true." He picked up his rum and drank it all at once.

Theodore released Ramón's wrist and signalled for another round of drinks.

Sauzas came back to the table and said with a smile: "What do you know? The Acapulco police knew already that Infante was dead! They sit here gathering news from their informers and never stir off their backsides! . . . Would you gentlemen like a room for the night in the hotel where I am staying? You have no hotel, have you? . . . Well, I know I can get you some rooms where I am, because the manager is a crook of the third or fourth order and is being investigated by both the *policía* and a couple of insurance companies. He will do anything for me, even throw the President out to give me a room!" Sauzas chuckled and slapped Theodore's shoulder.

"All right. We'll accept. Thank you," Theodore said.

"It's a very comfortable hotel overlooking the bay. A marvellous view day and night. And after we go and wash up, I'll invite you both to dinner! With your permission again, I'll call——" He broke off, staring in the direction of the sidewalk.

Isabel Hidalgo was hurrying towards them.

Theodore and Ramón got to their feet.

"I've been looking everywhere for you!" she said with a frantic glance that took them all in. "Inocenza told me you were here," she said to Theodore.

"Sit down, Isabel!" Theodore said, offering her his chair.

She sat down and looked at Sauzas. "He is here. I came with him yesterday afternoon—because, after all, I'm his wife," she said with a quick, proud glance at Theodore and Ramón. "He is in our hotel room, and he wants to give himself up." Her shoulders drooped as if this had taken her last strength to say.

"To give himself *up*? It's true, then, Isabel?" Theodore asked, as astounded by her words as if no suspicion had crossed his mind before.

Isabel was nodding, nodding miserably.

Theodore dragged up an empty chair to sit on.

"Thank you for coming to us, señora." Sauzas touched her arm compassionately, but he had time to look at Theodore and there was triumph in his eye. "Now what hotel is he in?"

"He told me to tell you everything—how he cut her with the knife to make it look like a maniac's crime. He hit her first, then he got afraid because he thought he'd killed her. That's what he told me," Isabel said in a quick, soft voice. She stared at the table edge in front of her. "He said he got the knife from the kitchen—and he threw it away when he went out. He knew about the muffler then, but he was afraid to go back."

"Is this the muffler, señora?" Sauzas asked, reaching for it from Theodore.

Theodore pulled the muffler from his jacket pocket and put it into Sauzas's hand.

Isabel looked at it and nodded. "Yes, it's the one I gave him on New Year's. I remembered—— I really remembered when you asked me, but I wasn't sure. . . . Oh, Teo!" Her hand slid towards his on the table and stopped.

279

Theodore patted her hand, and felt a terrible pity for her. He stared at a pattern of thin blue veins in the back of her hand. The hand slipped from under his and brushed back her disordered hair.

"There's nothing more, is there? Just go and get him," Isabel said to Sauzas. "He wants you to come."

"I shall, I shall," Sauzas said. "Now which direction is the hotel in, and what is its name?"

"Hotel Quinta Antonia—just a little place, here to the left. Perhaps three streets—or five. But not far," Isabel said, her voice shaking with tears. "Oh, what's he done, Teo? Done to you and Ramón and all of us? He said he was in love with her and yet he did—*that*."

Theodore was remembering the way Carlos had used to help Lelia on with her coat, the way Ramón and he had joked with her about liking Carlos, and Lelia had said: "Not in a million years", or something like that. Lelia had said to Ramón, in his presence, that he had nothing to worry about from Carlos, and of course there hadn't been anything to worry about—except that Carlos finally killed her. "You'll come with us to our hotel tonight, Isabel," Theodore said. "There you'll be able to rest."

Ramón, silent and pale, stood up as Sauzas did.

"You want to come, too?" asked Sauzas.

Ramón hesitated. "No. I believe. And maybe if I saw him, I would kill him, too."

Sauzas smiled at Theodore. "Why don't you wait here for me, señor? I should not be more than ten minutes, if he's co-operative."

Theodore walked with Sauzas towards the front of the place, unwilling to let him go without another word, and yet he did not know what the word ought to be, either from him or Sauzas.

On the sidewalk, Sauzas lifted his arm at a passing *libre*, which went on by without noticing him. "You know, Señor

Schiebelhut, you showed great faith in your friend Señor Otero. Some people thought the police stupid not to hold on to a man who confessed to stabbing a woman to death. But we did know something that you didn't know. From the autopsy, we found that Señorita Ballesteros died from a heavy blow on the back of her head. We think her head struck— with great force—the back of her bed. . . . Ah, here's a *libre*. The knifing came later, and we thought we knew why. Well, we *did*!" He beamed and opened the door of the *libre*. "Until a few minutes, señor! *Adiós!*"

As he walked back into the restaurant, a shocking picture came to Theodore's mind—Lelia hurled to the bed by Carlos Hidalgo, who wouldn't take no for an answer. He stopped a waiter and told him to bring some more hot tea and another cup. Ramón and Isabel were talking, Ramón leaning towards her, Isabel with her head higher now, and apparently in better possession of herself. Theodore sat down quietly.

Ramón looked at him and said: "If Carlos were to walk in here now, I think I would wring his neck and nobody would be able to stop me, not even bullets."

But Theodore did not think he would. Ramón's vindictiveness was all but spent, first against himself and then against Salvador Infante. At that moment, Theodore supposed that he himself carried a greater charge of hatred and vengeance against Carlos than Ramón, but the conviction that it, like most passions, would eventually abate kept him sitting in his chair, while Sauzas went to get Carlos. "Don't imagine it. Don't imagine what you haven't done. You are always doing that, Ramón." He glanced at Isabel.

A strange, gentle smile had come to Isabel's colourless lips, as if somehow her senses had vanished, at least for these few moments, and her tormented mind was enjoying a brief peace.

"It's like a game in which nobody wins, isn't it, Teo?"

Ramón said. "Neither you nor I nor Carlos nor Salvador Infante—only Sauzas. Only the *policia*."

Theodore did not answer.

A silence fell among them. None of them stirred, and Isabel sat like a smiling statue that did not even breathe.